DEATH WITH ALL THE TRIMMINGS

A Key West Food Critic Mystery

Lucy Burdette

AN OBSIDIAN MYSTERY

OBSIDIAN
Published by the Penguin Group
Penguin Group (USA) LLC, 375 Hudson Street,
New York, New York 10014

USA | Canada | UK | Ireland | Australia | New Zealand | India | South Africa | China
penguin.com
A Penguin Random House Company

First published by Obsidian, an imprint of New American Library,
a division of Penguin Group (USA) LLC

First Printing, December 2014

Copyright © Roberta Isleib, 2014

OBSIDIAN and logo are trademarks of Penguin Group (USA) LLC.

ISBN 978-0-451-46590-0

Printed in the United States of America
10 9 8 7 6 5 4 3 2 1

PRAISE FOR
THE KEY WEST FOOD CRITIC MYSTERY SERIES

Murder with Ganache

"Gourmets who enjoy a little mayhem with their munchies will welcome Burdette's fourth Key West mystery."
—*Publishers Weekly*

"One crazy adventure ride. This page-turner kept me up half the night—I had to finish reading this book. Lucy Burdette does not disappoint. . . . So, if you like your mystery with a little Key West style, then you should be reading *Murder with Ganache*."
—MyShelf.com

"Sprightly and suspenseful, *Murder with Ganache* has a unique piquancy. Like a gourmet meal, it will leave you wanting more."   —*Fort Myers Florida Weekly*

"[Lucy Burdette] once again crafts a complicated mystery that incorporates delectable descriptions of Key West cuisine."   —Kings River Life Magazine

Topped Chef

"Burdette fills *Topped Chef* with a fine plot, a delightful heroine, a wealth of food—and all the charm and craziness of Key West. You'll wish you could read it while sipping a mojito on the porch of a Conch cottage in mainland America's southernmost community."
—*Richmond Times-Dispatch*

"In addition to a compelling murder mystery, readers are treated to a dose of spirited competition, a pinch of romantic intrigue, and a hearty portion of local flavor. It's enough to satisfy both casual readers and cozy fans alike, though be forewarned: You'll be left craving more."
—Examiner.com

"The characters remain as fresh as the breeze off the ocean, as does the plot."   —The Mystery Reader

continued . . .

"This third mystery in the series . . . again delights. . . . The descriptions of the coastal cuisine, snappish and temperamental cheftestants, and drag queens all combine to make this a very well-written and tasty mystery, sure to please fans of food, reality shows, and mysteries."
—Kings River Life Magazine

Death in Four Courses

"[A] yummy sequel to *An Appetite for Murder*. . . . Anyone who's ever overpaid for a pretentious restaurant meal will relish this witty cozy." —*Publishers Weekly*

"Breezy as a warm Florida Keys day, *Death in Four Courses* is a fast-paced mystery that easily combines food and writing with an intricate plot to create an engaging mystery. Lucy Burdette is skilled at creating interesting characters who are very real and familiar. . . . Lots of food talk, a tropical setting, and a hunky detective provide the perfect backdrop for the second Hayley Snow mystery." —The Mystery Reader

"This book was a quick, fun read that held my attention from the beginning. . . . I will eagerly await other releases in the Key West Food Critic series!"
—Fresh Fiction

An Appetite for Murder

"What fun! Lucy Burdette writes evocatively about Key West and food—a winning combination. I can't wait for the next entry in this charming series."
—*New York Times* bestselling author
Diane Mott Davidson

"For a true taste of paradise, don't miss *An Appetite for Murder*. Lucy Burdette's first Key West Food Critic mystery combines a lush, tropical setting, a mysterious murder, and plenty of quirky characters. The victim may not be coming back for seconds, but readers certainly will!"
—Julie Hyzy, national bestselling author of the White House Chef mysteries and Manor House mysteries

"When her ex-boyfriend's new lover, the co-owner of *Key Zest* magazine, is found dead, Hayley Snow, wannabe food critic, is the first in line on the list of suspects. Food, fun, and felonies. What more could a reader ask for?"—*New York Times* bestselling author Lorna Barrett

"Burdette laces *An Appetite for Murder* with a clever plot, a determined if occasionally ditzy heroine, and a wealth of local color about Key West and its inhabitants. You'll eat it up."　　　—*Richmond Times-Dispatch*

"Florida has long been one of the best backdrops for crime novels—from John MacDonald to Carl Hiaasen—and Burdette's sense of place and her ability to empathize with a wide strata of Key West locals and visitors bodes well for this new series."　　　—*Connecticut Post*

"An excellent sense of place and the occasional humorous outburst aren't the only things *An Appetite for Murder* has going for it, though: There is a solid mystery within its pages. . . . Not only does Burdette capture the physical and pastoral essence of Key West—she celebrates the food. . . . Although you might want to skip the key lime pie, don't skip *An Appetite for Murder*. Let's hope it is just an appetizer and there will be a feast of Food Critic mysteries to follow."
—The Florida Book Review

"Burdette cleverly combines the insuperable Key West location with the always-irresistible hook, food. . . . Hayley is a vibrant young character to watch, and she writes scrumptious food reviews as well."
—*Mystery Scene*

"Hayley herself is delightful. Exuberant and naive, rocking back and forth between bravado and insecurity, excitable and given to motormouth nervousness, she's a quick study who has a lot to learn. I'm sure that many readers will be happy to make her acquaintance and follow her through future adventures."
—*Florida Weekly*

Key West Food Critic Mysteries
by Lucy Burdette

To Paige and Sandy this time,
with gratitude.

ACKNOWLEDGMENTS

I owe many thanks to the folks who stood by me as I wrote this book. Angelo Pompano and Chris Falcone are so generous with their time, reading and brainstorming every step of the way. My fellow writers in the mystery business, including Hallie Ephron, Susan Hubbard, and my wonderful blogger friends at Mystery Lovers' Kitchen and Jungle Red Writers, are always there with a word of encouragement and a good idea. Thanks to Paige Wheeler for her friendship and dedicated work as my agent, and to Sandy Harding, my talented editor. Whew, you can't imagine how much better a draft is after she's made her editorial suggestions. Thanks to all the folks at New American Library, from fabulous cover designers to copy editors to the marketing department, to everyone who has a hand in bringing the books to print.

Thanks to Steve Torrence for help with police procedure. As always, mistakes are mine, not his. And while we're on the subject of Steve, thanks to all the folks who allowed me to use their names in the book—the names are real but the characters are definitely fictional. And, oh, how lucky was I to meet Chef Norman Van Aken just as I was desperate for details about a real chef's life? Thanks, Chef!

I'm grateful for every reader and librarian and bookstore owner—without you, there would be no point.

Thank you for reading and thank you for spreading the word—take Charles Pigaty in Milford, CT, for example, who decided he could hand-sell one hundred copies of *An Appetite for Murder*. And he did!

And to my family, especially John, the biggest thanks of all.

In theory, we've come a long way from the notion that a woman's place is in the domestic kitchen, and that the only kitchen appropriate for a man is the professional one. But in practice, things can be pared down to the following equation: woman : man as cook : chef.

—Charlotte Druckman, *Gastronomica*

1

Approach love and cooking with reckless abandon.
    —Jackson Brown and H. Jackson
Brown Jr., *Life's Little Instruction Book*

My cell phone bleated from the deck outside, where I'd left it to avoid procrastinating via text messages, Facebook updates, or simply lounging in the glorious December sunshine with our resident cats, watching the world go by. The biggest interview of my career as a food critic was scheduled for this afternoon and I wanted—no, needed—to be ready.

Miss Gloria, my senior citizen houseboat mate, hollered from her rocking chair overlooking the water. "It's your mother. Shall I answer?"

"Mind telling her I'll call back in an hour?"

Miss Gloria would relish the opportunity to chat with her anyway, and maybe her intercession would slash my time on the phone with Mom in half when I returned the call. I am crazy about my mother, honest. But it had still been a shock when she announced she'd rented a place in Key West for the winter season.

Wouldn't it be so much fun to spend Christmas in paradise together? And New Year's . . . and Martin Luther King Day . . . and Valentine's Day? You get the picture. Mom had followed Diana Nyad's attempts to swim from Cuba to Key West with rapt attention. When Diana overcame sharks, jellyfish, rough water, and advancing age to complete her 110-mile swim on her fifth try, at age sixty-four, Mom took it personally.

"Diana says we should never give up," she announced on the phone a couple of months ago. "*Why not 'be bold, be fiercely bold and go out and chase your dreams'?*"

My mother had been a little down since the summer because her fledgling catering company had not taken off the way she'd hoped. Although she's an amazing and inventive cook, the business part of owning a business eluded her. For her first five catering events, cooking with only the highest-quality ingredients, she'd lost money rather than made it. A lot of money. Even her newish boyfriend, Sam, who was supportive beyond any reasonable expectation and categorically opposed to meddling, had suggested she take a few steps back and reconsider her plan.

"Why not? You should go for your dream, too," I remember saying. "That's exactly what you told me when I lost my bearings: Keep putting yourself out in the universe, and eventually the wind will fill your sails." I stopped myself from trotting out more metaphysical tropes. I hadn't wanted to hear too much advice when I was feeling down; Mom probably didn't want mine, either. "What do you have in mind?"

"I'm thinking of coming to Key West for the winter!"

Whoa. If that was her dream, who was I to stop her? But my big solo adventure on this island was about to turn into *How I Met Your Mother*.

Half an hour after the phone call, Miss Gloria came inside to report on her conversation with Mom, our two cats padding behind. I stroked my striped gray boy, Evinrude, from ears to tail, his fur warm from basking in the sun. His purr box caught and sputtered to life.

"She's hoping we can swing by in half an hour to look at her condo and have a little lunch," Miss Gloria said. "Sam is flying in later tonight, so this may be her best shot at girls-only time for a while. And then she starts her job with Small Chef at Large on Monday. Jennifer's already assigned her to head up a couple of the Christmas parties they're catering."

Exhibit two: my mother's new job with Small Chef. You had to give her credit for sheer brass guts. How long had it taken me to land my position as food critic at *Key Zest*? A couple of months at least. And lots of groveling and dozens of sample restaurant reviews. Key West is chockablock with talented, overqualified folks who swarm every decent job opening like roaches to crumbs. And yet my mother had landed a position with the premier caterer in town after meeting her once, at my best friend Connie's wedding reception last spring. She'd been here only a week, but I suspected she was already best friends with half the natives on the island. She'd probably be designated an Honorary Conch at the next city commission meeting.

"Give me fifteen minutes to finish this up and we'll go," I told Miss Gloria.

Today I was interviewing Edel Waugh, chef-owner of the new Key West restaurant Bistro on the Bight. I skimmed the review her New York restaurant, Arnica, had scored in the *New York Times* last spring. Overall, the review glowed with praise, but Paul Woolston, the critic, had ended with this punch to the gut: "With bad blood between the ex-husband and -wife co-owners of Arnica, one wonders when—not if—their personal poison will seep into their food."

I tweaked the list of questions to ask Edel when we met later, then changed out of my sweats and into a pair of slim-fitting black jeans and a red swing shirt that drew the eye away from the waistline and matched my sneakers. Christmas, just two weeks away, was the one time of year that I broke my own rule about not wearing red because it clashed with my auburn hair. Miss Gloria was waiting for me on the deck, dressed in the first of a deep rotation of Christmas sweatshirts, this one spangled with sequins and glitter-dusted reindeer.

"You look so cute!" we said at the same time.

We locked the cats up in the houseboat—things get a little dicier on the island during the high season, with an uptick in partying visitors and in the homeless population—and headed down the dock to the parking lot, where I keep my scooter. Miss Gloria began to sing "I Saw Mommy Kissing Santa Claus" as she fastened her pink helmet and swung her leg over the bike. As we puttered down Southard Street to the end of the island, Miss G pointed out which Conch houses had been newly decorated for the season. The specialty here, of course, being white lights wound around the trunks of the palm trees. Who could be grumpy on a day like this?

Ten minutes later, we rolled past the wrought-iron gates and the guardhouse that mark the entrance to the Truman Annex complex, and took a right onto Noah Lane, the last developed street before the Navy's harbor, aka the mole. My mother could not have afforded a seasonal rental in this neighborhood, except that her boyfriend, Sam, had gotten excited about a winter getaway and bankrolled a nice house just blocks from my ex Chad Lutz's condo. When the gates closed at six p.m., there was only one way out of the neighborhood; it would be hard to avoid him. If I wasn't already inured to running into Lutz the Putz, I would be by Easter, when Mom headed north.

Mom came bursting out of the front door onto her new home's wide wooden porch and hugged us both. "My two favorite ladies," she yelped. "I've made chicken salad and cupcakes. Come on, I'll give you the grand tour and we can eat out by the pool."

"I can't stay long," I told her. "I have an interview set up with the chef at Bistro on the Bight."

"The restaurant opening on the harbor!" Mom said. "I read about it in the *Citizen*. I can't believe my favorite chef in the world will be right here in Key West. I'm dying to eat her food again. Any chance—"

"Sorry, Mom." I cut her off and grinned. "I'm happy to share a lot of things with you, but not my job."

I'm the food critic for the Key West style magazine *Key Zest*. It's complicated because we have only four people on staff. One of them, the co-owner Ava Faulkner, despises me and would happily slash me from the masthead at the first opportunity. Next is Danielle, our administrative assistant, who manages all the online intricacies of the magazine and scrambles to keep the whole project from sinking under the weight of Ava's negativity. And last but not least is my editor Wally Beile, who makes my heartstrings and other body parts twang in a most unprofessional way. Though with his own mother dying of cancer, I hadn't seen much of him lately.

Afraid I'd hurt my mother's feelings, I sputtered a little more explanation. "I don't think bringing my mother along on the interview would give the appearance that I know what I'm doing."

"That's okay, honey," she said, "I don't have time,

anyway. I'll catch up with her another time." Then she gripped my shoulders and looked into my eyes. "I swear, Hayley Catherine Snow, I will not cramp your style while I'm here."

"Thanks, Mom. I'm sure there's room for two Snow women on this island." I wasn't sure, really, but I was going to try hard to make it work. Because the truth was, she had always been my biggest fan, and she was a lot of fun besides. And, let's face it, utterly out of my control.

She spun away, leading us into a spacious living room furnished with expensive rattan furniture, cushioned with pillows covered in pale linen fabric patterned with palm fronds. The kitchen was even more magnificent—a bright yellow-and-white-tiled space that included a six-burner gas range, two dishwashers, two ovens, a wine chiller, a bread warmer, and a center island topped in green granite that made me vibrate with envy.

"You could throw one heck of a party here," I said, as we followed my mother onto the back porch. White rattan chaise longues overlooked a perfect little dipping pool shaded by palm trees with an elegant waterfall at the far end.

"Wait until you hear how many events Jennifer has me working," Mom said. "She wants me in the kitchen a couple of days a week, of course, but she's already put me in charge of two parties. I'm developing the menu for tomorrow—a Southern belle's Christmas luncheon. I'm thinking curried chicken salad with grapes and pecans, and a green salad, and then for the ladies who don't eschew carbs, big buttermilk biscuits and maybe Scarlett O'Hara cupcakes."

"Oh swoon," said Miss Gloria. "No one in her right mind is going to eschew those carbs. What is a Scarlett O'Hara cupcake?"

"It has to be red velvet, don't you think?" I asked.

"Maybe with raspberry cream cheese frosting? That's what I tried out this morning. We'll see if you approve." Mom led us to the table, which she'd set with shimmery gold place mats, tan polka-dot napkins, and white plates. A bright orange bird of paradise swooped from a clear glass vase at the center for contrast.

"Watch out Martha Stewart," Miss Gloria said with a cackle. "You are so clever. It already looks like you've lived here forever!"

We loaded our plates in the kitchen and brought them out to the poolside table. Mom slid a platter of the pink-icing-slathered cupcakes in the center, to remind us to save room. I spread a thin layer of honeyed butter onto a warm biscuit, admiring the tiny flecks of green scallion in the dough, and then bit into it.

"Oh my gosh, these are the best," I said, and then tasted the chicken. "And the curry is exactly right—a little bite but not enough to put anyone off."

Miss Gloria only rolled her eyes and moaned with pleasure.

"Oh for heaven's sake," Mom said when we were halfway through lunch. "I almost forgot to tell you the other news. You remember my cousin Chuck? His daughter, Cassie, is a pro golfer. She and her husband are popping down to the island for a couple of days this week and I've insisted they stay with me. And weren't you going to make a dinner reservation at Latitudes when Sam's here this weekend? Would it be a problem to add two more people?"

"Not really," I said, though more people made it challenging to concentrate and harder to manage. "As long as they don't mind me ordering and tasting their food."

Latitudes is the restaurant on Sunset Key, the small

private island a stone's throw from Mallory Square, at the very bottom of Key West. Dinner guests have to make a reservation well ahead and then take a water taxi to the island. For me, this dinner would be work more than pleasure, as I'd been assigned to review the restaurant for the next issue of *Key Zest*. I couldn't afford to take a second trip over—I had to get what I needed in one visit.

"I know they'll get a kick out of a little window into your world," Mom said. She bit into one of the cupcakes, sighed with satisfaction, and patted her lips with her napkin. "I also set up a tee time at the Key West golf course for Cassie and her husband, Joe, and Eric and you. I invited Eric because he and Joe are both psychologists so I figured they would hit it off. I know Eric played a little as a teenager. Your muscle memory doesn't forget that kind of history, right?"

This was crazy in so many ways that I was struck dumb. Well, almost dumb. "Back up a minute. *I* don't play golf," I managed to squeak, because I couldn't say the things that really came to mind. Out loud. To my mother. In front of Miss G.

Mom laughed, a silvery peal that meant she'd started marching down a path and would not be deviating from it. "How hard could it be? And, besides, Cassie's a pro. I'm sure she'll be happy to give you some pointers."

2

Revenge is like serving cold cuts.
                                    —Tony Soprano

As you might expect from our island's near-Caribbean status, Key West restaurants tend to be casual, with wide-plank floors, doors thrown open to the outdoors, and waiters with tattoos, cutoffs, and weathered faces. Bistro on the Bight had not adopted this trend. The designers had set the eatery apart with clean, spare decor heavy on stainless steel, copper trim, and leather. Orchids bloomed purple and pink on every table, and I noticed no funky odors—almost unavoidable in a humid climate when a place had been around awhile. I jotted a few notes on my phone and waved to the server, who emerged from the swinging door that I figured must lead to the kitchen. He was clean-shaven, dressed in a full-body white apron with all black underneath, as though he might have just flown in from New York City. Black is not big on this island.

"I have an appointment with Ms. Waugh. I'm Hayley Snow."

"The chef is expecting you," the server said, and led

me to a table for two in the far corner of the room, near the kitchen. "Can I bring you a beverage?"

"No, thanks," I said, pointing to the BPA-free water bottle clipped to the side of my backpack. I was still swimming from a second glass of my mother's Arnold Palmer—half lemonade, half iced tea, and one of the drinks in the running for her southern Christmas party menu. "I'd love to look at the menu while I'm waiting, though."

He crossed the room to the hostess stand and returned with a crisp linen folder.

"She'll be with you shortly."

As he exited through the swinging door, I heard a voice from the kitchen, feminine yet husky with intensity: "This is not rocket science. You need to prepare it exactly as I showed you yesterday. Our customers don't want a new adventure every time they order a dish—they want what they loved last time and the time before. Exactly as the recipe is written. Do you understand?"

"Yes, Chef," chorused a few voices.

I began to peruse the pristine pages of the menu and was immediately drawn to the shrimp salad with fennel and orange and a roasted chicken served with pommes aligot, a recipe featuring potatoes mashed with heavy cream, garlic, and cheese. My mouth began to water even though I'd just eaten.

The kitchen door swung open again, banging against the pickled wood trim on the wall. A petite woman with a pink face, rosebud lips, and a mass of black curls escaping from her toque barreled over to my table. She thrust her hand at me, and when I took it, squeezed mine like a lemon pinched in a vise.

"Edel Waugh," she said. "You must be Ms. Snow. I appreciate you taking the time to write the feature."

"Delighted to meet you," I said. "Please call me Hayley. I have some questions prepared, if that's okay." I tried to hold my voice steady and not show how nervous I felt—of course she would expect me to come with questions. Besides, I had the sense that this small, fierce woman would roll right over me if I didn't take the lead. She nodded, sat down across from me, and crossed her arms over her chest.

"You developed a very successful restaurant in New York. Why not stick with what you've already got humming? Why Key West?"

She flashed a quick grin, rubbed a finger over her chin, which had a spot of something on it—grease? Gravy? Though I couldn't think of any dish I'd seen in her repertoire that involved gravy. Which seemed a shame, really. My stomach gave a little rumble of agreement.

"New York is fabulous in December—the lights, the crowds, the festivity. January and February? Dead. I'm an ambitious person," she said, rapping her fist on the table, which bobbled a little from the force of the impact. A frown crossed her face and she snapped her fingers and called for the waiter who'd greeted me. "Leo?" He trotted across the room. "As soon as Ms. Snow and I are finished, you need to look at this table," she told him, rocking it for emphasis. "Our diners should not have to endure an unsteady eating surface." He backed away with a sheepish look on his face, and she returned her attention to me.

"Truth is, as in many arenas, a female chef has to work harder than a man to get to the top levels. The work is brutal—long hours, heavy lifting, staffing issues, money problems. Of course, male chefs have those challenges, too, but women are assumed to be less creative than men, less driven, less than men in actually any way you can imagine. But I don't buy that."

She stared me down.

"As I'm quite sure you know, the New York restaurant was developed with my ex-husband. This is my chance to prove that my food and my restaurant are equal to anything a male chef might invent." Her eyes blazed with intensity.

Who would dare consider her less than a man?

"I have gathered some information to share with you that you might do well to read before you write your piece. Menus, of course, but also my training manuals for kitchen and front-of-house staff." She pushed a folder across the table. "Let's go for a spin around the kitchen—assuming you're interested?"

"Of course."

She whisked me through the gleaming kitchen, which smelled amazing—onions frying, sauce simmering, chicken roasting—and introduced me to a few of the staff: the head sous-chef, two line cooks, the pastry chef, even a dishwasher. They all struck me as professional, if a bit harried. In each case, Edel's staff tightened visibly under the glare of her examination, almost flinching as she approached. There was no question about who would be in charge of the dishes coming out of this kitchen. She would be watching every detail from the amuse-bouche to the cleanliness of the glassware to the size of the carrot chunks in the stew to the herb sprigs garnishing the dinner plates.

After we'd finished the tour, Chef Edel walked me out through the restaurant to the dock along the water. "Before you write anything up, I'd like you to come back, spend a few hours in the kitchen. I think you'll understand what we're trying to do here in a way you can't by listening to me talk—or even the brief visit we just had." She cocked her head and narrowed her eyes. "Honestly? I'm not quite sure that Key West will be able to appreciate my kind of food—the islanders may be too provincial. I mean that literally and figuratively," she added.

I gaped at her, unsure what I could possibly say. Maybe she didn't realize that a large chunk of this population came from points north, including her own New York City. It was a peculiar blind spot, to say the least.

"How would tomorrow around four p.m. work in your schedule? We are treating tomorrow night as our soft opening. I'd like you to join us for our staff dinner before the restaurant opens."

I agreed without checking my phone because nothing felt more pressing than the opportunity to watch this whirlwind chef in action.

"There's a reason I asked for you to write this piece," she said.

She'd asked for me? I thought my boss had come up with the idea.

"What's that?"

She fidgeted, gazing over the horizon for a moment—the first time I'd noticed her looking insecure about anything—then swung those intense brown eyes back to me. "Some things have started to go a little wrong."

Now I was really puzzled. And curious. Surely she wasn't looking for my culinary expertise. I'm an accomplished home cook, but certainly no gourmet chef—my tweaks on her recipes could not be welcome. "What kinds of things?"

"Recipes altered. Things gone missing. Like that. I could use another pair of eyes. I'll discuss it with you after dinner service tomorrow. The soft opening is less than twenty-four hours away and my staff is acting as though they've never set foot in a professional kitchen."

"I'd love to help if I can. But why me?"

"I've heard about you. You've gotten involved with other mysteries on this island. People say you're good with puzzles. And fearless. To the point of being a little stupid."

Which struck me almost dumb, for the second time that day. If she was trying to butter me up, her technique needed honing in a way I was certain her knives did not.

3

Chestnuts roasting on an open fire . . .
                    —Mel Tormé and Robert Wells

Although it had been Ava Faulkner's idea for *Key Zest* to have a presence in the Hometown Holiday Parade, which helps mark the launch of the Christmas season, I wasn't surprised that she turned the actual work over to the rest of us. Wally managed to scrounge a banged-up golf cart with three bench seats for the base of the float, and we'd been brainstorming ideas for the past couple of weeks by e-mail. Santa . . . elves . . . key lime pie . . . palm trees . . . margaritas . . . key deer . . . At the last go-round, we were basically nowhere. Pretty much the only part we had nailed down was that Wally would dress as Santa, Danielle and I as elves. We'd blocked out late this afternoon and this evening to firm up a theme and begin production, as the parade date was caroming in our direction.

Parades are big business on this island. The grand-daddy of them all, Fantasy Fest, takes place during the week leading up to Halloween and features a different theme each year. And lots of costumes, which in Key

West means the skimpier, the better—right down to body paint only. In the presence of an excellent paint job, it might take the onlooker five minutes to realize she's staring at a stranger's bare breasts. Maybe painted to simulate Mickey Mouse or an antique car or a bunch of grapes, but bare all the same.

Fortunately, dressing as an elf would not involve exposing a lot of skin.

I parked my scooter at the back of a conch house in New Town, where one of Wally's pals let him store the cart for the week leading up to the parade. The sounds of Bruce Springsteen crooning "Santa Claus Is Coming to Town" wafted out from the stand-alone garage. Lights twinkled inside and I heard Danielle singing harmony to Bruce's baritone. My heart was pounding a nervous rat-tat-tat-tat. It felt like forever since I'd really talked with Wally and even longer since we'd spent any time alone. Last spring all signs pointed to the possibility that love was about to blossom. But then his mom's stage-four cancer was diagnosed. Understandably, the other concerns in his life fell away to the shadows. He'd been working from her home in Delray Beach for months and months while she suffered through surgery and chemotherapy. Her health seemed to be on a slight uptick—at least in the short run—so he'd taken the opportunity to come back down to Key West for the holidays. I'd watched this progression once already when my friend Connie's mother died during our freshman year in college. Losing your mother too soon—watching her waste away in pain—was just about the worst experience I could imagine.

I pulled in a big breath of balmy air, arranged a cheery smile, and headed in. Wally was wiring two dashing reindeer that looked like stolen lawn ornaments to the front of the golf cart. A sign hanging from the deer's necks proclaimed them to be carrying Santa and his cutie pies.

"Santa and his cutie pies?" I yelped over Bruce's song.

"Danielle thought of it." Wally, wearing a faded green T-shirt and worn jeans that showed a little flash of thigh through the thinnest places, hopped off the cart, slung an arm around my shoulder, and pecked my cheek. I hugged him hard. He looked and felt thinner than he had last time I'd seen him. Danielle turned down the volume so we could talk normally.

"Do you get it?" Danielle asked, pointing to the cart. "Do you see? The rest of the cart will look like a giant key lime pie when we're finished." She had laid out another sheet of thin plywood and blocked out in bright paint TO SAMPLE THE BEST OF THE ISLAND, VISIT KEY ZEST. She was in the process of tacking white lights to the cursive lettering that spelled out *Key Zest*. But my attention leaped to her costume: a Santa hat, black leggings, and a bikini top constructed out of red faux fur outlined in more blinking white lights. The outfit made the most of her considerable assets.

"Hayley, wait until you see this," she said, demonstrating how the blinking *Key Zest* sign would hang from the cart's roof. "The most important thing is lots of lights—and we put together a sound track that has all the best foodie Christmas carols on it." She began to warble "Rockin' Around the Christmas Tree." She grabbed my hands. "Do you know how to dance swing? I was thinking we would pop out of the pie whenever the parade slows down and then dance! Maybe toss out candy canes?"

I eased my fingers from her grip and backed away. "This all sounds great. Sort of. But please don't tell me you want me to wear that." I pointed at her fuzzy, blinking brassiere. "An elf costume is bad enough . . ."

"Come on, it's cute. It's Key West. Skimpy costumes are the norm. And it will draw attention to our float."

"Believe me, you don't want the kind of attention I would draw."

Wally crossed the garage and tousled my hair, a big grin on his face. "She's pulling your leg. She figured once you saw what she had on, the striped tights and red elf skirt would start to look good." They both started to laugh.

"So I'm modest," I said. "I'm from New Jersey." Which only made them laugh harder.

I began to help Danielle tack lights to the wooden board, and then duct tape swirls of lights on the body of the cart. Finally the whining of Wally's band saw wound down.

"Did you get a chance to meet the new chef at the Bight?" Wally asked.

"Did I ever," I said. "She's as tough as my grandmother's cast-iron frying pan. But I liked her. In fact, she's invited me to have the family meal with the staff tomorrow and then spend a couple hours in the kitchen. It's their soft opening."

"Do your best work," Wally said, "because Ava fought me tooth and nail about assigning this to you."

"I'm your food critic. Who else was going to write it?" I asked, indignant. I spend a lot of time feeling indignant when it comes to Ava Faulkner.

Danielle piped up, "She said, and I quote, '*We have half a dozen new restaurants debuting in Key West every season. Let's concentrate on the ones that make it, not waste space on some damn fancy-pants New Yorker who wants to make a big splash by dragging her old ideas to a new location.*'" She wagged a finger and pinched her lips in an excellent imitation of my nemesis. Except for the gorgeous cleavage, which Ava lacks.

I sighed. "She's such a pain. Do you think anyone would notice if we fed her rat poison?"

"Maybe something a little more subtle, considering that her sister was murdered," Danielle said, and grimaced. "Besides, rat poison makes an awful big mess. And how would we get it into her? She hardly eats anything and she certainly wouldn't eat something you cooked."

"So true." We worked a few minutes in silence, attaching the gigantic pie shell to the sides of the cart and installing the blinking KEY ZEST sign on top.

"Why do you suppose Edel Waugh wanted to open a restaurant in this town?" Danielle wondered, when we stopped for a break.

"You know, I asked her that question, but she never really answered. Other than talking about how grim New York is in January. And she did say this was her chance to prove herself separate from her ex-husband."

"All the biggest chefs want to expand their domains," Wally said. "It's like a McDonald's franchise, only different. And much, much better. Design a menu and a concept that diners love, then set up another one just like it, somewhere else. Double the reservations, double the money, double the name recognition. People want familiar yet fresh. In this case, New York food with Key West flair."

"But you can't cook in two kitchens at once," Danielle said.

"I don't know how much she cooks at this point— she's the grand director and idea woman. But imagine training the staff in two places—that must be a major headache," I said. "Making sure the dishes are the same whether you order them in New York City or Key West. Maybe that's why she was yelling at the staff."

Danielle looked at her watch. "Oh shoot, I have to

run home and get changed. My date is picking me up in an hour."

"Why don't you wear what you have on?" I said. "You'd sure make a big impression."

She grinned and blew me a kiss, then gathered her things, turned off the bare bulb hanging from the ceiling, and trotted away. That left Wally and me alone in the shadows of the garage, now lit only by the twinkling of a thousand little white fairy lights. He switched on the Christmas music soundtrack, which began to play "I'll Be Home for Christmas," and started around the golf cart toward me. My heart thumped and skin tingled as I anticipated his embrace. Eight months since he'd declared he might have feelings for me and we still hadn't figured out how to handle them in public. Or really in private, either. He reached for my hands and pulled me closer.

"Helloooo!" called a voice from the yard outside. The dreaded Ava Faulkner. We sprang apart and Wally yanked the chain of the overhead light, shocking the room with the sharp brightness of the bare bulb. I busied myself cleaning up scraps of wood and paintbrushes and hammers so Ava wouldn't see what I was certain was my tomato-red face.

Wally began to yammer about the design of the float and explain how the elves would come bursting out of the pie to distribute candy canes emblazoned with the *Key Zest* Web address. Ava looked unimpressed.

"I didn't even think to ask," he added, eyebrows lofting. "Would you like to be an elf, too?"

"You're kidding, right?" she asked, a look of horror on her face. She turned to me. "Could you excuse us? We have some business to discuss."

This was vintage Ava—humiliating the minions by treating them like children or undervalued underlings.

But there would be nothing to gain by confronting her or refusing to leave, so I scurried to collect my backpack and helmet. "See you tomorrow," I said to Wally. Outside, I paused in the shadows by the open window to catch my breath. Which suddenly made eavesdropping irresistible.

"You wanted to talk?" Wally was saying.

"I'm not happy with how things are going," Ava said. "I'm sorry that your mother has been ill. And I've been willing to tolerate your absence over this period of months—but it was with the understanding that you would be sure the business was covered."

"I have made sure," Wally said in a firm voice. "I've said this every time you and I have talked. Hayley and Danielle have been handling the day-to-day issues and we have been in touch by e-mail and phone daily. I'm doing the best I can, considering that my mother is dying."

I would not have been that polite. I would have melted into a blubbering, outraged puddle.

"As I mentioned, I am sorry about your mother," said Ava, "but I beg to differ. Very little has been handled. Our subscription numbers have stagnated. I've picked up several phone messages from potential advertisers who have not been contacted—they are offering us easy money, and we can't be bothered to follow up. But worse than that is a lack of editorial direction."

I peered through the window into the garage. Wally had sagged against the workbench on the far wall, his arms crossed over his chest, his glasses pushed up to his forehead so that even from a distance the sadness in his eyes was clear. I wanted to rush in and hug him, and then lambast Ava for her insensitivity, which would only make things worse. Then I realized that if his job was in trouble, so was mine. Over and over, he'd protected me from her misplaced wrath. If he was going to be squeezed out, I was a goner, too.

"Do tell me about the problem with editorial direction," he said in a quiet voice.

Ava gave a quick nod. "I know I mentioned the piece about Bistro on the Bight. If Hayley Snow"—I flinched at the sound of my name barked from her scornful lips—"is supposed to be a food critic, then how can she possibly spend time in this woman's kitchen and write a puff piece on this supposedly up-and-coming chef and retain any scrap of impartiality? Can't you see that every restaurant on the island will be demanding equal treatment? And then every reader will assume that the chef has been greasing the skids to earn what is not a review but essentially a monstrous advertisement?"

"I don't agree," Wally said. "You've been saying for months that we need articles with more depth, more heft. Profiling new business owners is part of that. And Hayley is a consummate professional. She will not cross lines, nor will she produce a so-called puff piece." He pushed away from the bench and stood up taller. "What are your other concerns?"

Ava huffed and stalked around the golf cart to slap her bag on the workbench. "I've made a list," she said, as she pulled her iPad mini from the satchel.

I'd heard enough. Hell would be paid if I got caught listening in on her harangue. Besides, her insensitivity made me sick to my stomach.

One thing was certain: the more she insisted I should not interview Edel Waugh, the more determined I was to continue.

4

If you're cooking with love, every plate is a unique event—you never allow yourself to forget that a person is waiting to eat it: your food, made with your hands, arranged with your fingers, tasted with your tongue.

—Bill Buford, *Heat*

Before blasting across the island to the old harbor for my second visit to the Bistro on the Bight, I read over the document called "Do's and Don'ts for Servers" that Edel had e-mailed me last night. "Extremely detailed" was one way to describe the list. "Anal," "obsessive," "controlling," and "neurotic" were others. I concluded that it might be a miracle her staff hadn't bumped her off rather than simply played practical jokes or quit in droves. Or however else her problems had manifested themselves. By now I was extremely curious.

To be fair, I agreed with many of the items on her list: If she managed to keep her drill-sergeant proclivities confined to the kitchen and waitstaff, her diners would be in for an exquisite experience. Whoever had launched the trend of having waiters announce their names and proceed to treat diners like old maiden aunts deserved what they had coming. And don't get me started on staff sharing their own experiences with why they'd switched to gluten-free diets or the pounds they'd lost by eliminating carbs, or, worse yet, any white-colored food. Or clearing plates before everyone at the table was finished . . . or asking diners if they were "still working on" their meals, as though dining at that particular restaurant was a Herculean task rather than a pleasure. Servers could stumble into a lot of traps, and Edel seemed determined to sidestep all of them.

I parked my scooter in the pay lot near the old Waterfront Market, hoping the Cuban Coffee Queen was open. The CCQ, a concrete shack painted as though it's a giant postcard of Key West, dispenses some of the best coffee on the island. If Edel worked me as hard as she worked her staff, I would need every jolt of energy the caffeine offered.

Not only was the coffee stand open, but it was also jammed. I wended my way through a big family from India, a couple with two babies in strollers, and two workers from the Fury pleasure boats, probably headed to man the sunset cruises, which at this time of year cast off earlier and earlier. As I waited in line to order my Cuban coffee, one of the CCQ workers pushed out through the trailing strands of heavy plastic that separated the little kitchen from the outdoors. He offered a chunk of ham to a waiting Australian shepherd with spooky blue eyes, who snatched the meat and nearly took his fingers off.

I sat on the yellow bench to wait for my coffee, then recognized the man next to me as Wes Singleton, the former owner of a fried-fish-and-burger joint on the harbor. A funky-smelling bar can survive in Key West with the right music and the right party vibe, but a funky restaurant is a turnoff. Wes's place had finally succumbed to a series of bad customer reviews online and a brief shutdown by the health department. Rumor had it they'd found a horde of rodents in his kitchen. The restaurant had been in my queue of places to review; I was grateful that it had closed before I had to weigh in. Even though I recognize it as a necessary duty, I still despise writing negative reviews.

Wes lit up a cigarette and slurped a slug of his coffee.

"How's it going?" I asked, inching away from the smoke.

"Slowly," he said, blinking sleepy gray eyes. "Looking for work."

"Have you tried Edel Waugh's new place? I'm certain she's looking for experienced staff." Then I wished I'd kept my big mouth shut. Because of course Edel's restaurant had replaced his, after the little rhubarb with the health department and the financial problems that had followed.

He stared back at me. "Don't you think it would be a little weird to work for someone else in what should by rights be my space? Besides, I've heard she's hell on wheels." Then he cackled, and I laughed with him, because what else could I do?

"I hadn't thought of it that way. I'll let you know if I hear of something," I added, just to be polite. The worker at the cash register called my name and I said good-bye and eased through the crowd to collect my café con leche.

Inside Edel's place, I was greeted by the waiter I'd seen yesterday. "How did the dinner go last night?" I asked. "The soft, soft, soft opening?"

He held out his hands, palms up. "We were okay in

the front of the house"—he gestured to the empty tables and chairs—"some issues to work out in the back. But I'm sure Chef is all over it."

"We didn't meet formally yesterday. I'm Hayley Snow."

He shook my hand and smiled. "Leo McCracken."

"Do you hail from New York or were you hired here in Key West?"

"I'm down from New York for the high season. After that, we'll see." We both cringed, hearing a clang of pans clashing to the floor and a harried, screaming voice. "She said to send you in when you arrived," Leo said. "Good luck." He gave an apologetic smile and went back to folding crisp white napkins into neat triangles.

I trudged across the dining room and pushed open the swinging door. Edel was looking up at a tall man with a shock of white hair wearing a chef's toque and checkered pants. "Did you taste that before you added the salt?" Her voice was hoarse with fury. She grasped a big wooden spoon and stabbed it at his apron-wrapped belly. "Go ahead, taste it now."

The sous-chef dipped the spoon into the pot, sniffed the pale pink sauce first, and then took a sip. And instantly recoiled. "Oh my god," he said, clutching his throat, his eyebrows arched in horror.

"Explain," said Edel, squeezing her hands into fists. She was shorter than the sous-chef by a good eight inches, possibly even a foot, but in spite of his vantage point looking down on her, he appeared terrified. "Explain how our signature pasta sauce is so spicy and salty that no customer would eat it."

"I don't know." He shrugged helplessly. "It was fine when we made it. I'll start another batch right now." He turned away from Edel and called out to two of the other workers. "Mary Pat, get tomatoes, shallots, garlic, butter, and cream from the cooler. Rodrigo, get this shit out of here." He slammed the spoon against the big pot, splattering the ruined sauce around his station. A swarthy man with an impassive face who'd been washing dishes scuttled over to whisk the stockpot away.

Then Edel noticed me hovering inside the dining room door. "Come in," she said, waving me forward and mustering a smile. She wiped her damp face with the sleeve of her white coat. "I'm sorry for that introduction to our kitchen. Apparently, we've got soft-opening-night jitters."

Then she swept me through the kitchen and introduced me to the staff—the sous-chef she'd just bawled out was Glenn Fredericks. After Glenn, I met the line cook, Mary Pat; the pastry chef, Louann; and Rodrigo the dishwasher; and then I lost track. I perched on a stool and took notes as I watched them prepare everything that would be needed for the night to come.

"What's the best thing about Christmas in Key West?" Louann asked me. "Sounds like you've been around for a while."

"Hmm, so many choices. But probably my favorite event is the lighted boat parade. I've been invited to ride on my friend Ray's little Boston Whaler. He's going to have lighted reindeer and lots of chickens. I suspect we'll be the smallest boat in the harbor, but with the best seat in the house."

"Where should we watch if we don't have a boat?"

"Somewhere along the dock in front of Schooner Wharf," I said.

Edel stopped by Mary Pat's station and examined a pile of julienned carrots. "These are too big. These could choke a horse, not to mention a yellowtail snapper. They are meant to be delicate matchsticks, to garnish the dish. I thought we had been over these specials in detail, but apparently not enough detail."

The sous-chef stomped over, snatched the cutting board off the counter, and scraped the vegetables into a trash can, muttering something about idiots and bullshit. He sent Mary Pat back to the walk-in cooler for another enormous bag of carrots, and they began again, with Edel watching.

By five o'clock, the prep work was finished and the kitchen was filled with amazing smells—one of them I could have sworn was an Italian red sauce.

I stopped Edel after she'd delivered a bowl of key limes to the pastry chef. "What incredible dish am I smelling? I didn't see anything Italian on your menu, aside from the tomato-vodka sauce."

She broke into a wide smile and tipped her head at an enormous pot bubbling on one of the back burners of the farthest cooktop. "Bolognese sauce. My grandmother's recipe. We're serving it for our family meal— for good luck. You'll eat with us." A decree, not an invitation. But I wouldn't have missed it.

Fifteen minutes later, I was seated with Edel and her staff around a long table at the back of the dining room. Edel took the head chair, heaved a big sigh, and raised her glass of water. "To all of you who have chosen to travel with me on this new adventure, thank you." She looked as though she had more to say, but choked up. She waved to Leo, the head server, and he delivered steaming bowls of pasta smothered in red sauce to the table. "Eat, eat," she said. "We'll all need our stamina tonight."

I loaded a heap of spaghetti on my plate, topped it with shredded parmesan, and began to eat. "This is amazing," I told Edel. "You should put this on your menu."

"I'd vote for that," said one of the line cooks.

"Red wine and milk?" I asked, hoping she'd spill her recipe.

"Red wine and white," Edel said with an impish grin. "And milk. And that's all I am willing to say. A chef's recipes are her greatest assets. The jewels in her crown."

After twenty minutes, the bowls were empty, the plates cleared, and Edel clapped her hands. "I needn't tell you all how important this night is to me. I think you understand that. So I will say only one more thing: Never forget the people who will be eating the dishes we prepare. They are what matters—they are eating the products of our care and our love. If we cook with that in mind, our customers will feel it in their hearts." Her gaze swept the table, meeting the eyes of each of her staff members in turn. She gave a quick nod and then clapped her hands. "Let's go back in there and show them how great food can taste!"

I spent the next few hours glued to the stool in the corner of the kitchen, watching Edel's people work. For a new staff, they came together amazingly well. The restaurant was nonstop busy, but from what I could see, all the customers seemed to get a meal and pretty much what they'd ordered.

When the madness ebbed around nine thirty, I edged around the kitchen, watching the workers at each of the stations, from Rodrigo, the dark-skinned dishwasher who seemed to speak only Spanish, to the female pastry chef piping whipped-cream designs on her key lime parfaits, to the head sous-chef, who did his best to keep distance between himself and Edel since the scolding about the ruined sauce and the chunky carrots. For her part, Edel had shifted from irate to professional, flitting from station to station with suggestions, instructions, and even a few compliments . . .

Every half hour or so, Edel exited the kitchen to

make the rounds of the front of the restaurant, where her friends and invited guests were dining. I tasted whatever was offered to me and found every item delicious. Even the signature vegetarian dish—Edel's takeoff on the more commonplace Key West shrimp and grits, only without the shrimp—which I would not have thought to order—was stunning. Lightly stir-fried vegetables—small carrot coins, bright green spears of broccoli, wedges of red onion, and purple radishes—served over cheesy polenta and garnished with golden Parmesan crisps were sublime.

I was perched back on the stool near the grill when Edel came tearing in from the dining room, barreling toward Mary Pat at the salad-prep counter and brandishing a white plate.

She slammed down the plate and the salad flew over the counter. A few pieces stuck to Mary Pat's apron and a shred of carrot clung to her cheek. "What kind of dressing did you use on this?"

"That's our standard mixed-green salad with the house vinaigrette." She swiped the carrot off her face and flung it to the floor.

"Take a whiff," Edel said. "Does it smell like balsamic and olive oil to you?"

Mary Pat picked the plate up and sniffed. "Something smells a little off." She crossed the aisle to the station where the vinaigrette had been made, picked up a large bottle of oil, and sniffed that, too. Looking puzzled, she lifted her shoulders. "There's something different—this doesn't smell like olive oil. But I made it exactly the same way as I did yesterday and the day before and the day before that. You told us no variations. You said people want to know what they're getting."

"It doesn't smell like olive oil because, dammit, it's peanut oil." Edel's voice had risen to a shriek. "You understand that this could ruin me, right?"

"But I didn't use peanut oil." Mary Pat hurried to the pantry and hauled out an enormous white plastic bottle of oil. She unscrewed the cap and took a whiff, then passed it to Edel, who had the red face of someone on the verge of stroke.

"Peanut oil here, too. You can clock out right now," Edel told her. "I'll let you know whether to come in tomorrow." Her hands shook as she picked up the jug of oil and carried it back into the pantry. When she didn't come out for several minutes, I poked my head in.

"Is the taste between the two oils so different? I suspect most people won't even notice the difference," I said, knowing I shouldn't butt in, but hoping to calm her down. Her reaction to the salad dressing had seemed severe. Possibly even paranoid.

Edel stared at me and then shook her head slowly. "It's *peanut* oil. One of the customers felt his lips begin to swell and itch and so he asked the server to remove the salad. He's highly allergic to peanuts and he knows what happens when he eats anything containing them— he's suffered several trips to the emergency department."

I nodded with sympathy.

"All I need is one case of anaphylactic shock in my customer base when I've insisted that we don't use nuts in our mirepoix. Or in our pastry cream. Or especially not in our vinaigrette. We don't chop nuts on the same cutting surface; we don't even use the same pans. I put all this in writing on the bottom of every menu— *we will tell you if we use nuts in a dish. We are scrupulously careful about our customers with allergies.* And yet somehow"—she swabbed the perspiration off her face with the back of her hand—"somehow someone substituted peanut oil in every dish we cooked tonight."

"Every dish?"

"All the oil in here smells like peanuts."

"But wouldn't your chefs have noticed the bottles?" I asked.

"I'm saying someone poured out the canola and olive oil and replaced it with peanut. Sabotage, pure and simple."

She sank onto a stool, a twin to the one on which I'd spent most of the night, watching the buzz in the kitchen.

"We should talk about your staff, how long you've known them—"

"Not tonight," Edel snapped. Her head drooped and she buried her face in her hands.

5

*So many relationships have been ended by
metal utensils in nonstick.*
—Nicole Cliffe

My psychologist friend, Eric, had insisted on picking me up and driving me out to the golf course on Stock Island, once he heard my tirade against my mother and her crazy plans, my second cousin and her professional golf career, and wasting a day by humiliating myself with a game I couldn't bear to watch and had no interest in playing.

"I can see you'll need a personal shrink on board today," he said, laughing as I waited for him to unlock his Conch car, a convertible Mustang painted with undersea and other tropical scenes by a local Key West artist.

"Since when do you play golf?" I asked, flouncing into the passenger's seat and clipping on my belt.

"I caddied as a kid," Eric said. "They let us caddies play for nothing on Mondays when the course was closed for maintenance. Sometimes the pro would come out with us and give us tips."

"Did you like the job?" I asked, a note of disbelief, and, yes, horror in my voice. "I thought you preferred your adventures in your mind."

Eric laughed. "Oh there was plenty of mental adventure to be had. You need to be something of a psychologist to carry clubs for rich guys playing a tough course. I never could understand why they expected to be good at something when they spent so little time working at it. Lots of them thought that with the right cutting-edge equipment and the right caddie, they'd be brilliant. But golf doesn't work like that."

We crossed over the bridge to Stock Island, and Eric took a left at the first light. This road leads to just about all the landmarks of Stock Island—the sheriff's department, the county prison (which also serves as a local jail), the community college, the animal shelter, the Quonset hut–style homeless shelter, Mount Trashmore (aka the dump), and the Key West golf course. Where else in the world would golfers share space with gators, egrets, prisoners, and homeless folks? Eric pulled into the farthest space in the golf club's parking lot, to minimize the chances for scratches and dents on his hand-painted car. My mouth felt dry and I fought to keep from hyperventilating.

He patted my knee. "Remember, you can't expect anything of yourself if you've never played." He glanced over at me and frowned. "It's not so much about the golf, is it?"

I yawned, trying to relax my jaw and pull in some air.

"Cassie?" he nudged.

I nodded. "I've only met her a couple of times. The last was the worst."

"What happened?"

"I was maybe ten, still loved playing with Barbies.

Mom had given me Barbie's Dream Kitchen that Christmas." I sighed, remembering the excitement and pleasure. "The package was wrapped in green polka-dotted paper with a big red bow. It was under the tree for almost a week. When my parents weren't in the room, I'd shake the box until the little timer chimed. I couldn't wait to open it." I grinned. "No surprise I'm in the food business, right? The kitchen had a little pink oven and a pink stove, and somehow it all smelled like chocolate-chip cookies. It came with miniature cake mixes and pans, and Mom had sewed me a little apron that looked exactly like Barbie's. I was so excited to show my big cousin everything." I lapsed into silence, remembering the acute embarrassment that had followed.

"But?"

"But she was sixteen, way past dolls. And not the least bit interested in pretending to make cakes. She looked at the kitchen for about two minutes and then spent the rest of the visit hitting golf balls into the woods behind the house. My father was ultra impressed with her focus. *'You need to find your passion. And then work at it like your cousin. You don't want to turn out like your mother. Making dinner is not a career.'*"

"He said that?"

"Yup, that's what he told me. They were on the verge of a divorce, only she didn't see it." My voice trembled and I took another deep breath. "I didn't, either."

"There was a lot more going on that day than a visit from Cassie," Eric said. "You sensed that something ugly was brewing between your parents. All that angst got associated with your cousin's visit."

I grimaced and flounced out of the car. "Thank you, Doctor. She could have at least pretended to be interested in my kitchen. It was really very cool."

He laughed and got out of the car, then popped the trunk and fished out a set of golf clubs in a red plaid bag.

"You own golf clubs?"

Before he could answer, a text message came in from my mother.

Tell everyone that I moved the dinner reservation up to seven so Cassie and Joe can see the cat man before we eat.

I groaned. This was turning into the day that would not die.

We headed toward the clubhouse, an inviting white building with a metal roof, green shutters, and rocking chairs on its wide covered porch. "Suppose I wait for you all here? You can pick me up when you're finished playing."

He poked me in the back. "Let's go. This will be good for you. What if you marry a guy who loves golf and you have all this baggage around it? This outing will help you decathect from the game, but in a good way."

I bugged my eyes at him. "Decathect from the game? If you say so."

The pro behind the counter set me up with a battered bag of rental clubs and half a dozen balls, and Eric loaded my pockets with tees, plastic ball markers, and two stubby pencils. We began to argue about the need for golf shoes, which would have involved shelling out sixty dollars for saddle shoes with plastic spikes on the soles that I never would have worn again. Ever. My cousin and her husband arrived in the shop.

"Ix-nay on the hideous shoes," I hissed at Eric, then turned to hug Cassie. We assured each other how great it was to meet again; then I introduced the men.

"Eric has a therapy practice here in Key West," I said. "And Joe Lancaster is a sports psychologist on the LPGA tour."

"Specializing in my neurotic brain," Cassie said with a laugh. "When we started working together, I was definitely sliding downhill fast toward a job as an assistant pro on a nine-hole course."

"You weren't that bad," Joe said, tousling her hair. "Your mind was on a lot of things besides golf."

The men began to chat like old pals while we stood by awkwardly. Cassie looked smaller and less imposing than I remembered—shorter than me by a couple of inches, her brown curls streaked with blond, her body muscular and tanned. She was athletic like a pacing jaguar, not pudgy and soft like an indoor house cat. Like me.

"Are you guys ready? They want us on the tee in ten minutes," Cassie said. She glanced at my rental bag, and then began to paw through the clubs. "Looks like they've set you up with some antiques."

"It won't really matter," I said. "Apparently Janet failed to mention that I don't play at all." I never call my mother by her first name unless I'm truly annoyed with her. This nightmare qualified; the closer we got to the first hole, the tighter I felt.

"Don't worry about it," said Joe. "Just swing a few times to advance the ball. If you start to slow the foursome down, pick your ball up and drop it on the green. No one's worried about scoring today, anyway."

How did I explain that it wasn't slow play I was worried about, it was making zero contact with the ball and looking like a fool? I'd been the kind of girl who was chosen last on every schoolyard team—T-ball, volleyball, soccer, field hockey. Cassie, I was certain, would have been first. Probably ahead of most of the boys.

I was hoping to ride with Eric, but Joe loaded my bag on the back of Cassie's cart. "It makes more sense for you women to ride together. Not that Cassie will be playing from the ladies' tee." Joe laughed. "But I'm dying to hear about Eric's practice, and I know you girls have years to catch up on."

Behind Joe's back, I made googly eyes at Eric and then shrugged. "Sure."

If such a thing was possible, the first hole went even worse than I had feared. After Joe, Cassie, and Eric had teed off, I grabbed my rental driver out of the bag. It had an enormous silver-and-blue head, with THE TERMINATOR written along the length of the shaft. I stood on the tee, feeling dizzy and helpless.

"Hold it like a baseball bat and swing nice and easy," Joe said.

After three whiffs, I hit the ball. It caromed off at a ninety-degree angle and smacked the golf cart where my cousin waited. "Sorry!" I yelped.

"No problem," she said, faking a smile.

By the time we reached the first green, I'd had enough. I'd been forced to play dodgeball back in grade-school gym class, but I didn't have to do this.

"I'm done playing," I said, jamming the Terminator into my bag. "I'll drive the cart the rest of the round." No one argued.

I tried to distract myself from that failure by noticing little bits of nature. Fat ducks waddled along the fairway, then took off in formation, as if to find their winter "V." I hugged the cart path, which ran not two feet from someone's condo. A rosemary plant flourished in a pot on the porch. Next to the steps sprawled a stand of mother-in-law's tongue that would have been a showcase houseplant back home.

On the third hole, which paralleled Route One, I parked in the shade of a coconut palm. The other three walked to the tee. By now I'd calmed down enough to realize that I wasn't the only one having trouble. In a soothing, low voice, Joe began to list the thoughts Cassie should and should not allow into her mind before she swung.

"Remember, think while you're at the driving range, but just feel on the tee," he told her. "Soft hands and let it flow."

She teed up a ball and took a vicious cut. Her ball sailed out almost longer than I could see, then bent to the right, careened over the chain-link fence, and headed toward the highway.

"Wow," said an astonished voice from the bushes on the other side of the fence. "She whacked the hell out of that one." A weathered figure in faded jeans and an old baseball cap with a fish on it emerged from the palmettos, a cigarette in one hand and a beer in the other. My homeless friend, Tony. He did a double take when he recognized me. "Hayley? What the hell are you doing out here?"

"Good question," I muttered, and waved him to silence.

Eric dropped back a few yards to stand with me while Cassie and Joe discussed how she was holding the club. "Strong thumb," "backspin," "closed face," "upright stance," "lateral movement"—their voices grew louder and the lingo more foreign—a language I didn't know and didn't care to learn.

"She's got a little glitch in her game," Eric whispered. "Joe was hoping that playing a casual round on a strange course would help her settle down."

"Not sure that's working out so good," Tony piped up.

Cassie turned around, glaring at Tony. He lifted his brown bottle in salute and winked. She stalked down the fairway. Eric hurried to his cart to pick up Joe, and the men followed her.

"Nice going, Tony," I said, but couldn't resist snickering. "Guess I'd better go get her."

"Wait," he said. "What the hell's going on with the Bistro on the Bight?"

I turned back to him, my face guarded. I was sure Edel Waugh wouldn't welcome gossip among the Key West homeless. "What do you know about it?"

"This week I've been swinging by the kitchen at the end of the evening. A couple of the staff are good guys. They hand out leftovers that didn't sell but won't keep." He coughed and then dragged on his cigarette. "That lady can cook. Even better than my ex."

All the times I'd chatted with Tony over the past year, I hadn't thought about him having an ex. Or a job or a house or kids. Hadn't considered what twists in his life might have led him to drinking beer in the palmetto bushes before noon. Eric whistled and waved to me from the fairway ahead.

"And last night?" I asked.

"Last night I didn't get a single bite. Rodrigo, the dishwasher, he told us the boss made them throw everything out. Even the chicken and rice dish with sausage and shrimp." His stomach gurgled as if in protest and he put a hand to his belly. "I was looking forward to that ever since I read it on the menu."

"Peanut oil," I said, and scrabbled through my golf bag's pocket until I found the granola bar I'd stashed there for emergencies. I handed that and an apple over the fence to Tony.

"Gotta go," I said. "Will you let me know what you hear? You have my phone number, right?" He nodded, and I drove off.

After nine holes, we visited the clubhouse to use the restrooms and grab drinks and snacks. An apple and almonds for Cassie; a hot dog, a Coke, and peanut M&M's for Eric and me. Then I changed my mind and ordered a Miller Lite and picked up a glazed doughnut with hideous pink icing and multicolored sprinkles from a box lying open on one of the tables.

"You eat like Cassie used to," Joe said with a strained laugh.

We motored down the tenth hole toward the water tower and heard dogs yapping from the animal shelter just past the green. Cassie grabbed her putter and rolled her head from one shoulder to the other, trying to work out some tension. She yelped and pointed to something moving in a tall pine. "What the heck is that?"

"Iguanas," said Eric. "Wait until you see them on the sixteenth green. It's like they think that pond is their personal beach."

"Eric was telling me a little about the new restaurant on the harbor and how you're trying to lend a hand to the chef," said Joe to me, when they came off the green. "You know, Cassie was quite a sleuth back in the day."

"I wouldn't exactly call myself a sleuth," I said.

"What do you call a lady who solves four murders and counting?" Eric asked, and they both laughed. "The culinary Miss Marple."

"Not funny," I said.

"The Nancy Drew of the foodie set?"

I made a slashing motion across my neck.

Cassie really looked at me for the first time all day. "It's not fun, finding the dead. But how can you look the other way? Sometimes the professionals who are supposed to be solving the crimes don't care about these people as much as they should. And sometimes a person outside the criminal justice profession has a knack for noticing things that other folks don't see."

"But in the end, all this murder stuff messed with

her mind," Joe said. "She even started to think I was after her." He grinned.

"Not funny," Cassie said, a flash of anger in her eyes.

Before I could thank her for understanding or ask about her experience, she stomped off toward the next tee. A flock of curlews took off in front of us, wailing a mournful cry.

6

A cook is a man with a can opener. A chef is an artist.

—Georges Auguste Escoffier

We filed onto the shuttle boat for Sunset Key at the dock outside the Westin resort. The night was perfect for dinner on the beach—warm, with a star-studded sky, and a breeze strong enough to ruffle hair but not to blow out candles.

"What a glorious evening," my mother said, and then to Cassie: "I'm so glad you're here. Since your father refuses to leave California, I'd have to fly to the West Coast and make a tee time at his golf course in order to see him." She squeezed Cassie's hand and flashed a brilliant smile.

"Apologies for him—he's constitutionally unable to relax," Cassie said with a grin. "My focus didn't come from nowhere," she added. "I'll tell Dad you miss him." A large yacht motored by and she clutched her stomach as our boat pitched in its wake.

"Almost there!" my mother sang out. "Even people with the weakest stomachs can make it to Sunset Key.

There's nothing else like it near Key West—a ten-minute ride but you'll feel as though you're in another world." She turned to Eric. "How was your golf game today?"

"Great fun," he said. "Cassie gave all of us tips and saved me about fifteen strokes around the green." He refused to meet my eyes. No amount of tips would have helped me today. In fact, any minuscule natural talent I might have started the round with had been squeezed out by an accumulation of tension and resentment twenty minutes later.

I flounced off the boat before the rest of the gang and trotted up the gangway toward the restaurant as fast as my tired legs could take me. This island is as manicured and sedate as Key West is noisy and raunchy. For Christmas, garlands of greenery studded with red bows and twinkling with tiny white lights had been looped around the handrails that bordered the ramp. Manufactured beauty is not usually my style, but the night was ideal for eating outside. And aside from the deck at Louie's Backyard, Sunset Key has to be the most beautiful setting in the county.

I stopped at the receptionist's stand. "We have a reservation for eight. In the name of Snow?"

The brunette behind the podium tapped on her computer screen, then nodded and smiled. "We saved a table as close to the water as you can be without getting your feet wet. Is the rest of your party here?"

I smiled, jerked a thumb behind me, and rolled my eyes a little. "They're coming—you can't miss 'em."

As my gang clattered in, giddy and boisterous, I spotted a small woman with corkscrew curls and bright pink cheeks alone at the bar. Edel? I followed my group to the table.

"Thank you so much," my mother said to the hostess. "This is stunning. Now, let's see. Joe should sit next to Sam and Bill so they can get acquainted. And Cassie right here in between me and Miss Gloria." She patted the seat beside her with the best view of the open sea and the stars winking over the water. The torches around the edges of the patio flickered softly.

"I think Edel Waugh is at the bar," I muttered to my mother. "I'm going over to say hello. Order me a glass of Albariño or Sauvignon Blanc when the waitress comes around?"

"See if she'll come over and say hello," Mom begged. "I'm dying to meet her."

I shrugged. "I'll try." I wove among the other tables and went inside. Edel was slumped on her stool, both elbows on the bar. Looking like maybe she didn't want company. But too late, she had spotted me.

"Beautiful night," I said, patting her shoulder. "I'm surprised to see you here."

"Monday," said Edel. "We're closed on Mondays," she added. "Or we will be. Even though we haven't officially opened, I needed a few hours off before the opening-night madness."

She picked up her empty highball glass and signaled the bartender. "Hit me again, Glenfiddich and soda. And something for my friend here, too."

I shook my head. "Can't stay. I'm here with some friends and family—"

"They'll wait," Edel said. "What will you have?" Before I could protest again or even answer, she turned to the bartender, a thin woman with a long black braid and perfectly shaped eyebrows. "Make her one of your Bloody Marys. Good vodka and kick-ass spicy.

"Sorry about the big scene in the kitchen yesterday about the peanut oil," she continued, swiveling back to me. "I warned you there has been some excitement. But I'm sorry I lost it." She crooked a half smile.

I nodded and climbed onto the stool. "Do you have any theories about what happened?"

"Not really," she said, her chin sinking to her palm. "I can't imagine anyone—my ex-husband excepted—who has it in for me." The bartender exchanged her empty glass for a full one, and Edel took a swig. Then she held her glass up and tapped it on the Bloody Mary that had been delivered to me. "*Sláinte*. To your health."

I sipped my drink, which was the right kind of spicy—just this side of singeing my throat as it went down. "You were right. This is delicious. Is your ex in town?"

"He wouldn't be caught dead in this backwater. Any place with a population under a million isn't worth his bother." She swigged an inch of Scotch, shook the glass until the ice cubes clattered, and then drank again. "I'm not worth his bother, either."

I thought of the discussion on the golf course earlier this afternoon and Cassie's question about whether Edel had brought staff with her or hired them new from the Key West pool. "I know your head waiter, Leo, came down from New York. How about the other staff?" I asked. "Are they locals?"

Edel sighed. "My sous-chef is from New York. I've worked with him for ages. Most of the others we found here."

"Would all of them have had access to the pantry?"

"I suppose anyone could have come in early without getting noticed. As you saw, the place was a madhouse. We have to settle this," Edel said, her words beginning to slur. "I cannot have negativity in my kitchen. I cannot have staff members who are against me—or even neutral. They need to be playing on the team, not hooting on the sidelines." She plucked an ice cube from her glass and began to chew it. "I'm probably doomed.

Somebody wants to ruin my business before it even takes off."

"Maybe it was an honest mistake," I said, trying to sound a hopeful note. "But shouldn't you call the cops if you really think it was sabotage?"

Edel straightened on her barstool, her eyes glassy and her cheeks burning. "No cops. Period. I can't risk bad press right now. This opening is too important. It's hard enough to be a woman in this business—I don't need press that paints me as hysterical and paranoid. It's not like other businesses, where bad press is better than no press. Bad reviews here turn diners stone-cold. But you know that. You've done it to restaurants yourself."

I opened my mouth to defend myself. And say what? In the end, she was right. I hated writing negative reviews. Hated it. But as Wally reminded me, it was part of the job. If I didn't have the stomach to tell the truth when it needed telling, my words would be worth nothing.

My mother appeared on the other side of Edel, grinning from ear to ear. She thrust her hand out. "I'm Janet Snow, Hayley's mother. I'm so thrilled to meet you in person. We trekked into the city from New Jersey for many special occasions at your restaurant. I can still taste your lobster thermidor." She closed her eyes and patted her stomach, then clapped her hands together, startling both of us. "I simply can't wait for Bistro on the Bight to open."

"Mom's a foodie," I told Edel apologetically. "She's working for one of the local caterers for the season."

"Pleased to meet you," said Edel, looking a little shell-shocked, which wasn't unusual for a person hit by the whirlwind that is my mother. "Our menu here is not so classically French."

"You could prepare dog food and I bet it would be delicious," Mom said, and then added to me: "Sorry to interrupt, but the natives are getting restless. And we didn't dare order the main courses without you. Would you care to join us for dinner?" my mother asked Edel. "Absolutely my treat."

"Thanks, but no," Edel said, as she slid off the stool. "I was on my way out." She leaned over to whisper to me. "No cops. Will you come tomorrow?" Her eyes glittered. "I need someone looking out for me."

"I'll be right over," I told my mother, and gave her a gentle push back toward our table on the beach. I considered Edel's request for a moment. Hadn't I already crossed the line from food critic to amateur investigative reporter? Why act as though I was half in? Why ruin her dream to try to salvage my own neck? "What time?"

"Four o'clock?" Once Edel had hugged me and staggered off, I returned to my tablemates. Seven sets of curious eyes stared at me.

"I hope you don't mind," Mom said finally, when I offered no explanation for my absence. "I chose some appetizers for the table. The lobster bisque—that's their signature, so a must-try, the burrata cheese, the Sunset Key shrimp, the duo of tuna, and the beef carpaccio."

"Perfect," I said. "Sorry to hold things up."

"Is everything all right?" Mom asked.

"I think it will be. She's stressed out by her opening—putting a lot of pressure on herself."

"Did you see the article in the *New York Times* last week?" Mom asked. "All about whether women chefs are not getting the press they deserve. Some men claim they aren't getting attention because they don't deserve it."

"That's ridiculous," I snapped. "She's a genius in the kitchen."

"And no press probably means fewer investors," Eric said.

"I'm sure she worries about that," I said. "Besides wanting to cook and serve the best food ever, she's got to keep the people backing her happy."

"It's pretty much like that in the golf world, too," Cassie said, straightening in her chair.

"The prizes and the TV coverage for the men's tour are much, much larger than those on the LPGA tour," Joe added.

"How's life going out there?" Sam asked. He pantomimed a golf swing, holding his fork like a club.

Cassie managed a smile. "I won't complain. No matter how hard it is, tons of girls would give anything to take my place."

Joe took her hand and rotated her diamond ring around her finger. "She's very modest. She won two tournaments this past season and tied for second and third in two others. But the rookies on the tour are younger and younger. And many come from Korea or Japan and barely speak English, though they've played all their lives. Things seem a lot different from when we began."

Cassie nodded and pulled her hand out of Joe's grip. "I'll say. The girls I started out with—Kate Golden, Donna Andrews, Lisa Hackney Hall—are retired for the most part. Poor Lisa fell apart for a while and lost her momentum when her mind took over her swing." She looked around the table. "She had to work really hard to get it back. People wonder how hard it can be to swing a golf club."

"Plenty hard," Joe said, and tucked a strand of hair behind her ear. The tension in her shoulders gave way a little.

"I suppose it's challenging at the top of any profession," Eric said. "Although not always as physical as golf."

"And all that traveling," Sam said.

"It's got to be murder on the girls who want to start a family," Mom added.

Cassie said nothing. The waiter arrived with our appetizers and placed them in the center of the table. We began to sample them and I made notes as I ate. The house-made burrata was fresh and light—unlike any other mozzarella cheese I'd eaten in the Keys. As I took my first spoonful of rich bisque, I noticed a woman lurching through the other tables toward ours. Edel.

"The Bistro's on fire," she said in a panicked whisper, holding up her phone and blasting me with a whoosh of alcohol-sodden breath. She definitely shouldn't be driving.

"Oh, honey, no!" said my mother, starting to rise out of her chair. "Can I—"

"Let me handle it," I told Mom. And to Edel: "I'll run you over there. My scooter is parked right near the dock." I stood up and turned to my mother. "Take some notes on the rest of the food?"

Then Edel and I hurried toward the dock and its waiting tender.

7

Oh please don't go—we'll eat you up—we love you so!
    —Maurice Sendak, *Where the Wild Things Are*

The sound of sirens, the whoosh of a crackling fire, and the smell of charred wood overwhelmed us as I roared up Caroline Street toward the harbor, Edel clutching my waist. I took a quick right past the Key Lime Pie Factory, decorated like a gingerbread house for the holiday season, the words from the owner's canned advertisement blaring from the television on the outside wall. A dull orange glow came into view and Edel's breathing grew faster.

"Oh god, please don't let it burn down," she moaned.

A police car, lights flashing, was parked catty-corner across the street, and a uniformed officer waved us away. Edel sprang off the back of the scooter as soon as I rolled to a stop.

"You can't go down there, miss!" the cop yelled. But she dodged around him and kept running. He barked into the radio clipped to his shoulder—a rat-a-tat-tat of

cursing and then something about the madwoman barreling toward the fire.

I dragged the scooter onto its stand on the sidewalk
near where the harbor's lit Christmas tree had been
constructed of ropes and buoys. When the officer
turned to yell at some other tourists, I darted after Edel,
down the dock that ran along Schooner Wharf and behind the old Waterfront Market. More police cruisers
and several fire trucks were already on the scene,
crowding as closely as they could to the alley leading
to Edel's restaurant. Beyond them, a circle of curious
spectators tried to push even nearer. Smoke swirled
thickly and I coughed and buried my nose in my sleeve.
A burglar alarm howled intermittently.

"Clear the area," hollered a muscular man in a gray
T-shirt and a police cap. "People, it's not safe here." He
blocked the way of a tall man who tried to push past him.
The man stumbled back, nearly falling over his golden
retriever. Down the alley behind the restaurant, firemen
in tan suits with orange stripes and yellow helmets wrestled with two enormous hoses, training fierce streams of
water onto the fire. I heard the sizzle of water meeting
flames, then saw a cloud of smoke and steam. Keeping
my mouth and nose covered, I edged around the perimeter of the fire zone, looking for Edel. She wasn't hard to
spot, tussling with two of Key West's finest.

"Ma'am, you can't go any closer." A burly cop
stepped in front of Edel, then grabbed her wrist as she
tried to duck around him. "You need to clear out."

"But it's my restaurant," she shouted.

He shook his head and nudged her back. I wormed
through the crowd to collect her and drew her back
from the hot cinders and billows of smoke that eddied
around the back of the restaurant. Tears welled in her
eyes as she watched.

"Listen. There's nothing you can do to help," I said. "You have to let them put it out."

My friend Lieutenant Steve Torrence materialized from the crowd and I waved him over.

"This is Edel Waugh," I told him, placing my hand on her shuddering back. "She's the owner."

"I need to get in there," she said, waving at the flames.

He gripped her shoulders, his eyes comforting but hands firm. "It's not safe to get closer. They're very skillful—they will get the fire under control. Why don't you ladies come with me and we'll see what we can find out?" He raised an eyebrow at me and I looped my arm through Edel's and half dragged her back to his cruiser. He settled the weeping chef in the passenger's seat, handed her a bottle of water and a box of tissues, and went off to consult with one of the firemen. I couldn't think of a thing to say that wouldn't come out like pablum. Finally her sobs slowed to hiccups.

Torrence returned some minutes later. "From what I can tell, I don't believe there will be serious damage to the restaurant. The fire seems to have started in the trash in the alley behind the kitchen—possibly in your storage shed. Your fence around the patio is probably totaled and the shed is, practically speaking, destroyed, but the building itself should be fine."

She slumped against the headrest. "Oh thank god." She took a deep breath and sank back, her eyelids fluttering closed. Then her eyes snapped open. "Who could have done this to me? I can't fail. I just can't."

Torrence motioned me a few steps away from the police car. "A friend of yours?"

I nodded. "New friend. I'm writing a piece on the restaurant for *Key Zest*." I paused, wondering how much to say. "She'll kill me for this, but you should know she's been worried about someone sabotaging her place."

His eyebrows drew together in one dark line. "What kind of sabotage? And who?"

"She doesn't know who. Things like changing the ingredients in her recipe bible."

Torrence looked puzzled.

"That's the book with instructions of everything they make in the restaurant. She's a fiend for wanting everything to come out the same each time they make it."

"Oh you mean a cookbook."

"Sort of. A cookbook on steroids. With a lot of extra instructions and anal details." I coughed as the wind gusted and thick, smoky air swirled around us. "And this might sound minor, but it's actually even worse, because it's dangerous: substituting peanut oil for canola. Which she only discovered when a diner's throat swelled after he ate his salad." I shrugged and looked down at the sidewalk. "She didn't want any cops involved. She's big on control. She likes to handle things herself."

"It's a little late for that now," he said, mopping his forehead with his sleeve. "What was she planning to do, run over with a garden hose and put the fire out herself? She should have told us. You should have told us. Someone could have been seriously injured. Or worse." He stomped back to the cruiser.

"Do you have any reason to believe this fire was not accidental?" he asked Edel.

"Are we going to be able to open as planned?" she fired back without answering his question. She'd pulled herself together, looking fierce now instead of sad.

"That is not our top priority," he said. "But I very much doubt it."

Her face flooded a deep red and she leaned in as if she was about ready to light into him. I melted away to give them some space, lurking at the edge of the crime-scene tape that now blocked the alley.

But what was I looking for? Shady characters carrying cans of gasoline? A familiar face from the restaurant, looking guilty?

Three firefighters went running toward the ruins of Edel's shed, shouting and waving. An ambulance tooted its horn in several mournful whoops, pushing through the crowds to the parking lot behind Edel's place. Torrence's radio crackled and he, too, ran down the alley, closer to the fire.

"What's wrong?" I yelled, trotting after him. He waved at me to back off.

The wind shifted; sounds of a band singing Buffett music floated over from one of the party boats on the harbor. And over top of the music and the clanking of hoses and the crowd, a man's voice yelled, "There's someone in the remains of the storage shed. Make room for the stretcher."

Edel's face went ash white.

More men came running. A gurney pushed by two firefighters was whisked into the back yard of Edel's restaurant and then out again, this time carrying a body wrapped in a silver space blanket.

As the ambulance roared off with the gurney and the body, Torrence finally returned to where we waited near his cruiser.

"Who was it?" Edel asked, her face pale and lips quivering.

Torrence just stared at her and shook his head.

"Can I go onto my property now?" she asked.

"Certainly not," he said. "They're looking for hot spots. Besides, it's considered a crime scene now—until we figure out exactly what happened. We'll need you to

come down to the police department in the morning
for follow-up questions."

"Who was it?" I asked, feeling stupid with shock.
And then: "Crime scene?"

He shook his head again. "We don't know yet."

"But were they all right?" Edel asked. She grabbed
his arm as if to shake him.

He detached himself from her grip. "Honestly, we'll
call you when we know something definite. Best thing
you can do is go home and get some rest."

When it became absolutely clear that she wouldn't be
allowed onto her property, nor would the cops give us
further information, I whisked her back to the Westin
boat dock, where she'd take the shuttle boat back to her
condo. My family and friends were just getting off the
Sunset Key tender with a crowd of tipsy diners.

"Is everything okay?" Mom called. "We were so
worried when you didn't text."

With a grim look on her face, Edel hurried past them
onto the boat without speaking.

"What in the world?" asked my mother, then turned
to me, her forehead creased in puzzled furrows.

"I'll tell you later," I said.

"You missed a great meal," said Miss Gloria. "We
packed some things up for you to try." She pointed to
a brown paper bag that Eric was carrying. Incredible
odors of grilled meat and fried onions and ginger
wafted up and I realized how ravenous I was.

Mom took a step closer to me and sniffed. "You
smell like smoke." She brushed the hair away from my
neck. "Come over to our place. You can eat something
and tell us what happened."

"Do you mind?" I asked Miss Gloria.

"The night is young," she sang out with a smile.

"We're headed home," said Eric. He leaned in to kiss

my cheek. "The dogs have been waiting for hours and I have an early appointment. Call me tomorrow?"

Within ten minutes, the rest of us were settled at my mother's kitchen table. Mom set out a plate of emergency cookies and put water on for tea, and I prepared to work my way through the leftovers.

"Eat first and make your notes," Mom said. "Then you can tell us. No matter what else is going on in her life, a food critic has to eat."

I took a few bites, then felt a wave of nausea that left me weak. I couldn't get the image of the body—wrapped in a silver blanket, lugged out of Edel's back yard and shuttled into the ambulance—out of my mind.

"The grouper was better piping hot," Mom said. "But isn't the texture of the coconut with the bok choy amazing? And I love the ginger-mango flavor—it's subtle, but it pops."

I shrugged, tried to smile, put my fork down on the plate.

"Tell us what happened," Mom said. She brought a mug of Red Zinger tea laced with honey to the table and reached for my hand. "It must have been bad. The way Edel looked— and now you."

I described the scene when we arrived, and how the fire had finally been extinguished, and how, in the end, Torrence had reassured Edel that it looked as though the damage was contained to the alley behind the restaurant's kitchen—the fence and the shed. "He wouldn't let her go anywhere near it—too dangerous. It was a mob scene there—a blazing wall of testosterone. Every firefighter and cop on the island must have showed up. And all those gawkers wanting to get closer."

"But then what?" Mom asked.

"Then they were checking to make sure the cinders

were out and they found a body in the storage shed out back. Anyway, I'm almost certain the person was dead."

Miss Gloria gasped. "Oh good lordy, lord. Not again!"

"Who was it?" Cassie asked.

I pushed my hair out of my eyes. "If they knew, they certainly weren't telling us."

"Had someone broken into the restaurant?" Joe asked.

"The alarm was blaring and there were glass shards all over the alley, but I can't be sure." I looked around the table, at the people I could trust with most anything. I hoped. "Edel's broken up, naturally." I bit my lip, paused a few seconds. "She thinks someone has it in for her new restaurant."

"What do you mean?" Cassie asked.

"Who, and why?" Mom asked, a beat later. "Does she think the fire and the death are related?"

"Lordy, lordy," said Miss Gloria. "That's a rhubarb!"

I shrugged. "If she knows who's involved, she isn't sharing it with me."

"Motives never really change." Joe ticked off the possibilities on his fingers. "Love, money, fear, greed, power. Does she think the attacks are personal? Or professional?"

"She hasn't said."

"To scare her? Or really do some damage?"

I shrugged again; it was becoming clearer and clearer how little I did know. "And why hurt her business?"

"Don't underestimate her competitors," Cassie said firmly. "Someone who's surging to the top is always going to be envied by the people she's barreled past. I can tell you from experience"—a look of sadness and anger crossed her face—"the envious can be vicious."

"Said from a woman who knows what it's like to be on top," Sam added with a grin.

He loved Cassie already. And I couldn't help feeling a twinge of envy myself. I wouldn't be surprised if he was out on the golf course with her by the end of the weekend. I wished I didn't care, but he'd begun to feel like another father figure to me. Being an only child, I wasn't the best at sharing.

Especially with someone whose first impulse was to clobber the competition to a pulp. I excused myself to head for home, and Mom walked me and Miss Gloria to the door.

"Have you spoken with Lorenzo lately?" she asked.

My favorite and almost always reliable tarot card reader.

I shook my head. "No. But I'm not sure I could face more bad news."

8

*I always think there's something rather
foreign about high spirits at breakfast.*
        —Mr. Carson, *Downton Abbey*

After spending more time than usual fixing my hair
and planning my outfit (how much could a girl do with
jeans and the yellow *Key Zest* shirt—who was I kidding?) in anticipation of seeing Wally, I went into work
early the next morning. I needed time to write up the
Latitudes review before Wally and Danielle arrived.
Writing a review based on takeout leftovers and my
family's opinions was not a restaurant reviewer's best
practice, but I didn't have the time or money to repeat
the visit. Besides, I had bigger worries—like holding
my job when my investigative-culinary-reporter piece
had disintegrated into arson and a hysterical chef. And,
worst of all, possibly murder.

Our office copy of the *Key West Citizen* lay on the
stoop, with a scary picture of Edel's restaurant fire
lighting up the night above the fold. I carried it up-
stairs, started a pot of coffee, and sat down to read.

KEY WEST DETECTIVE NATHAN BRANSFORD BAFFLED

BY APPARENT ARSON AT BISTRO ON THE BIGHT, the headline read. Below the fold was a photo of Bransford,
crouched at the entrance to the alley leading to the
restaurant, looking . . . hapless. He must have arrived
after Edel and I had left. I'd had a very brief romance
with the detective in question—long enough to realize
that he was utterly obsessed with his image and intent
on keeping it untarnished. He would go bananas when
he saw this headline.

I continued to read. No injuries had been reported.
Which did not exactly match what we'd seen at the site.
Did they have a reason to hide the discovery of the
body? Or had the victim survived without injury?
Considering the silver shroud I'd seen, I doubted that
outcome.

Investigators were looking for traces of accelerant,
and any witnesses to the fire were asked to come forward. The state fire marshal would be consulted. An
interview with the restaurant's chef/owner, Edel
Waugh, offered no comment on the fire, other than as-
suring future diners that she was pressing the police
department to allow the restaurant to open as planned.
On that, Bransford himself had no comment.

I poured a cup of coffee, added milk and sugar, and
retreated to my nook at the end of the hall to begin
writing. Forty-five minutes later, I had the bones of the
Latitudes piece roughed out, but my stomach was
growling so loudly I could barely think.

Then I Googled Edel Waugh's restaurant, Arnica, in
New York City's East Village. The critics were divided
into two camps: those who found the food to be inventive and delightful, and those who thought the restaurant tried too hard with its combination of cutting-edge
and classically French food.

I heard signs of life in the reception area and the coffeemaker began to gurgle again. Fingers and toes crossed that it was Danielle with doughnuts or pastries. She and I took turns launching, embracing, and abandoning diets, so we both welcomed the days when all good intentions failed.

I came down the hallway sniffing. "Do I smell doughnuts?"

Danielle grinned and flipped open the top of a big white box. "Right out of the deep fryer at the Glazed Donut. I figured Wally could use some cheering up. And you have never turned down fat, yeast, and sugar in the year I've known you."

I laughed, chose a plain glazed, and started to eat, savoring the sugary coating, nibbling the featherlight dough so it would last as long as possible. Hoping that way I wouldn't be tempted to reach for a second.

"And besides all that," Danielle said, but this time with a frown that she smoothed away as quickly as it appeared, "Ava's bringing in some possible investors this morning. I guess Wally forgot to tell you."

"Investors?" I grimaced. "I guess he did."

"Don't feel left out," Danielle said. "He's so worried about taking time away from his mom that it's been hard for him to focus. And Ava is pressuring him big-time about everything you can imagine."

As I popped the last bit of doughnut in my mouth and began to lick the sugary glaze off my fingers, Ava crashed into the office. Two people followed in her wake: a man in a gray suit, a starched white shirt, and a pink tie; and a woman with über-short, spiky red hair, high heels, and skintight black jeans. If she'd been a bird, she would have been a woodpecker.

Ava glanced at Wally's darkened window, the mini blinds still closed. She swung around to glare at Danielle. "He's not in yet?"

"He called. He'll be here in fifteen," Danielle chirped. "There's a jam on Roosevelt—apparently two cars and a scooter got tangled up. You know that narrow place where the road drops off—"

Ava tried to cut her off, but Danielle kept yakking.

"I brought doughnuts," she said to the two strangers. "And the coffee is fresh and hot. Let me get you settled in Wally's office." She flashed a two-dimple smile and they couldn't help smiling back. "Follow me."

Ava trailed after them, a sour-persimmon expression on her face. In Wally's office, Danielle flipped on the lights and set up the wooden TV trays that leaned against the wall. Then she brought in the doughnuts, arranged on a lacquered tray depicting a Winslow Homer seascape. "These are local—you actually watch them as they are lifted from the deep-fat fryer. The most adorable young couple owns the place. I chose some plain glazed, in case someone doesn't like the fancy flavors," she told the visitors. "But these others are key lime, chocolate, and a couple with maple frosting and candied bacon."

Bestowing another big smile on Ava's guests, she hurried back out to the front room to fetch their coffee.

"Let's get started," I heard Ava say, closing the blinds so we could no longer see into the office. I strained to hear the conversation. "Wally can catch up when he gets here. Our readership has exploded over the past six months," she explained.

Which I'd certainly never heard her say to me. Whenever I'd sat in staff meetings with Ava, she'd only complained about drooping numbers and receding shares of the marketplace.

"I realize that it's not fashionable to move from online to print," she continued, "but this is an unusual community and we have an unusual opportunity. We get a population of visitors who would gladly pay for a classy guide to what's what on the island."

"What's your competition?" asked the woodpecker lady.

"The Sunday living section of the local newspaper was dropped entirely this past year," Ava said. "It was called Solares Hill, named after the highest point on the island. It turned out not to be such a high point after all."

"Which might be interpreted as the last gasp of print," said the man in the suit.

"I don't think so," Ava said. I could picture her wagging a finger. She hates to be contradicted. "I think it points to a failure of their imagination. There are other weekly newsies, but not of the quality we intend to produce. Of course, we intend to make some changes in our staff. I can assure you that you'll see a higher level of professionalism."

"How many staff do you have currently?"

"Wally, myself, and two three-quarter timers. My vision is to hire three half-time people, which eliminates our obligation to provide benefits."

The woman murmured a question that I couldn't make out.

"Our staff has gotten lazy," Ava said, and now I could picture the curl in her lip. "But imagine if we pruned the deadwood, leaving us with three part-time writers pitching ideas against each other. The creative juices would definitely surge."

I sank lower in my chair, wishing I could creep back to my office but afraid to draw Ava's attention—and her ire. Danielle made monkey faces to try to cheer me up, aping Ava's thin lips and overplucked brows.

We heard quick steps on the stairs and Wally burst into the office.

"Crap," he said. "Traffic was a nightmare. Are they already here?"

"Ava's busy poisoning them," Danielle said in a soft voice. "She's pretty much already promised to fire us. We need you in there." She placed a steaming mug in his hands and he marched into his office.

"I'm Wally Beile. So sorry to hold you up. I want you to meet our other staff. If you stay around for the parade tonight, you'll see them dressed as elves." He stepped back out of his cubicle and motioned for us. "That's one way of saying they are flexible and fun-loving, along with being supremely talented."

With a hand on each of our backs, he pushed us into the room. "Danielle is our administrative assistant. She's the brains of the organization and she knows Key West in and out, as she's lived here forever. She makes a mean cup of coffee and she has her finger on the pulse of the pastry business on the island." He gestured at the plate of doughnuts, and Danielle waved.

"I can't help it," she said. "It's a gift. I have a nose for sugar and fat." Everyone laughed, except for Ava.

"Hayley Snow is our food critic," Wally said. "She has a finely tuned palate and she's a fabulous writer—a combination that doesn't come along very often. And she's flexible and fast. She can write about anything, not just food. She wrote a piece on the Hemingway cats last spring that made a major splash in the annual Sunshine State Awards for professional journalists—in their features division. Trust me, it's difficult to break in there."

"Thanks, boss," I said, blushing. "I love my job."

"What are you working on now?" asked the woodpecker woman.

"This morning I roughed out a review on Latitudes, an upscale restaurant on Sunset Key. Later today, I'm planning to visit Kojin, the noodle shop on Southard

Street, which is more down-market but with amazing Vietnamese food. I try to alternate fancy places with street food so there's something for everyone. My motto on reviews is *tough but fair*."

Ava looked up from her iPad mini and snorted, but Wally was nodding so I kept going.

"I'm also doing some research on a piece about a new restaurant opening later this week. The chef was highly regarded in New York City, so it's actually quite a coup to have her here."

"What kind of food?" asked the suited man.

"She owned a restaurant in New York with her husband. The menu was cutting-edge—a mix of classical French and molecular gastronomy, but on steroids. I think that was her ex's influence—he trained with Thomas Keller and Grant Achatz. He wanted to cook like them, only become more famous and land farther out there with his menu. In any case, now that she's local, the chef is cooking food that's a bit homier and with a Caribbean flair. It should be comfortable for folks who don't necessarily want a fine-dining experience. Not everyone is interested in dishes that challenge them."

The woodpecker lady smiled—I would have picked her for foie gras delivered in a steaming tube, but maybe she was mac and cheese all the way. I kept my gaze focused on her and continued to blab.

"In fact, I tried the spaghetti Bolognese that the chef made for her staff dinner, and, to my mind, it would rival the dish any Italian grandmother could prepare." I saw instantly from the look on Ava's face that I had stepped in it. How could I explain why I'd been eating dinner with Edel's staff without coming across as supremely unprofessional?

A loud banging sounded on the outside office door

and I thought for a moment that I was saved. Danielle hurried out to answer.

"I need to speak with Hayley Snow," said a familiar deep voice. "I'm Detective Bransford from the Key West police."

9

All the stories that had made me apprehensive about the restaurant business were true: the grueling hours, burns and cuts, screaming chefs, coming home greasy and stinking of fish. But I also acquired a skill that I had sorely lacked my entire life: I learned how to suck it up.

—Ivan Orkin, *Ivan Ramen*

The chatter died and all eyes turned to me. "Excuse me," I said, and bolted out of Wally's office. "What do you want?" I hissed at Bransford.

He narrowed his eyes and glanced at the gathering in the office. "Where can we talk privately?"

"My office." Which was a cubicle, really—much closer quarters than would feel comfortable to be jammed up with him. But at least it had a door that closed—an advantage, given that my bosses and our potential investors were fifteen feet down the hall. Wally and the others gawked as we trooped by.

I pointed to the folding chair by my tiny window. The colored Christmas lights we'd installed last week blinked cheerfully, a blue, a red, and a green dolphin leaping in succession. Once Bransford sat, I perched on my desk and shut the door, feeling slightly claustrophobic. I could smell his aftershave—or shampoo, maybe?—a lime and coconut blend that I didn't recognize. His ex-wife had probably chosen it to mark her territory. He, on the other hand, could probably smell my fear.

"I've been trying to reach you," he said.

"I was in a staff meeting. I didn't have my phone with me because it was the kind of meeting that might make or break your job," I added, pointing to the phone, which I'd left on the desk. I had a bad habit of reading e-mail and texting while half listening to Ava, which she despised. But that little bit of distraction kept me from wanting to leap out of my chair and strangle her. "What's up?"

He sighed heavily. "As you may be aware, our arson investigators found a body in the shed behind the restaurant last night. At this point, although the investigation isn't complete, the fire does not look accidental. And that suggests we may well be dealing with a murder."

Which confirmed my worst fears. And then the real meaning of the news punched me a little harder. "My god, who was killed? What happened? How did they end up in the burning building?"

"I thought perhaps you could help us answer that. Ms. Waugh is down at the station right now, being questioned again. But I'd like to hear your side of things."

He stared me down, like I was responsible for the uptick in Key West crime over the past twelve months. Which it did feel like sometimes, if I was completely honest.

"I wouldn't say that I have a side," I said softly, hoping he'd lower his volume too. Hoping Ava and company couldn't hear the conversation through the flimsy hollow door.

Bransford frowned. "Let me say it another way. Why were you at the fire last night? And what is your relationship with Ms. Waugh?"

Breathe in, breathe out, I told myself. I hadn't done a thing wrong, no matter how his questions made me feel.

"Edel asked me to help her watch over things at her restaurant a little. She seemed to be anticipating trouble during this opening. And she'd heard that I'm nosy." I snorted with laughter, hoping he'd join me. Hoping that the tension would ease out of the room like a boiling pot removed from the burner. But he didn't.

"Did you not consider reporting the trouble to the police before it got this serious?"

"That's something you should ask her," I huffed. "Were you thinking I should report every curdled cream sauce in every kitchen I visit? There's a big difference between sabotaging a meal and setting fire to the restaurant and killing someone."

I felt claustrophobic and physically uncomfortable perched on my desk, the corner pressing into my flesh. But it would be hard to adjust my position without bumping into Bransford. He was doing the man thing—spreading his knees as if anyone else in the room would accommodate him. Or maybe it was a police thing. Either way I felt crowded and sweaty. I grabbed a tissue from the box on my desk and wiped my face.

"How well do you know Ms. Waugh?" he asked, after a pause.

Which was actually a very good question. "I met her

three days ago—that's it. But I like her very much—
even though she's a bit prickly. And her food is amazing." I tapped my fingers on the desk. "My mother ate
at her restaurant in New York City many times. It's
hard to stand out in that city, and yet she and her husband managed to do it."

"Her husband?" Bransford asked.

I gulped, wishing I could learn to filter my words
before I blurted them out. "They're no longer together.
This is her solo restaurant. He's not in Key West. As far
as I know."

"Tell me about the sabotage she claimed to be experi-
encing," he said, with a special emphasis on "claimed."

So I reviewed the two incidents that I'd witnessed,
the ruined sauce and the peanut-oil substitution. Bransford's eyebrows lifted.

"Let's start with the sauce," he said.

"I can tell that you think it's not important, how her
sauce tastes. But this is the basis for the restaurant's
signature seafood dish. That means tons of people order it—they want to experience the finest of what the
chef has to offer." I fell quiet for a minute, thinking how
to best put this in words, especially to a man who
didn't care much about what he ate. Food was fuel for
him, that's all. "And for Edel, the dish is a very personal extension of her. If the diners don't like her tomato vodka sauce, they don't like her." My words
trailed off. "At least I think that's what she feels."

"So, you don't know her well. In fact, you hardly
know her at all. And yet she wanted you to solve her
problems. Did you ever think to ask 'Why me?' I mean,
what is your stake in all this?" The eyes that had looked
like the color of moss when we were dating looked
more like pond algae right now. He despised this side

of me—the urge to get involved in dangerous situations that weren't my responsibility. Or, really, any of my business.

"She said she'd heard about me. How I was involved in other cases and solved some mysteries," I finished weakly, feeling my lips quiver, not wanting to meet his eyes. I did not bother to add the part about being fearless to the point of stupid.

"I bet she heard," he muttered. "Does the name Glenn Fredericks mean anything to you?"

"He's her main sous-chef," I said. "He's the one who got yelled at about the ruined sauce. But why do you ask? Did he have something to do with the fire?"

Bransford ignored the question. "So, back to the sauce . . . In your professional opinion, who might be interested in ruining her food?"

"I only know who works for her. I have no idea if they'd want to torpedo her new place."

"Names?" he asked.

I listed off all the folks I remembered from my evening at the Bistro—Glenn, Mary Pat, Rodrigo, Louann, Leo. And with regret I described the details of the arguments I'd overheard in Edel's kitchen and her tendency to blow her top with her staff. "I had agreed to spend this evening at the restaurant, too," I said. "What are the chances she'll be allowed to open?"

"Not good," he said. "Until we have more answers, the place is still considered a crime scene. She certainly won't be using the back yard anytime soon."

His expression softened a little. "I know you mean well, but you're in way over your head. Did it ever occur to you to wonder why she didn't call the police if she felt someone was threatening her restaurant or her food?"

"I asked that," I said sharply. "I'm not an idiot." I paused, waiting for confirmation that did not come.

"She didn't want bad press before opening night. You know how gossip spreads in this town."

Bransford stood up. "Well she's got bad press in spades now, doesn't she?"

I smirked, remembering the headline. "Your press wasn't that great either: Bransford Baffled—"

He cut me off, looking incensed. "This is not funny. A man was killed. And we had a near miss with the city's diesel tanks, which are located right behind her restaurant. Can you imagine what might have happened if they'd caught fire?"

He towered over me—so close I started to hyperventilate. "No," I squeaked. "But why are you asking me? I wasn't there when the fire started. I only gave Edel a ride to the harbor because she was drunk." Oh lord, I wished I hadn't said that. "I mean, she wasn't—"

"Let me tell you what would have happened: There would have been a massive explosion. Most of the buildings in Old Town are made of wood. Old and dry, seasoned like firewood. A big blaze could have wreaked havoc, like the Duval Street fire, before your time. The one and only reason it stopped burning was the fire reached the end of the block. Here? All the buildings and boats in the harbor could have been burned to rubble. Many casualties in terms of businesses and, more important, people." His face was flushed and he was practically shouting.

Underneath his rant, I heard a tapping on the door. With a whoosh of relief, I pushed it open. Wally. And behind him, heads poking out from his office, the curious faces of the two investors.

"Is everything all right?" Wally asked, bracing himself, legs wide and fists on hips.

"The detective was just leaving." I gestured to the hallway and Bransford stomped out, passing Wally's office without acknowledging the audience.

"I'll text you if I think of anything else," I called. The door slammed shut behind him.

I tried to smile reassuringly at Wally. "This was about the fire at the Bight last night."

"He's a bully," Wally said, frowning. "I don't like to see him push you around like that."

"You may be right, but I'm okay," I said, and nodded my thanks. "Someone died. He's doing his job. And he was mortified by the headline in this morning's paper."

"Still," he said as he started down the hall to his office. "I don't like him." He turned around again. "I wonder whether this is about something else entirely. Maybe he wants to get back together with you."

I blushed and hissed and waved his suggestion away. Then I sank into the chair where Bransford had been sitting, still feeling shaky. And a little weirded out, as I noticed the body heat that had seeped into my battered leather chair. Bransford was right about one thing: Last night could have been far worse than I'd imagined. I jotted down the names of the workers in Edel's kitchen and ran my finger over the list, wondering if there might be one who'd be willing to talk about what he or she had noticed over the past few weeks.

The phone rang and Mom's name came up on the screen. "Jennifer from Small Chef just phoned. Two of her workers called in sick for the Christmas luncheon at the Truman Little White House. Any chance you'd be willing to help? The pay is decent and we'd have a ball. I know you were going to Edel's place, but it doesn't look like they'll be opening. And, to tell the truth, I'm in a panic. Do you know anyone else who might help? It's my first gig and I'm in over my head."

Like mother, like daughter, I thought. "Sure. What time and where?"

10

Food meant love and comfort and even peace in my family. Quite natural that I'd crave something good to eat when I felt a little sad or angry, or like now, a lot of both.
—Lucy Burdette, *Murder with Ganache*

I waited for Ava and the visitors to clear out before packing up my stuff. Not a good time to look like a slacker. So I tweaked the Latitudes review and shot it off to Wally, who would edit for content, and Danielle, who was deadly with fact-checking and spelling mistakes. Then I would have one more chance to polish until it gleamed.

Once I heard Ava and company leave, I grabbed my backpack and stuck my head in Wally's office on the way out. "You look a little shell-shocked," I said. "Thanks for sticking up for me with Bransford."

"I can't stand that guy," he said. "He acts like he has it in for you. But I don't think he's come to terms with your relationship being over. How else would you explain that intensity? Unless he's just an ass, which is certainly possible."

I grinned. "We never really had a relationship. It's more like a love-hate thing, with the hate part much more prominent than the love," I said, and smiled again. Then, seeing the sick look on Wally's face, wished I hadn't mentioned love. Change the subject, Hayley. "What's with these investors?"

Danielle popped out from behind her desk in the reception area and walked over to stand behind me.

"I'm sure you heard some of it," he said. "Ava wants to go big with the magazine. And I can't say she's all wrong. The town is thriving. Real estate has gone crazy. The arts scene has never been so strong." He scowled and ran his fingers through his hair so it stood up like somebody's overgrown Bermuda grass lawn. "Even if Edel Waugh's restaurant never takes off, just the fact that she came down from New York to try something here means a lot. We're not just a sloppy little backwater anymore. But, Hayley"—he looked at me—"it's not often that I agree with that detective, but I agree about this: You need to step back from the Bistro."

"But—"

"But nothing. That assignment has been canceled. Take the rest of the day off. We'll see you tonight at the parade."

"But who are these people?" Danielle asked. "If they're friends of Ava's, they're probably not friends of ours."

Wally sighed. "One of the hardest things about starting a small company is knowing when to sell, when to let some new people in. The owner of a start-up is by definition overinvested in the company. Of course I think *Key Zest* is great. And I think you're both great, too. Amazing, really. But this may be an offer that's too good to refuse."

"So, they are not really investors. They want to buy us out," I said. Realizing as I said it that there was no us.

"They aren't giving me a lot of choice," he said. "If I don't agree to sell, Ava's going to leave and team up with them, anyway—"

"Yes!" Danielle yelped, pumping her fist.

Wally's face twitched into a small, pale smile. "The trouble is, if I don't go along with them, she plans to start a new style magazine, something they could back. And they have unlimited funds. And lots of big ideas. They could squeeze us out in a heartbeat." He sighed and dropped his head against his chair back. "I have to admit that turning over the day-to-day headaches to someone else has its appeal. Then I could concentrate on the editorial side of things, the side that I'm good at."

"Will we lose our jobs?" Danielle asked. Her lip quivered and her eyes looked shiny, as if she might cry.

"Not on my watch," said Wally, but without much conviction.

Now that I was paying attention, I could see the exhaustion in his eyes; I thought about how much his mom's struggle with cancer must have drained him. How much fight did he have left for our magazine? Maybe it was the end of an era. A short era, in my case. Things turned over quickly in this town—go big or go home.

But home to what? My mother's spare bedroom?

Definitely not. I loved living on this island. I loved eating and writing and helping people choose where to spend their money and finding new places to try. I loved the palm trees and the blue, blue water and the rhythm of the seasons, from steamy summer to stormy fall to glorious, sunny winter and tourist-crowded spring. I looked the three of us over, in our silly matching yellow shirts. I loved both of them, too. I had to get out before I started to blubber.

"Mom needs help with a luncheon she's catering," I said in a bright voice. "So this little break is the most perfect timing ever." I didn't mean it, but I wasn't going to let Wally see how worried and sad this potential change made me.

11

Failure is the condiment that gives success its flavor.

—Truman Capote

I whisked down Southard and through the gates that marked the entrance to the Truman Annex, slowing enough to wave at the guards who lounged in the little gatehouse. Hanging a right on Emma Street, I buzzed over several blocks to the Truman Little White House, one of the island's biggest historical attractions. The building is quaint and adorable, with white shingles and louvered slats covering the second story, and red, white, and blue buntings hanging from the first-story windows. When not in use for official business, the grounds are in high demand for weddings and other parties.

The rental company had already begun to set up tables and folding chairs on the lawn behind the white house. Tourists in bright clothing with buttons on their shirts that identified their cruise ships relaxed in white Adirondack chairs, filed in and out of the gift shop, and gawked at the party activity. Mom, wearing a crisp white blouse, black pants, and an apron, was talking with a tall man near the back gate that led to the Harbor Place condos, where I'd lived for six weeks when I first arrived on the island. Pushing away my misgivings, I veered over to get instructions.

"Did you know that seven U.S. presidents either used this building to do the business of the White House, or arranged for peace talks to take place here? Harry Truman, of course, spent many weeks on these grounds during his presidency," said the man, whose voice sounded altogether too familiar. "These flags"— he gestured at a set of six flagpoles—"represent the nations who attended peace talks with Colin Powell in 2001. The countries whose flags are on either end, Armenia and Azuriastan, were the warring factions."

Yep. Same sandy hair and broad shoulders. Same professorial tone. Same phony heartiness reserved for people he wished he didn't have to waste time on. I had to bite my tongue to keep from blurting out that there was no country called "Azuriastan"—it was Azerbaijan.

"I could go on for hours about the history of this place," the man added.

And, of course, he could have. Leave it to Mom to find my ex, Chad Lutz, aka Lutz the Putz. He loved knowing more than the person he was talking with— which I'd judged adorable in the early, rosy days of our short relationship. Later on, not so much. My heart banged and a sheen of sweat broke out on my upper lip. I mustered an enthusiastic smile so fake he could surely see through it. But he looked almost as uncomfortable as I felt.

I slipped my arm around Mom's waist and squeezed.

She smooched me on the cheek. "You'll never guess who I ran into!" she said. "I almost didn't recognize him because he looks a little more substantial than I remembered." Mom's not so subtle way of saying he'd gained a spare tire. "Chad was just telling me about the history of the Little White House."

"Nice," I said, baring my teeth. I hadn't seen him face-to-face since the day I'd rescued him from a would-be killer, shortly after he'd thrown me out of his penthouse. The reunion felt about as horrendous as I'd imagined—a dead romance full moon dragging in a tidal wash of insecurity and humiliation.

When I failed to produce any small talk, Mom continued in a chirpy voice. "He says business is booming these days." Chad was one of the premier divorce lawyers on the island, known for his relentless and ruthless attacks on the opposition.

"You can always bet on relationships going sour," I said. "If that's the way you choose to live." I grinned to soften the sarcasm, hoping to avoid a scolding from my mother later. She believed in bringing enemies to their knees with kindness, rather than making a frontal assault.

"Hayley is doing so well in her food critic job," my mother said, words hushed now, as if sharing a precious secret with Chad. "And her social life puts those folks in the paparazzi gallery in the *Key West Citizen* to shame. I had to literally beg her to help me out with this party."

"I should let you get to work, then," Chad said, backing away. "Nice to see you both." He wheeled around and headed for the parking garage where he stored both his Jeep Wrangler—his beach car—and his Jaguar sedan, used for official lawyerly transportation.

"Such a twit," Mom said with a laugh as we watched him go. "Glad you scraped that guy off your shoes."

"Umm, I think it was the other way around."

"You would have gotten there, sweetie," she said, and pulled me into a quick hug. She clapped her hands. "I am so glad you're here. I don't know why I thought I could pull this off in forty-eight hours by myself."

We trotted over to the table where the bar was being set up. Mom's boyfriend, Sam, also dressed in black and white, was arranging champagne flutes on the table.

I gave him a kiss on the cheek and rumpled his salt and pepper hair. "She's got the whole family working."

"I should have known when she said she had a little project going today that I wouldn't be lounging around the dipping pool," Sam said. "Your mother does not know how to relax."

Mom hurried over, wiping her hands on her apron. "Maybe we should move the bar a little farther back to open up the circulation. I can pretty much guarantee our most popular drinks will be the Arnold Palmers and the champagne." She winked at Sam. "Ladies who lunch like to pretend they're not really drinking." She turned to me. "Can you start unloading the coolers from the van?"

Within half an hour, white cloths covered the tables and Mom had arranged glass cylinders filled with limes and pine cones in their centers. We scattered dozens of tea lights and ropes of gold beads around them. The places were set with white china and silverware, and red-and-green-plaid napkins tied up with gold mesh ribbons. Sam and I had lugged the coolers full of chicken salad, green salad, and cupcakes to the serving tables on which we'd arrange the plates.

"Here comes the boss," Mom said.

A white SUV roared up and parked on the sidewalk. Jennifer Cornell—a blond whirlwind—hopped out. A strong young woman with dark hair pulled back into a ponytail got out of the passenger's side.

"I've brought reinforcements," Jennifer told Mom. "This is Mary Pat Maloney. She fills in for me in the high season and emergencies. Luckily she has a few days off from her day job."

I recognized her immediately as Edel's irreverent line cook, the woman who'd made faces behind Edel's back but worked as hard as anyone in the kitchen. Would she be willing to talk about Edel? Or why Glenn Fredericks was on Bransford's mind? Something told me she'd have some interesting theories.

Mom fanned her face with her hand and hugged Mary Pat. "You're a lifesaver, honey. I'd feel awful if I flubbed my first assignment."

Jennifer's gaze swept over the tables. "It looks lovely so far," Jennifer assured my mother. "If everything is under control, I need to head back to the kitchen to work on tonight's event."

"You're working tonight, too?" I asked.

"Nothing too fancy, just a Christmas-cookie nibble at Schooner Wharf after the parade," she said. "Come by if you can."

Mary Pat and I began to arrange the green salad and chicken salad on plates as the women attending the luncheon filtered in, dressed in flowing pantsuits or short dresses, with a few wide-brimmed hats and lots of chunky jewelry. Not much like the crowd I ran with.

"Any more news on the fire at the Bistro?" I asked Mary Pat, once we had all the salads served and had passed the baskets of piping-hot biscuits.

"We're hoping to open the restaurant by the weekend," she said. "All the fish we ordered has been sitting for too long, so it will have to be trashed and replaced. Edel's apoplectic about the stone crab claws. The harvest is way down this year and prices have skyrocketed. She paid a bloody fortune for what's now essentially cat food. Any felines who frequent the dump will be in heaven."

"Have you seen Edel?" From Mary Pat's report, it didn't sound like she'd heard about the death.

"I rode my scooter over this morning to check on things—she was there arguing with the fire marshal, and then the good-looking detective." She paused to study me. "He's a friend of yours, isn't he?" She wiggled her fingers—quotation marks around "friend."

I felt my eyes go wide. By now it shouldn't have surprised me how much people knew about everyone else's business on this island. "I wouldn't say we're friends. But not exactly enemies, either. We've had a few dustups, that's all. Were they able to identify the body in the fire?"

Mary Pat's turn for wide eyes. "There was a body?"

I blew out some air and nodded. "If it's confirmed that the fire was arson, the death could be a murder."

"OMG, that's horrible," she said. "I'm surprised Edel wasn't completely off her rocker. How in the world does she think we can open the restaurant under those circumstances?"

"She's hoping it will all be wrapped up quickly," I said, "though I'm not sure how exactly."

Seeing Chad Lutz had gotten me thinking about divorces, nasty divorces in particular. How much bad blood could be generated when two people who thought they loved each other realized the love had run cold—that it had in fact frozen into icy hatred? "I hope you don't mind if I ask: Have you met Edel's ex?"

She looked at me as though I was about five steps behind a normal person's thinking. "Of course I've met him. I worked with the two of them for years. But, honestly, I don't think he's been down here that much lately. At least not since their wedding—and that's got to be ten years ago. He certainly wouldn't torch her restaurant."

"Wait. They were married in Key West?"

"Oh yeah," she said. "They spent their honeymoon here, too. I think that's when they came up with the idea of the Bistro."

More surprises. "They came up with the idea together? I thought it was Edel's baby."

Mary Pat shook her head. "They did everything together until all hell broke loose."

"All hell?" I asked.

"The divorce, I mean," said Mary Pat. "Last summer."

"What about Glenn?" I asked. "What's his role in the restaurant family? Edel was pretty hard on him the night I visited your kitchen."

My mother signaled us from across the lawn and we began to clear the tables, scraping the leftovers into a gigantic trash bag and stacking the plates. A tiny white-haired woman in a white jacket and gold pants stood up, replaced her straw hat with a Santa hat, and addressed the lunching ladies. "Thank you so much for your support for our holiday fund-raiser. We've amassed two thousand dollars so far . . ."

"Edel's a perfectionist," Mary Pat whispered. "It's not just Glenn—it's anyone who doesn't measure up to her standards."

"Is her ex involved in the finances of the Bistro?" I asked.

Mary Pat stopped her work to stare at me, her cheeks pink from both exertion and the sun, which had come out from the morning clouds and glared down on us full strength. "I very much doubt that. But I'm not privy to the accounting side of things," she said. "I work in the kitchen."

"Sorry," I murmured. "I know I sound nosy. I'm just concerned about what's going wrong over there. And with the fire and the death, I'm afraid someone's upped the ante."

"Unless it was a homeless guy trying to keep warm," she said. "Not that that's not terrible, too. But just suppose he gets sloshed and crawls into Edel's back yard to spend the night. Because where else is a guy with no money gonna sleep? But then he feels cold. He lights some trash on fire, and things get out of control and he's overcome with fumes and doesn't get out in time. Maybe he never even wakes up."

Which all seemed quite logical, even if I didn't quite believe it happened that way.

"Good point," I said. "I'm always curious about how folks end up on this island and how long they've been here. I didn't realize that Edel had her heart set on a Key West restaurant ten years ago."

"We all start out with dreams," Mary Pat said. "Some of them get trampled." She shouldered a tray of my mother's gorgeous raspberry red velvet cupcakes and marched off to deliver them to the ladies.

12

*If you want to become a great chef, you
have to work with great chefs. If you are
gonna be one, be one.*
                                    —Dana Herbert

When all the women had teetered away from the luncheon and the Little White House grounds were restored to their pristine condition, I took off on my scooter for Houseboat Row. Mary Pat had clammed up completely for the remainder of our shift, as if she could sense my intense curiosity about her crushed dreams. She wasn't about to tell me anything more about them.

I had an hour before I was due to don my elf costume and show up at the Bayview Park public tennis courts where the holiday parade route began. I planned to spend some of that time Googling Edel's husband and Mary Pat Maloney. But before investing too much time in an Internet sinkhole search, I checked the *Key Zest* Web calendar to see what Wally had laid out for the next few weeks. I preferred to get a little ahead on my assignments by planning my restaurant meals and drafting some of their history before I visited. Other than the Latitudes review, which I'd already submitted for editing, and the feature on Edel's restaurant, which had been postponed indefinitely, there was nothing listed. For me, anyway.

Wally was assigned to write a piece on finding a great Christmas dinner in Key West if you weren't cooking, as well as a story on art openings during the holiday season. Ava was doing a roundup of musical events in the month of December. Ava? Writing? Since when did she do anything for *Key Zest* aside from boss the rest of us around? Even *Danielle* was writing a piece on last-minute gift suggestions. Possibly the busiest time in our calendar across the whole year and I had zero assignments. Zilch, nothing, nada.

Pushing back a cloud of foreboding, I went to the deck to visit with Miss Gloria. Our home rocked gently in the wake of a large motorboat and a snatch of "The Holly and the Ivy" drifted from the boat's radio. At home in New Jersey, at this time of day, it would have been dark already—and freezing. Miss G was stretched out on a chaise longue, a cat tucked under each arm, a pink fuzzy afghan over her legs. Wisps of white hair stuck out from the green-and-red elf hat on her head. From the next boat over, our four-legged, gray-furred neighbor yapped at me, but without much energy. Miss G put the newspaper down and grinned.

"Heaven, isn't it? Even Schnootie is relaxing."

"Heaven," I agreed as I sank into the chair next to her.

"What's wrong?" she asked. "You look glum."

"I suppose I am." Miss Gloria hated it when I treated her like a fragile old lady and held things back that might upset her. On the other hand, she wasn't young. And, besides, whatever I told her would make its way back to my mother sooner or later. Not that she intended to tell secrets, but she sometimes forgot that's what they were.

I settled for this: "I'm worried about work. Worried about getting fired. Worried about the magazine getting bought out. Worried that Wally's been too distracted by his mother's illness to stay on top of everything. And worried about him, most of all—he seems tired and unhappy."

Miss Gloria's forehead wrinkled right up to her elf hat and she remained quiet for a minute. "Wally's a smart man. But don't underestimate the effects of cancer. Everything about it is hard—the diagnosis is terrifying, the treatments are arduous, and the process strains even the closest relationships. Not to mention destroying the feeling of invincibility most of us carry around before this nasty disease sweeps in. My sweet husband battled cancer for almost ten years until it finally got the best of him. I'm sure there were things that slipped through the cracks while our attention was on his sickness."

Which made me feel terrible—sad for what she'd endured and sad for the loss of her husband. "I'm so sorry you had to go through that. I hate cancer!"

"Me, too. But they weren't all bad times," she said. Evinrude butted her hand and she stroked him until he purred. "It brought us closer together in some ways." Her eyes narrowed. "Is he letting you in?"

"Excuse me?"

"Wally. Is he sharing his feelings?"

I shook my head. "Not really. But we haven't had any time alone to speak of."

"Everyone reacts differently," she said. "I saw that during my husband's treatments. Some people—men especially—don't want to talk about any of it. But holding it in can make the process so isolating." Now she stroked Sparky's head with one hand, and Evinrude's with the other. "Just make sure you offer him the opportunity."

"Thank you. You're so smart," I said, coming over to kiss her forehead, and then straightening the elf hat, which had slipped to a rakish angle, almost covering one of her eyes. "You look like you're ready for the parade."

She patted her hat and grinned. "Your mother and Sam are picking me up in a little while and we'll watch it from the vacant lot in front of Bare Assets." We both giggled, because the idea of watching a Christmas parade from the vantage point of a strip-club parking lot seemed so nutty.

I went back inside to my cabin to dress for the float. The costume fit a little more snugly than I'd expected, which should not have been a surprise, given than Danielle had done the ordering. With her deep experience on the bench as a bridesmaid, she'd assured me that one should always order a size down or risk an unflattering, baggy fit. I squeezed into the red-and-green tights, added an inch to the skirt's waistband with the judicious use of a giant safety pin, and Velcroed the pointy, felt elf shoes over my red sneakers. Then I pulled on the hat—similar to the one Miss Gloria was wearing, only taller and with more bells—and jingled out to the deck. Schnootie began to bark furiously and flung herself to the end of her leash. She choked and sputtered and started to bark again.

Mr. Renhart, who had been sleeping in a hammock on their boat, struggled to sit up, finally tipping out of the sling and slamming onto the deck. "Shut up, damn dog!" he yelped.

Mrs. Renhart rushed out to check on the commotion.

"What's the problem, silver beastie?" she asked as she scooped up the dog and buried her nose in her fur. "Did Daddy scare you?"

Mr. Renhart struggled to his feet, scowling, and stomped back indoors. Schnootie tried to wiggle out of her arms, still barking. Mrs. Renhart looked over at us.

"Schnootie," she said, "it's only Santa's elves. Were you a good doggie this year? Mommy's going to take you to the drag bar later to have your picture taken with Santa and those great big pretty ladies." She cracked a huge smile. "That's going to be our Christmas card photo this year."

Miss Gloria burst out laughing. I bit my lip to keep from joining her, not wanting to hurt our neighbor's feelings. But Schnootie posing with drag queens? I started to giggle.

"Anyway, so sorry about all the ruckus," Mrs. Renhart said. "Schnootie didn't recognize you in those outfits. She must have thought you were men. She doesn't even like Mr. R., especially since he's started growing that silly beard." She ducked her chin at the door through which her outraged husband had retreated.

Schnootie wasn't the only one with mixed feelings about Mr. Renhart. Still chuckling, Miss Gloria and I both removed our hats and the dog quieted immediately. Mrs. Renhart motioned good-bye with Schnootie's paw and returned to her houseboat's cabin.

"I'm off to Bayview Park," I told Miss Gloria. "You'll recognize our float when we go by—I suspect we'll be the only elves dancing in a key lime pie."

I drove the short blocks to the tennis courts, which were jammed with frolicking parade participants waiting to take their places. With the police presence prominent, the homeless fellows who often gathered in the park at night had settled elsewhere. As I found the *Key*

Zest float, the parade marshal blew a whistle and announced the start. I hopped into the back of the golf cart with Danielle and we headed out.

Wally glanced over his shoulder. "You ladies look adorable. If I were Santa, I'd be very happy with my staff."

"You are Santa," Danielle said with a laugh.

I tried to look and act lighthearted, stopping myself from asking the obvious question: Was he happy with us as his staff at the magazine, even though Ava obviously wasn't? Now was not the time for a serious conversation.

For the next half hour, the parade lurched down Truman. We grabbed handfuls of candy from our burlap sacks and distributed them to the kids clustered on the sidewalks. When the action slowed, we danced to "Jingle Bell Rock" in front of the cart. In the parking lot of Bare Assets, I spotted Tony with a small group of homeless men, drinking beer and smoking.

"I'll be right back," I told Danielle and darted into the crowd.

Tony did a double take when he saw me. "Wow, nice duds," he said.

I jingled my bells. "I guess you heard about the fire on the bight." Of course he would have heard about it—everyone would. In the flickering red-and-green lights flashing on the Metropolitan Community Church float as it rumbled by, the expression on his face shifted from friendly to guarded.

He pulled on his cigarette and blew out a cloud of smoke. "We heard," he said. "Cops have been all over us, wanting to know if we know the guy who died. Are any of the homeless guys missing? What did we see? What did we hear?" He jutted his chin out and then spat on the sidewalk behind me. "We don't know. None of us. People come and go in this town, and they don't sign out on some damn master attendance list. None of us saw anything, either." He dropped the burning cigarette and ground it into the pavement. "You working for them now?"

"The cops? Hardly," I said. "Only trying to help a friend. And keep my job." I sighed and turned away. No point in pressing any harder—he wasn't in a sharing mood. His reaction did raise a question, though: Why were the police pressing the vagrants so hard? In my experience, it took a lot to piss Tony off. A man couldn't afford to be too sensitive, living off the grid in Key West. I trotted back to the parade and hopped in the cart just as Wally took off again.

"Everything all right?" Danielle asked, a worried frown on her lips. "He didn't look very happy with you. That face he made was scary."

I shrugged. "We're all under pressure right now."

Wally slowed down the cart and looked over his shoulder. "I'm sorry about the scene in the office this morning. I know you two are concerned about the direction we're going with the magazine. I'll do everything I can to make this a win-win-win-win."

Danielle grabbed for the seat back in front of us and screeched, "Watch out!" Wally jammed on the brakes, nearly missing smashing into the float just ahead—a flatbed truck loaded with kids and adults wearing flannel pajamas, gathered around a chimney and waiting for Santa. Then I spotted my mother with Miss Gloria, Sam, Cassie, and Joe. And right in the middle of all of them, Edel.

I hopped back off the cart, distributed a dozen candy canes, and waded through the crowd to my family. "You're the cutest elf in the whole parade," my mother said. "Come meet us for a drink at the Turtle Kraals when you're finished? I promised Sam steamed shrimp and grilled wings. And look who we picked up." She tousled Edel's hair as only a mother could get away with.

"See you there," I said, and returned to our mini float. The parade lurched off Truman onto Duval Street, where the crowds were massive. Danielle and I took our sacks of candy and walked ahead of our cart. I waved and passed out candy and yelled "Merry Christmas" to the onlookers—feeling both part of something big and at the same time, part of nothing. Quicksand, that's what my life felt like at this moment.

I reminded myself that many of these tourists would give their grandmother's secret recipe for sugar cookies to be in my position, living in paradise. Something would work out with *Key Zest*—it just had to. And if my job was cut, I'd find something else to do. Even if it meant cleaning houses for a while, as I'd done when I first moved here. Wasn't a little bit of hard labor supposed to be good for the soul? That's what my father used to say when he told me to take out the garbage. And if things didn't work out with Wally, well, there were other men in the world. Lots of them. Maybe not as sweet and cute, but my mother would jump on that challenge like white on rice.

We made our final turn onto Eaton Street and Wally pulled the cart over to the curb. As Danielle and I packed the candy away and gathered our belongings, Ava and her two investors materialized beside our float. "I'd like to take our guests out for a bite. Can you come?" she asked Wally, not even looking at Danielle and me.

He squinted uncomfortably and fumbled for the right words. "Can you make room for Hayley and Danielle?"

I cut him off, forcing a big, regretful smile before Ava could say she'd make room for us at her table when hell froze over. "I'd so love to join you, but I'm meeting my family for a drink in a few minutes."

"And I," said Danielle as she twirled her cap and swiveled her hips, "have a date."

"Settled, then," said Ava to Wally. "I'll text you about where we are."

The three of us watched her go.

"She's the rudest person I've ever met," said Danielle. "She was probably a mean girl in junior high school   and a cheerleader. The kind of girl who invited other cool kids to her birthday party right in front of the dorks and geeks. And her parents probably let the kids drink in their basement when they were in high school. And the girls went to third base and ruined their reputations, and she's spent the past fifteen years trying to prove she really is worth something more than a quick poke in the cellar."

Wally looked stunned.

"Thank you, Dr. Danielle," I said with a snicker. "You've nailed her psyche. We should remember that it's not about us; it's about her insecurity. Do you want help putting the cart away?" I asked Wally.

"I'll be fine," he said. "I'll park over by the harbor and then drive back to New Town when we're finished." He shrugged apologetically. "She is rude. And ordinarily I would have told her to invite all of us or stick it. But I'm afraid to leave her alone with those people. You know what they say. . . ."

Danielle finished his sentence. "Keep your friends close and your enemies closer."

13

Why—at this point in history—do we need a "Best Female Chef" special designation? As if they are curiosities?
        —Anthony Bourdain on Twitter

I jingled through the crowds that had flocked to the harbor, trying to enjoy the party atmosphere and the twinkling holiday lights wound along the railings of the docks and in the shop windows and on the masts and sails and booms of boats. Only Edel's restaurant was dark, still reeking of charred wood. An official-looking paper from the state fire marshal had been pasted to the front door, informing potential customers that the establishment would be closed until further notice. I hoped that my mother had walked a different route with Edel to Turtle Kraals. The sight of her restaurant—boarded up instead of bursting with opening-night excitement as had been planned—was utterly depressing. And I wasn't the one watching my reputation and money sink into the depths of the harbor. If I felt a little discouraged tonight, imagine how it would feel to be Edel. How desperately she would be wishing for things to work out, especially if she'd been circling the drain in New York City before she came south.

I passed the pile of lobster pots stacked into the shape of an enormous Christmas tree and reached the Turtle Kraals restaurant, only yards from the dock where we'd landed in Ray's motorboat with my injured stepbrother last spring. Standing at the entrance to the restaurant, I scanned the buzzing crowd, searching for my family. Sam stood up and waved from the corner near one of the windows open to the harbor.

"The parade was wonderful this year," said Miss Gloria when I reached their table.

"Just charming!" said my mother, as I took the only empty seat in between Cassie and Joe. "Key West at Christmas is simply magical. I can't think of anyplace else in the world I'd rather be. And your outfit is adorable."

"Thanks. Doesn't rank high in comfort, however." I grimaced and adjusted the skirt, which was seriously annoying by now—both the scratchy fabric and the big safety pin cut into my waistline, reminding me there was a little more flesh than I'd like there to be. "I'd like to loosen the waistband, but I'd lose the whole dang thing altogether."

The waitress swung by long enough for me to order a Key West pale ale and a second platter of steamed shrimp. The first order had been decimated to a pile of shells and bay leaves by my family.

Mom lowered her voice and leaned in. "We were just discussing Edel's fire. The cops still don't have a bead on who did it. And they refuse to release the name of the person who died." She patted Edel's hand and then touched her flushed cheek. "It's very hard to live with this much uncertainty."

"It may be a matter of informing the next of kin

first," said Sam. "No one wants to read about the death of their loved one in the local paper."

"You're totally right," said Mom. "They need to do things in the right order."

"So, there had been incidents in the kitchen before the fire," Cassie said to Edel. "Tell us again about what happened."

Edel's gaze swung over to me, glowering.

"I'm sorry," I said. "I shared a few things with my family. They know how to keep a secret." Which they didn't.

Mom nodded with encouragement.

Edel slumped, her elbow on the sticky table, her chin in her hand. "Several of the recipes in the bible had been changed." She looked exhausted, the skin under her eyes dark like the color of an approaching thunderstorm. "I know you're going to ask which ones, but they won't let me into the damn kitchen so I can't tell you a lot more. I've been so tired and so upset, it's hard to think straight."

Cassie sat up, suddenly attentive. "You must have had a gut reaction when you saw the desecration of your recipes. And, chances are, remembering that reaction, those feelings, will bring back the memory of what was destroyed."

Sheer gobbledegook, I thought unkindly.

But Edel appeared to be buying it—studying Cassie's face and nodding. "It wasn't an old standby, like the spaghetti Bolognese. That I could make in my sleep. And, besides, I would rarely think of serving that to paying customers."

"They would find it worth every penny," I inserted.

She gave a distracted smile, then focused back on Cassie. "I think it had more to do with temperature." Her face lit up. "Like the stir-fried spring vegetables on cheesy polenta. What makes that dish completely special is the Parmesan crisps."

My mother moaned with pleasure. "If only we could have a few bites of that now."

"Instead of four hundred degrees, the recipe called for four hundred seventy-five," Edel said. "Which would have baked the crisps to cinders before the chef even thought to check on them. Of course, someone not so familiar with the recipe . . ."

"Someone in a hurry, as restaurant chefs so often are," Cassie added, "might not notice before it was too late."

Edel grinned. "You really understand food. Thank you."

I had to pinch myself to keep from saying something crusty. After talking with Eric on the golf course, I realized that my feelings had to do with old memories. And that Cassie had probably matured—and hopefully I had, too. But, honestly, my cousin understood nothing about food and cooking. Even her own husband had admitted yesterday that the sole dish she knew how to make was hot dog casserole, in which the secret ingredients were ketchup and canned beans.

"And then there was doctoring of the sauce," Edel continued. "Hayley was there for that." Her gaze flickered over to me. "All the regular staff were there. Same with the canola caper. The peanut oil switcheroo." She barked a mirthless laugh.

"So, you're thinking one of the staff members might have been behind those things," Joe said. "Someone who knew his way around the kitchen. The fire, too?"

"Torching my restaurant takes this vendetta to another level altogether," said Edel.

"You should try not to take it personally," Cassie said. "I've learned the hard way that people who try to take down other people do so because of their own issues, and because their envy poisons them. It has nothing to do with who *you* are."

Edel nodded sadly.

"I remember the back door to the kitchen was open both of the days I visited," I said, picturing my view from the perch on the stool. "It was hot in there."

"Goes with the territory," Edel said. "That's why we have those big fans running all the time. No air conditioner in the world could run hard enough to cool the kitchen, so I keep the screen door open so we can breathe. And, besides, the dishwashers are running in and out with sacks of trash. And half the workers are smokers." She wrinkled her nose in disgust. "It's Grand Central Station in that back courtyard and the alley."

"But would you notice if someone you didn't recognize slipped into the kitchen?" Cassie asked.

"I'd like to think I would," Edel said. "But I spend time in the dining room, too. It's also my job to schmooze with the diners." She sighed heavily. "Frankly, I'd much rather think the arsonist was someone I didn't know. Not someone close to me. Someone who knows how much this restaurant means to me but who tried to destroy it anyway? That would break my heart."

My mother put an arm around her shoulders.

The waitress delivered my beer and the basket of steaming shrimp. Suddenly starving, I reached for the top shrimp and began to peel away the skin. I dunked it into the spicy cocktail sauce and popped the whole thing in my mouth. Across the table mom's eyes widened, and I glanced over my left shoulder, still chewing.

Wally had gotten up from a table at the other end of the bar and he was heading toward us. Seated at the table behind him were Ava and the two investors. The woman, still dressed in her woodpecker attire, waved at me. The man, who had changed out of his suit into khaki shorts and a loud red-and-green Hawaiian shirt, did not. Wally stopped beside me; his hand brushed the back of my head and rested for a moment on my neck. This felt like the kind of intimate gesture that went along with two people who were involved. Cassie raised her eyebrows. I flushed.

"So nice to see you all," he said, grinning around the table.

"Come over here and give me a hug," said Mom. She popped out of her seat and folded him in close, then held him out at arm's length, her hands gripping his shoulders. "How in the world are you? And how is your mother?"

"She's holding her own, and thanks for asking." He patted her arms and took a step back. "We finished the third round of chemotherapy and we won't have to return to the doctor for a while. She'll go in for tests after the holidays, so she's trying to enjoy life and not think too much about the future. So it's a respite."

Sam clapped him on the shoulder and gave him a hearty handshake. "We're glad you're still standing."

Wally nodded, and glanced around the table at the others.

"This is my niece Cassie and her husband, Joe. You must know Edel Waugh." Mom pointed at the chef.

Wally's eyes widened and he forced a smile. "So nice to meet all of you. I'd better get back to my group." His fingers brushed my neck again, but this time the contact didn't feel so friendly. "Hayley, could I speak with you for a minute?"

I stood up and followed him a few steps away.

"Not such a good idea to be out with her," he whispered through gritted teeth. "It doesn't look right." He jerked his head toward Ava.

"It wasn't planned," I shot back. "My folks met Edel on the parade route and invited her for a drink. I had no idea she'd be here. And how was I to know we'd see you?" I swallowed, feeling furious with Ava and disappointed in him. To be honest, I felt more than disappointed. I was angry with him, too. What had happened to the boss who'd go to the mats for his employees if that was needed? What happened to the man I thought would be my boyfriend? All of that, gone up in smoke like Edel's restaurant.

"I went online and noticed that you've given me no more assignments," I said. "It looks an awful lot like you're rolling over and allowing us to get fired. It's not like you," I added. "At least have the courtesy to tell us the truth so we can look for other jobs. So we can look out for ourselves."

Wally groaned. "I'm dancing as fast as I can. Right now I don't have that much leverage. You need to do your part, too, try not to antagonize her every time you cross her path." With a grim expression on his face, he started back to Ava's table.

I wheeled around and returned to my family, my appetite evaporated. It was going to be impossible to pretend that everything was fine. I needed to get out.

Edel stood up. "I'm going to walk over to the restaurant and see if there's any news. Maybe I'll get lucky and they'll let me into my own place." She grimaced and then reached to shake my mother's hand. But my mother ignored the hand and hugged her instead. "Thanks for inviting me. Turns out I'm not much in the mood for a party," Edel said, once she'd pulled away.

"I'll walk over with Edel," I told Mom and the rest of the gang. "I'll catch you guys tomorrow."

Then I marched out after her, glaring in the direction of Wally's table. Whether he approved or not, I refused to have my actions dictated by Ava. Nor was I going to sit in this restaurant and pretend Ava wasn't there, discussing my future with my boss. The anxiety generated by the whole scene was turning my neck into a concrete pillar. And my heart along with it.

14

*Rage as clear and clean as grain alcohol
poured through her, burning everything un-
necessary away.*
　　　—Barbara O'Neal, *The All You Can
Dream Buffet*

Edel and I wove through the throngs of holiday cele-
brants crowding the docks and walkways along the
harbor. Drunken, naughty-worded versions of Christmas carols drifted out from the bars, and the lights on
the boats shimmered on the water. As we approached
the Bistro on the Bight, its windows black, Edel grew
ghostly pale, her eyes looking even sadder than they
had in Turtle Kraals. The darkness must have reminded
her, if she needed reminding, how much business she
was losing this week by not being allowed to open. She
had a grim look on her face and a slump to her shoulders. The official notice was still taped to the front door.

"I'm going to look in back," she said.

I trailed along after her, the smell of wet, charred
wood getting stronger as we approached the rear patio.
Several lengths of crime-scene tape flapped from the

blackened remains of Edel's fence and storage shed. But a path of sorts had been cleared to the back door.

Edel pulled a ring of keys from her pocket. "I'm going in," she said. "I need to see what's what inside."

"Wait until they give you a formal nod," I warned her. "I've had too many run-ins with this police department." I bit my lip—how did I say this delicately? Nothing came to mind. "They're a little bit, well . . . Neanderthal in their approach to solving crimes. Or should I say thickheaded and clumsy?" Which wasn't exactly fair or accurate. But I couldn't think of another way to slow her down.

I laughed, but Edel shook her head and marched toward the back door. She paused to take a deep breath, then inserted a key into the lock and disappeared inside. I backed away into the alley's shadows to keep an eye out for trouble.

Minutes later, I heard a loud argument between a man and a woman on the dock in front of the restaurant, followed by a big splash. Rubbernecking had become an instinct for me lately. I dashed down the alley. By the time I reached the water, a large man was scrambling up a ladder attached to the pier, sopping wet and laughing. The woman who had apparently shoved him was laughing, too. They staggered off in the direction of Duval Street, clutching each other and howling, their argument forgotten.

But then down Edel's alley, a siren whooped. I hurried toward the noise. Two police cars had pulled into the alley leading to her restaurant, their blue lights flashing. I arrived just in time to see the cops tumble out of the car with their guns drawn.

"Get out of here," one yelled at me, a short, stocky woman with short black hair and intense brown eyes. "Police! Get back!" She waved me away as they side-stepped toward the back door and plastered themselves flat to either side.

"This is the Key West Police," she shouted, toeing the door open and pointing the gun inside. "Come out with your hands up."

A third cruiser raced up the alley and a burly cop I did not recognize burst out of his car and barreled across the patio to join the others. Within moments Edel stumbled out of her restaurant, her hands on her head and her eyes wild. A fourth car surged up to the scene, this one unmarked. Lieutenant Torrence was driving and Detective Bransford rode shotgun.

Bransford leaped out of the car. "What's going on here?"

"It's only Edel Waugh. She owns the place," I piped up from my corner in the shadows.

Bransford whirled around. "What the hell? What are you doing here?"

My knees felt wobbly and my heart rate soared. "This is a terrible mistake. She didn't do anything wrong," I began to explain. "She didn't break in; she has a key. You have to understand that this is the busiest time of the year and this restaurant is her livelihood. She needed to find out what shape her kitchen was in. How much damage has been done with the beef and fish and all that, because it will affect her ability to open."

"A man has died in a fire that was purposely set," said Bransford, his eyes narrowing to slits. "We closed off access to the property because it's a damn crime scene. And she wants to look over her ground beef?" He spat on the ground and spun away.

Edel was steered to the nearest cruiser and instructed to put her hands on the roof. The female officer patted her down. "Clear," said the officer in a curt voice. Then she opened the back door of the cruiser and prodded Edel to take a seat.

"Are you ready to talk?" Bransford asked.

"I've been cooperating with everything so far." Edel scowled, clenching her hands into fists. "Perhaps there's a better question. Like, can't you and your people solve a simple crime so the rest of us can return to work?" Edel stood up and crossed her arms over her chest, which didn't do much to dispel the impression that it was one small woman against the big fierce Key West Police force.

"Where were you between noon and eight o'clock Monday afternoon?" Bransford asked.

"She was in the Latitudes bar on Sunset Key in the evening," I pitched in. She needed someone, anyone, to stick up for her. "You can ask any member of my family. We all saw her there."

Bransford turned around to stare. "I don't recall asking you anything," he said.

He pivoted back to Edel. "Does the name Juan Carlos Alonso mean anything to you?"

"I wish it didn't," Edel said, her face tightening and her lips quivering. "I'm certain you're already aware that he's my ex."

I stared dumbly. "Your husband was killed in the fire?" I asked.

Edel refused to meet my eyes.

"Have you known all along that the victim was your husband?" I couldn't believe I'd spent this much time with her, trying to support her, and she'd held back this crucial, critical, astonishing, disturbing piece of information.

"No, I did not," she squawked.

Bransford repeated, "Where were you Monday afternoon?"

The air seemed to leak out of Edel like runny frosting from a pastry bag. She slumped into the cruiser's open door, collapsing onto the battered black upholstery, her face in her hands. Her shoulders heaved as though she were weeping. But then she straightened up and looked him square in the face.

"I was here. Getting ready for the opening on Tuesday."

"I'd like you to come down to the station for a chat."

Edel said nothing, but angled her legs back into the cruiser. The lady cop slammed the door shut and got into the passenger's side of the vehicle and they backed away. Bransford and Torrence headed to their car.

"This isn't your business, Hayley," Torrence said over his shoulder. "You need to stay out of it."

So much for having a sympathetic friend with an inside track.

I started the long walk back to my scooter, which I'd left at Bayview Park before the parade, trying to puzzle out what could have happened yesterday. Could Edel really have torched her own restaurant and killed her ex? That seemed to be the working theory of the KWPD. The possibility made me feel physically ill—it was too much to keep to myself.

Several blocks from the tennis courts, I called my mother. "The cops just took Edel off." I explained the rest of what had happened. "The thing is, she didn't even put up a fight. She hardly looked surprised." I tried to picture the expression on her face after Bransford mentioned her husband's name. "More like she'd been waiting for them to figure this out and track her down."

My mother was silent for a moment—not her natural state. "In truth, we really don't know her all that well. We like her. And we love her food. But I suppose anything could have happened. Maybe she was way underwater financially and this was the only way she saw out."

"Roasting her ex was going to solve her money problems?" I asked, my voice squeaking into soprano range with outrage.

"You're right, honey. That sounds ridiculous. But people don't always think clearly when they're stressed. Eric or Joe could tell you that." She covered her end of the phone and spoke to someone, then came back on the line. "We're headed back to the Truman Annex for Christmas cookies and tea. Want to swing by?"

"No, thanks. I'll see you soon." I hung up, wishing I didn't rely on her so much. And feeling dissatisfied with the conversation, but not sure what I'd wanted her reaction to be, either. It boiled down to this: As furious as I'd been with Chad Lutz after he'd humiliated me and thrown me out, would I have burned him up? No way. I might have felt like it, but I'd have never followed through. What kind of woman would? I hated to think too much about the gruesome details. Honestly, I couldn't relate to that much rage. This was the kind of incident that had I seen the headline in the newspaper, I would have skipped right over it.

I finally reached my scooter and drove the rest of the way home to Tarpon Pier. The lights had been doused in Miss Gloria's bedroom, though our strings of Martha Stewart's best low-wattage white lights blinked cheerfully across our roofline.

I glanced up the finger, hoping for a nightcap and someone to share it with. Connie and Ray waved from the top deck of their houseboat. So I dropped off my helmet and backpack on our boat, grabbed a half bottle of white wine from our refrigerator, and went up the dock to join them.

"Mind if I come up for a few minutes?" I called.

"Come on. We haven't seen you in ages."

I bounded up the inside stairway and out to the deck. My friends were sprawled in low beach chairs, surrounded by the potted banana trees that Ray was trying to cultivate. They were drinking beer and holding hands—their own slice of paradise.

"You look kind of dragged out," Connie said. "Rough day?"

I sank down onto a weathered teak bench and poured myself a glass of wine. "I've been spending some time with the chef-owner of that new restaurant that's supposed to open on the bight."

"The one hit by the fire," Ray said, nodding. "I biked by the place. It could have been much worse than it was. Most of those buildings along the harbor are wood. Plus all those boats with gas tanks . . ."

"Were they able to identify the victim?" Connie asked.

I swallowed hard and grimaced. "Apparently it was Edel's husband. Though actually, he was her ex. Judging by the way the cops were treating her tonight, I'd say they think she was responsible."

Ray rubbed his fingers across his chin and took a swig of his pale ale. "She burned down her own restaurant to kill him?"

"It doesn't make sense, does it? Unless she killed him and then attempted to hide the evidence." I tried to put myself in her place, imagine how I'd feel if I'd killed a man I used to love. Maybe even still did. Horrified. Shocked. Sickened. Scared witless. And terrified of getting caught. "I suppose if you were desperate about what you'd done, setting a fire could seem like a solution. On the other hand, she's also desperate about her restaurant succeeding—and the fire and the death are definitely not advancing that cause."

"Desperate?" Connie asked.

I nodded. "And driven."

Ray shifted taller in his low chair and dropped Connie's hand. "This is not to excuse someone hurting anyone, or especially not murdering someone, but . . . Key West is a hard place to be as an artist. And I imagine that goes for chefs and restaurants, too." He began to peel the label off his bottle, the expression on his face stony.

"The town appears so artsy and low-key and easygoing. And welcoming. Of course, the idea of getting away from an icy winter and plying your art in paradise is practically irresistible." He tapped two fingers on his lips and frowned, looking over the deck railing to the headlights blurring by on North Roosevelt Boulevard, aka Route 1.

The only way in to paradise. And out, too—should your dreams get busted, I could imagine him thinking. And I knew exactly how scary that thought felt.

He glanced back at us. "But underneath the surface, the competition is incredible. The established artists are trying to beat back the newer artists and they're all trying to hold their tiny bit of ground so the visiting muckety-mucks careening down from New York City don't push them out of the spotlight."

Connie took his hand again and squeezed. I sipped my wine and nodded sympathetically. I hadn't heard a lot about Ray's painting career lately. He'd made a big splash at the Gallery on Greene last spring, but no new shows since then. He hadn't shared anything much when I'd asked how things were going, so I'd been afraid to push.

"Why are you involved with her?" Connie asked.

"She asked for my help."

"Why you?"

I shrugged. That was the million-dollar question, wasn't it? I finished my drink, said good night, and trotted back down the finger to my houseboat, feeling bone tired but not sleepy. Going to bed would be an exercise in futility. Instead I booted up my laptop and curled on the couch with Evinrude draped over my hip. I typed in the names of Edel and her ex in the Google search bar. Several headlines popped up—reviews of their New York City restaurants, largely glowing, and, farther down, a headline from last summer in the Page Six section of the *New York Post*.

Juan Carlos Alonso Parties at Pop-Up Restaurant in Brooklyn.

The first paragraph read: *Juan Carlos Alonso doesn't appear to be pining for his partner and soon-to-be-ex-wife, Edel Waugh. He was photographed in the after-hours pop-up restaurant, Munchies, with singer/songwriter Hazel Hernandez. Hernandez is best known for hiking up her skirt and twerking à la Miley Cyrus during her appearance on the TV cooking reality show Topped Chef. She was eliminated from the chef competition after her performance. Alonso and Waugh have filed for divorce and are alleged to be in a bitter contest over ownership of their flagship restaurant.*

All of which, considering the source, I needed to take with a grain of salt. I typed in both of their names again, but this time adding "divorce" to the search terms. I clicked on the next article, a month after the first, which proclaimed that Edel and Juan Carlos were in a bitter custody fight over their brand as well as their restaurants.

Should you doubt the worth of a chef's brand, the author of the article wrote, *consider the losses faced by Nigella Lawson or Martha Stewart or, particularly, Paula Deen after missteps in their personal affairs. When celebrity chefs cut themselves with the sharp knives of their own bad behavior, they bleed money from their tarnished brands, rather than blood from their fingers.*

I wondered which one of them—Edel or Juan Carlos—had wanted the divorce. And how the split had affected their restaurant. And whether divorce law would have allowed Juan Carlos a percentage of a new restaurant if it had been started without him. Would it matter if Edel had moved to Key West? Would he still be able to claim a piece of her success?

One person I knew would have some insight. I had his phone number seared into my brain, like grill marks on a raw steak. Chad Lutz. He hadn't acted entirely unfriendly when we'd run into each other at the Little White House earlier, though that may have been the effects of my mother and Sam and his reluctance to be rude in a public setting. I fidgeted with my phone. He was a night owl—a text at eleven p.m. would not have been unusual or unwelcome. At least not from someone he liked.

Finally, I caved in to my curiosity and texted him the question.

I had a minute of uncomfortable waiting before the phone buzzed back.

I'll be at the Courthouse Deli at 9 am for coffee.

In Chad's usual terse style, he'd not invited me to meet him. But what else could that mean?

15

You can't microwave a career or a life.
                                    —Cal Thomas

My alarm buzzed at 7:30 the next morning, an hour before I was due at We Be Fit for my personal training session with Leigh Pujado. Not my idea of a great way to start the morning, but Leigh had convinced me that lifting weights was the only way to counteract the meals I was consuming—bigger muscles meant more calories burned. If I planned to stay on in my position as food critic over the long haul, she'd added. A big if, as things stood now. I had time for a quick cup of coffee, a bowl of cereal, and a glance through the *Key West Citizen*. I scanned the front-page headlines and opened the paper, skimming over the usual whining in the Citizen's Voice until my attention caught on the crime report.

Ex-Husband of Local Restauranteur Found Dead after Fire, the headline read. Key West detective Nathan Bransford reported that the body found at the Bistro on the Bight had been identified as Juan Carlos Alonso, former husband of restaurant chef/owner Edel

Waugh. No arrests had made in the death, and the police were still looking for witnesses. Persons who may have seen anything suspicious in the harbor area around the time of the fire Monday night were asked to come forward.

It must have killed Bransford to sound so uncertain in the paper, particularly after the other day's headline: BRANSFORD BAFFLED. At least it appeared that Edel's trip to the station last night had not resulted in her arrest. I scarfed down a bowl of homemade granola, grabbed my backpack and helmet, and raced out to my scooter. Leigh hated it when her customers showed up late for their appointments. Yes, the minutes came off our exercise time, paid for by our money, but she took it as a personal failure—her inability to properly motivate us.

I hurried through the small gym, dodging the clanking machines operated by customers who had arrived on time for their sessions. The place already smelled like sweat and wet rubber. Muscle-bound trainers barked out instructions to their grunting clients. In the background sounded the pounding beat of "I Shot the Sheriff." I dumped my belongings in the tiny ladies' locker room and hurried down the hall to the gym. Seven minutes late. Twenty-three to go.

"Morning," I called to Leigh. "I swear I'll do the repetitions I missed at home this evening."

Leigh snickered. "When have you ever done an exercise without me standing over you?"

I shrugged. "Caught me there."

I placed my phone on a little shelf by the door, picked up the seven-and-a-half-pound free weights as she directed, and began a series of lunges and squats that had my thighs burning within minutes. I stopped to take a breath.

"You looked cute in that elf costume," Leigh said with a sly smile, and then directed me to the low bar to begin push-ups. "Your Santa was cute, too."

"No comment," I said, and began to leverage my body up and down over the bar until my triceps and biceps had joined the screaming of the other muscles. I dropped to my knees, resting my head on the bar.

"Okay, I get it: no action on the romance front," she said, tapping comments into her iPad. These would show up later in my in-box—impossible to ignore. *Address left-side weakness in hip flexor, increase time lapse for planks, superset hamstring runners and split squats. More push-ups!* Enough to make you feel tired before setting foot in the gym.

"What's coming up in *Key Zest* this week?" she asked.

"A review of Latitudes," I said, heaving myself up to standing. "A place to take your sweetie for a big splurge. Pricey but delicious. And the view, of course, is priceless." I grabbed a stainless thermos of cold water and took a long gulp.

"Hamstring pull-ups next," she said, ignoring my groan. "What else are you writing?"

I shrugged. "That's it."

She raised her eyebrows. "Trouble in paradise?"

"Let's put it this way: If there's an opening for another trainer, let me know."

Leigh laughed out loud. "If we had a snack bar, you'd be a shoo-in. Weren't you writing a piece about the restaurant that had the fire?"

I nodded. "Edel's Waugh's place. Everything's on hold until the cops figure out what happened."

My phone buzzed and jumped on its little shelf and I excused myself to look. Edel.

I held up a finger to Leigh. "I need to take this—be with you in a minute."

"How are you?" I asked, sidestepping into the laundry room for a little privacy.

"Not great," she said, her voice brittle and shrill. "I need to talk. Do you have any time this morning?"

I thought about Wally's warning about keeping my distance and neutrality. And Ray's question about why Edel was reaching out to me, anyway. On the other hand, I was already meeting my ex to mine his expertise about the fallout of celebrity divorce. Edel's divorce. And I had nowhere else to be today. And maybe no job.

"Sure. I'm headed down to the Courthouse Deli in a few to grab a coffee with an acquaintance. I'll buzz over to the Westin marina after that and meet you at the boat launch? I'm glad to hear you weren't arrested," I added, hoping she'd tell me what had really happened.

"Not yet. But they're definitely not finished with me. The cop told me Juan Carlos was clunked on the head before the fire. I think they think I killed him." Her voice cracked and it sounded as though she'd started to cry. "Honestly, I need a friend. Not the boat launch, though. Too many prying eyes. I'll meet you in the bar at Kelly's Caribbean in forty-five minutes." She hung up.

"Everything okay?" Leigh asked as I returned and replaced the phone on the shelf.

I could have simply said yes. But Leigh's a smart cookie. And a foodie, always looking for the next great meal. We had that very much in common. She was very eager for Bistro on the Bight to open. And very good at keeping a secret. And tied into a huge network of local folks on the island.

"Not really," I said, lowering my voice to a whisper. "That was Chef Edel. The body they found after the blaze was her ex, and she's worried that they blame her for his death."

"Wait a minute," Leigh said. "They think she killed him? Couldn't the death have been a terrible accident?"

I shook my head and followed her to the last machine of the morning to do lat pull-downs. "He suffered a blow to the head before the fire, or that's what she was told."

"So, it's possible someone set the fire in order to cover up the death. Let's think like a jock for a minute," Leigh said. "If he was killed up close and personal, wouldn't the murderer have to be someone strong? From the picture I saw in the paper a couple of weeks ago about the restaurant opening, your chef looked tiny."

"She is," I agreed. "Small in stature but mighty in personality."

"What was he doing there, anyway? Is he involved in the business?"

"There's a lot I don't know," I said as I took a seat on the bench near the front of the gym and grasped the bars that hung above me. The outside door swung open and my cousin Cassie blew in. She pulled off her bike helmet and finger-combed her hair.

"I'm looking for Leigh?" she said to the man at the desk. He pointed to us.

"What are you doing here?" I asked. My mother would have assigned demerits for my abruptness.

She shrugged. "I needed a place to work out. And someone to help with my flexibility. I feel like my hamstrings and hip flexors have tightened up over the past few months. Maybe that's why my drives aren't going anywhere. Or maybe I need to beef up my strength training. Anyway, your mom said you love this place."

"I wouldn't describe it as love." I scowled. "Leigh's more like a necessary evil."

Leigh strode over to shake Cassie's hand. "Just finish up with two more sets," she called back over her shoulder to me. "Pull your shoulder blades together and engage your abs. Nice to meet you," she said to Cassie. "I'm excited to work with a professional golfer."

Once I'd done the final sets, I hurried into the locker room, feeling crowded—once again—by my cousin. But why should Leigh's enthusiasm matter? I was not an ideal gym rat. Often late, frequently grumbling, and with no goals other than avoiding the attack of the dreaded pudgies. Why shouldn't Leigh prefer working with a real athlete?

I glanced in the mirror and fussed with my hair, which had expanded into a mass of unruly reddish curls. My face was slick with sweat and red as a ripe tomato. Not my best look. Not that I should care what Chad thought, either. And maybe he'd be impressed with my so-called commitment to staying strong and healthy.

I buzzed down Seminary Street toward the courthouse area of Old Town. The MARC plant store a couple blocks away from the gym was doing a brisk business with last-minute Christmas tree sales. I veered around a Smart Car and an old VW van whose owners were tying fir trees on their car rooftops. The smell of pine needles made me feel nostalgic for a good, old-fashioned, cold-and-snowy Northeast Christmas. For about forty-five minutes. After that, I'd be yearning for palm trees and humidity.

16

Food celebrities are a bit different. They seem more accessible and, however falsely, we bond with them. Their books, shows and tweets purport to bring us into their kitchens and connect us to their traditions in service of that most intimate of activities— sharing food. And we bring them into our kitchens, too, turning to them to help feed our families. So when they step out of line, how they've sold themselves to us matters, probably far more than they anticipated.
—J. M. Hirsch, the Associated Press

Chad was sitting on the bench outside the Courthouse Deli, near two homeless men with worn backpacks and a small, shabby-looking dog nestled between them. He smiled and waved and held up a Styrofoam cup in greeting.

"One café con leche with one sugar, just as you like them, madam," he said with a grin.

Who was this man, who both remembered my preferences and acted on them?

"You said you have some questions," he said. "I only have a couple of minutes. My long-term client from Palm Beach is coming in. You may remember the guy with the yacht bigger than Tiger Woods's boat? He's divorcing his fourth wife."

I nodded. "I think he was only on number three when I was in the picture." Frankly, I thought the man's story was pathetic, a saga about a guy who learned nothing from his own painful history. A man who kept a divorce lawyer on retainer was no joke. But to Chad it was funny.

"My question has to do with community property across state lines," I said. "For instance, supposing the most valuable community property of a certain couple is the reputation of a store or restaurant. Supposing that reputation is worth a lot of money. Supposing one of the spouses leaves the state and starts another business. Would the other spouse have any claim to that business? Let's assume that some of its success rests on the brand that the two spouses built together, even though they are divorced now."

"So both of the spouses were instrumental in building the brand?" he asked.

I nodded.

"Then I think a case could be made for returning to court and claiming rights to the new property."

"What if one of the spouses is making a public ass of himself? Or herself?" I added quickly.

Chad tapped on his chin so I couldn't help noticing his manicured fingernails, buffed to a polish. I curled my own fingers into fists to hide the scraggly nails. I'd been way too busy and upset lately to worry about that level of grooming detail—which he would never understand.

"To land the best clients, a man must look like he's

worth every penny that he charges," I remembered Chad telling me when I remarked on his two walk-in closets full of carefully tailored suits. When most people on this island get by on a drawerful of T-shirts and a couple pairs of cutoffs. Possibly a sweater or two for the weeks when our winter cold front blows through.

"If this fellow is making a public nuisance of himself, his wife would have grounds on which to sue him for defamation of their jointly owned character." Chad removed his sunglasses and pinched the bridge of his nose. "Let's suppose that Paula Deen's spouse—if she had one—were filing for divorce. His lawyer could make the case that her actions were reducing the value of their joint property because they were at odds with the reputation of the Deen brand as homey, healthy, and honest." He slid the glasses back on. "This sounds like a juicy case." He wiggled his eyebrows. "Do either of them need a lawyer?"

I tossed my Styrofoam cup in the nearby trash can and grinned weakly. "I'm not that close to the situation."

"Just nosy, as usual?" He smiled to soften the barb.

"Thanks for the info," I said, ignoring the smart remark and standing up. "Give my love to Deena?" His secretary, whom he did not deserve. No matter how friendly he was pretending to be at the moment. Yeah, and why was he bothering?

"Listen," he said, catching my wrist as I turned to leave. "I'm glad you texted me. I've been thinking for a while that I never apologized for being such a wanker. You know, the bit about putting your stuff out on the curb."

I opened my mouth, then closed it. I couldn't think of anything to say in response. Finding my belongings dumped on the street in front of Harbor Place had been perhaps the lowest moment in a series of low moments. Although finding him in the sack with another woman was worse. He interrupted my gloomy memories.

"And losing your grandmother's recipes. That was mean, and I'm sorry."

"Ummm, thank you. I appreciate that." I pulled my wrist out of his grip. I still believed he'd destroyed them, not lost them. "And thanks for the coffee." I started across Whitehead Street, my nerves buzzing from the extra shot of caffeine and his unexpected mea culpa. I'd have to figure out later—in private—why he was bothering to apologize more than a year after he'd broken my heart.

My mother called minutes later. "Cassie said she had a wonderful workout with your trainer."

"That was fast," I said flatly.

Mom just laughed. "Listen, would you mind coming to dinner tonight? I know it's a busy time of year, but Sam dragged in an enormous Christmas tree and I need help decorating. And I couldn't get the idea of spaghetti Bolognese out of my head. I've made enough for an army. Miss Gloria's coming, too."

She was practically wheedling, which brought out feelings of guilt and sympathy. Besides that, what else did I have going on? Not much. And I really missed decorating a tree, no matter how brave Miss Gloria and I had been about being practical and skipping that tradition. "What time?"

I returned to my scooter and zipped over to Kelly's on Caroline Street, named after movie star Kelly McGillis, who was rumored to keep a watchful eye on the place. It was a cute white clapboard building with a sign in front proclaiming it to be the original home of Pan Am Airways. Behind the building was an open courtyard with tables for dining and stools for barhopping. I'd never been inside—though anytime I'd passed by at the end of a workday it seemed busy with a cheerful, happy-hour crowd, especially after sunset. And also during the lunch hour when the place appeared to cater to tourists and cruise ship visitors, looking for the "real" Key West experience. But Edel was right—in the midmorning, we were unlikely to find anyone we knew in this bar.

I went inside, pausing for a moment so my eyes could adjust to the dim light. Edel was sitting in a far corner of the room, nursing what appeared to be a bloody Mary.

"Can I get you something?" she asked.

I shook my head. "I'm overcaffeinated, and it's a little early for me to start drinking." I cocked my head, pressed my fingers to my forehead. "You said you needed my help. But I'm getting the idea there's a lot you're not telling me."

"There's no one I can turn to on this island," she said. "Who do I trust? Someone's out to destroy me and I don't know who it is. No one cares whether my restaurant makes it or not. But if it doesn't, I've got nothing. Nothing."

"And yet when we were discussing potential problems, you failed to mention Juan Carlos," I pointed out.

She looked up from her drink and blinked. "Okay, so I didn't tell you everything. That stuff is very personal. And painful."

I waited. If she wanted to play games, I would walk.

"I was working in the bistro all day Monday, just fussing. Getting things ready for the big day. Then Juan Carlos showed up out of nowhere and started arguing with me. I had no idea he was on the island. There was no reason for him to have come." Her bottom lip trembled and she pinched it between her forefinger and thumb.

"Why was he here? What were you arguing about?"

She ducked her chin, sipped her drink. "We fought about money and the New York restaurant, and then he left." Tears welled in the corners of her eyes, glinting in the Christmas fairy lights strung above the bar. "Actually, that's not all. He wanted to give it another chance."

"The marriage?"

She nodded.

"How did you feel about that?"

"I—I said I needed time to think. That now was not a good time to hash out personal issues. It was time to concentrate on my place. Do everything I had in my power to make it work." The tears tipped over the rims of her eyes, made runnels down her cheeks.

"But you didn't want him back?"

She wiped her face with the back of her hand, fanned her fingers on the table. "I don't know. Of course I still love him. But he completely humiliated me. And he risked everything we'd built." She touched the empty place on her left ring finger where a wedding band would have been. "Have you heard of Page Six in the *New York Post*? It's celebrity gossip. He showed up there with a girlfriend—flaunted his cheating in front of me and the whole world."

"That must have felt awful," I said, meaning it. I'd just been reminded of how bad it felt to stumble upon Chad in bed with another girl. Even now, a year later, the memory still stung. At least my shame had been mostly private. Juan Carlos's infidelity had been shockingly public.

"What was the purpose of the shed in back of the restaurant, where the fire started?" I asked. "Can you think of anything that your ex-husband would have been looking for?"

"Storage," she said. "I'd had an air conditioner put in—the shed would have been worthless without climate control. This way I could keep the prices down by ordering in larger quantities."

"So, what—cans of tomatoes? Baking supplies? What?"

"All of that stuff," she said. "Once we put the big coolers in the kitchen, there wasn't a lot of room for dry goods."

"Okay, so dry goods. I can't imagine Juan Carlos was looking for canned broth in your shed."

She squared her shoulders. "First of all, we don't use canned broth in my food." She barely smiled. "And second, no, I can't think of any reason he'd have been there. We'd fought hours earlier, and then I returned to Sunset Key to try to calm down. You saw me at the bar."

I nodded. "Do you keep money there? A safe?"

"No," she said. "I would never leave valuables on that property. Too many people passing through. And he was definitely not after my money, what there is of that. His family is filthy rich."

I sat quietly for a moment, wondering now whether they'd had a prenuptial agreement, and whether any of his family dough would be hers upon his death— probably not after the divorce. And trying to parse out what she wasn't saying.

Her eyes widened, big as pot lids. "I see what you're thinking. The same idea the cops had. That I needed money for the restaurant project. And that doing him in would do the job because I'd inherit."

I snorted. "I hope that's not the best theory they've got cooking. There are plenty of ways that plan could go terribly wrong. What do you think happened? Did the police tell you exactly how he died?"

The tears began to run down her cheeks again. "The blow to the head knocked him out but it appears he died of smoke inhalation. If only I'd gone back to the restaurant and found him, I could have saved him." She removed the napkin from under her drink and blotted her eyes.

"So, are you thinking maybe someone set the fire to try to cover up what they'd done?" I said, watching her expression closely to see whether this hit home for her. Nothing.

"Or else he was unlucky," I added. "Really unlucky." This time she winced.

"Any ideas about who set the fire? Did he have problems with any of the staff who were working with you at the new place? Any conflicts that could be construed as a motive for murder?"

She smoothed out the damp napkin on the tabletop, folded it until it looked like a paper fortune-teller, the origami finger toy we used as young teenagers to predict the names of our future husbands. Then she lifted her gaze to meet mine. "He fought with many people. You have to understand, he was intensely emotional, which came, I'm certain, from his mother. She's a hot-blooded Spanish woman who never has gotten over Juan Carlos marrying someone of Irish descent. Oh, how I dread seeing her."

"The funeral," I said.

She shook her head. "She's not intending to have a funeral. A memorial service in a month or so, so all his friends and relations have time to make reasonable travel plans. She may be a hothead, but she's practical, too."

"So, you'll see her in a month?"

"If I'm invited." She groaned. "But, worse than that, she's flying in this afternoon to claim his body. I told her I'd pick her up at the airport and then put her up in my guest room. She declined staying with me, but I insisted that we have dinner—after all, we were the closest women in his life. At least for a while. But I'm dreading this so much."

She looked as though she would cry again. I knew what my mother would have me do.

"Why don't you both come to my mother's place for dinner tonight? She's having our gang already. Two more will not matter to her. In fact, I know she'd insist." After a few more minutes of convincing, she agreed.

"Will you be involved in planning the memorial service?"

"She won't let me anywhere near it."

"But still, he was your husband . . ."

She rolled her neck toward one shoulder, then the other. "We were history, as far as she was concerned. It's not worth fighting her on this."

A million thoughts ran through my head. How tragic it was that she wouldn't be invited to her own husband's memorial service. How complicated their lives must have been, entwined in both love and work. How hard it must have been for her to wrench herself away. Had she been as successful at separating herself from him as she claimed?

"I wonder what will happen to his restaurant in New York," I said.

"No idea. I suppose it will depend on what instructions he left in his will. And what his mother wants to do. It would be a shame to see it go."

"How was the place doing after you left the city?"

"Of course there was a big burst of interest following the disgusting publicity in that gossip rag. And a lull after I left with a few of the staff. But overall fine, I suppose."

She looked deflated, like a cake pulled from the oven too soon. "I should go."

"See you tonight, then." I patted her hand, paid our bar tab, and then headed out into the day. Sunny but breezy—most of the locals were wearing sweaters; some even had moved to hats and mittens. With no real work to do, I would have considered going to the beach, but it would have been windier there. And, besides, my mind was absolutely racing. So I drove over to Southard Street and parked in back of the Preferred Properties Real Estate office and shot up to the third floor to *Key Zest*. Which, chances were, would not be my place of employment much longer. And that thought made me feel instantly sad.

Danielle was not at her station, but thin lines of light leaked through the slats of Wally's shutters. I crept closer, listening for voices, but heard nothing. So I quickstepped to the end of the hall and settled in at my desk. Think like an optimist, I told myself. And for ten agonizing minutes, I brainstormed hypothetical articles for my possible future. A story on the lighted boat parade with excellent photographs would be a must for *Key Zest*. Of course the other magazines in town would also be carrying pictures of the boats in the harbor, all strung with Christmas lights. Nevertheless, we couldn't ignore one of the most beautiful events of the season. And I already had a front-row seat booked on Ray's boat.

Then I roughed out a review of the Kojin Noodle Bar based on previous experience—its light and savory dumplings, irresistible cold sesame noodles with shrimp, and the more adventurous pho and dragon bowl. My stomach growled ferociously and it occurred to me that the gut was my ticket in to talk with Wally. I dithered for a couple of minutes—should I ask him or just order? I called in an order big enough for two and went back to my computer.

Minutes later, I phoned Connie to find out where Ray thought the best vantage point on land to see the boats tomorrow evening might be. When she didn't answer, I left a message with the question. Then I moved on to roughing out a story on the New Year's Eve day Dachshund Parade, which had to be the strangest parade in Key West. Which is saying a lot, as this is a town replete with strange parades. But two city blocks undulating with dachshunds, aka wiener dogs, dressed in costumes, and other dogs dressed as hot dogs to impersonate dachshunds had to take first place. Last year, a Chihuahua flash mob gathered together through Facebook joined the procession at the last minute.

Finally I couldn't stand it a minute longer—this pretending to be productive. I went out to pick up my food. Back inside, with two big steaming bags of noodles, I rapped on Wally's door.

"Come in," he said, sounding surprised.

I pushed open the door. "Listen, I suddenly had a fierce craving for noodles from Kojin." I held up the loot. "Hope you'll help me eat—I ordered enough for the whole office. Want anything special to drink?" I plopped the bags on the floor and clapped both hands to my head. "I'm babbling like a crazy person. Let me start over." I picked up the take-out bags, turned around, and walked out, closing the door behind me—feeling like banging my head against it. Or simply fleeing. Instead I pasted on a big smile and knocked again.

"Come in." He opened his door.

"It's me. Just wondering how things are going." .

Wally burst out laughing. "What about the noodles? Aren't you going to mention the noodles?"

I grinned. "I figured I'd just show up with them and you'd get interested."

"Sit for a minute, okay? I am sorry about the way things are going around here," Wally said. "It's a stressful time and I wish it wasn't spilling over onto you and Danielle."

"Can you tell me anything?" I took the seat catty-corner to him and put the bags of food on the floor, hating that I sounded like I was pleading.

Wally sighed. "Nothing's been decided for sure. We're doing a lot of talking. And, of course, I'm talking about you and Danielle as part of the package."

"And Ava?"

"Ava is a major pill. Nothing is going to change her opinion about you. Well, maybe if you win a Pulitzer. Or a James Beard Foundation award. Yeah, that's the ticket." He turned back to his computer and tapped through his e-mail in-box. "I know I got a press release about this earlier in the week. The entries close on December eighteenth."

"I'll do whatever you suggest, but the chances of me winning a James Beard award are like the chances of finding a steamed vegetable in Paula Deen's kitchen." I pulled the container of dumplings out of the bag, offered one to Wally, and then dragged another through a pool of spicy sauce and popped it into my mouth. Instant ecstasy. "Who are these people who are thinking about investing?" I asked when I'd finished my bite.

He rolled his neck in a slow circle and I heard the crackles of tension. "They're both from New York City, colleagues of Ava's when she worked in magazines there years ago. I'm not sure anything will work out with Marcus Baker; he's not really clicking with Key West. But Palamina, she loves the place. It's like she lived here in another life."

"Is Ava out with them now?"

"She set up a little mini tour for each of them based on their interests. I think Palamina was going to hit the Hemingway House and then the butterfly museum. Or was it vice versa? Ava's got other things to do today, so I'm meeting Palamina at the Banana Café at noon. And, no, I'm sorry you can't join us. And I'm sorry about all those noodles." He flashed a wry smile. "They smell delicious, but I need to save myself for lunch. Maybe you can take the leftovers home to Miss Gloria?"

I nodded, feeling a heaviness settle into my stomach. Feeling ridiculous and hopeless. "I roughed out some ideas for articles for this week and next," I said, trying to muster up some enthusiasm. "I've never been so productive."

He ducked his head, looked away. "Let's give it some time. See how things go."

I slumped back to my cubicle with the take-out food. Sometimes hard news makes me hungry as a bear bursting out of hibernation. Other times—like now—I lose my appetite completely. I checked my e-mail, scrolled through a dozen Facebook status updates about holiday baking and cat antics, considered calling my mother. Instead, I stashed the noodle-shop takeout in Danielle's refrigerator and left the office. I headed across the island on Duval Street, which, I had to admit, looked better than any other time of year, decked out in faux-fir garlands with red bows and lots and lots of lights.

If Duval Street were a woman, she was dressed to kill.

17

I had a lump in my throat the size of a bundt cake pan.
—Jessica Soffer, *Tomorrow There Will Be Apricots*

I parked in the open lot between Duval and Simonton streets and jogged toward the butterfly conservatory. Even if Palamina wasn't inside or even if she refused to talk with me, a visit with the butterflies would calm my galloping mind and soothe my spirit. I went into the gift shop crammed full of butterfly doodads and paraphernalia, bought a ticket, and stepped inside the double doors that protected butterflies from escaping to the harsh outside environment.

The temperature was warm, the humidity high, and the air permeated with the sounds of birdsong and bubbling streams; I could feel my blood pressure plunging. I stopped to admire two gorgeous striped butterflies feeding on fresh cantaloupe, and watch a school of pink fish dart through the pond shaded by tropical foliage. Each time one of my negative thoughts pushed into consciousness, I shoved back. *You're going to lose your job. Get lost. You don't have a boyfriend.* Not listening. *Your stepfather-to-be prefers your cousin.*

"Ridiculous!" I said out loud. My inner voice was sounding like the lament of a ten-year-old.

The woman ahead of me turned around. "Were you talking to me?"

Palamina. I would have recognized the patterned tights and the over-the-knee black boots anywhere.

I grinned. "I have the bad habit of muttering to myself and sometimes it gets louder than I expected." I thrust my hand at her. "Hayley Snow. We met yesterday in the *Key Zest* office."

"Of course I remember you," she said, clasping my hand between both of hers and shaking it warmly. "I love your reviews. I've been reading over all of the back issues, and I think you bring a special zip to the magazine. Aside from that, I can tell you truly love to eat. Nothing worse than an anorectic food critic who picks at her meals."

"I'm definitely not a picker," I said, grinning and patting my belly, feeling my cheeks flush. "Thanks for the nice compliment. I'm glad you think I add a special zip, because, to be honest, Ava Faulkner wouldn't always agree. In fact, she'd like to pull the zipper closed on my employment contract."

"Ava doesn't hold all the cards," said Palamina. But her face had tightened, the warm, welcoming smile faded. "This place is amazing," she said, pointing to a pair of flamingos who had waded out of the shadows of the pond. "Wally and Ava had some wonderful suggestions for visiting what they imagined might be my favorite things in this town. And they were spot-on. I'm going to see the Hemingway cats next."

I clapped my hands. "Totally my number-one happy place on the island. I take the tour at least every couple of months, because each of the guides adds his own twist to the Hemingway story. But sometimes I go just to sit with the cats. The cats are the best."

We began to wander through the rest of the conservatory, Palamina exclaiming joyfully at each new species of butterfly. "I wonder how they get here."

I shrugged and pointed out a pair of hummingbirds hanging over the flowers of a flashy red royal poinciana. "So it sounds like you've known Ava a long time. How did you meet her?"

"We were sorority sisters," she said. "Seems like a lifetime ago. After graduation I stayed in New York, where I've been working on women's magazines for the past ten years. And meanwhile Ava was smart enough to move to paradise." She held out her arms, as if she meant the butterflies, the conservatory, the day, the island. She seemed to have fallen in love with Key West even more quickly than I had.

"I'm not convinced my colleague is bowled over by this opportunity," Palamina continued, "but I love what you and the other staff have done with *Key Zest* so far."

I made a snap decision: There was no advantage to being coy. "Unfortunately," I said, "I suspect you'll find that you have to choose between Ava and me." I sighed. "Since she is the big boss, there's not much of a contest."

Palamina laughed, tossing her streaked mane back like the horse she was almost named after. "Don't give up yet. I do know how to deal with her," she said. "We worked together for years as copy editors and researchers and general magazine gofer slaves."

I left Palamina meditating on a small metal bench in a recess of the conservatory. Glancing back, I saw two or three butterflies had landed on her multicolored hair to check out the new territory. I felt a little better knowing that she admired my writing and my ideas, but I thought she underestimated the power of her former classmate's wrath.

Back outside I stood on the sidewalk, blinking, adjusting to the tumult of tourists and the bright sunshine. I walked to the parking lot where I'd left my scooter and noticed a police car idling near the corner of United and Duval. The door swung open and Detective Bransford got out.

"Oh lord, what did I do now?" I asked.

"Good morning to you, too," he said, cracking a grin. "I know I was a little rough on you yesterday," he added gruffly.

I couldn't see his eyes through his dark sunglasses but he still had a small grimace on his lips. I kind of enjoyed seeing him grovel. "You were." I waited him out, letting him sweat.

"I'm under a lot of pressure to solve both the arson and the mysterious death," he said. "You know as well as I do how much is going on in this town during the Christmas season. The Chamber of Commerce has made a huge push about the lighted boat parade and the Old Town harbor as a holiday destination. Christ, they've spent a small fortune on advertising, even placing posters in the New York City subway system. But I'm getting panicked phone calls from the bed-and-breakfasts in town that people are canceling because they're spooked by the fire."

He pushed his sunglasses up the bridge of his nose. "So, I'm sorry if I came on too strong."

"I get it," I said. "Okay—you're under a lot of pressure. But I have nothing to do with any of this. I don't have anything to add."

"You don't think you have anything to add," he said

abruptly. "But you spent a full day and a half in Ms. Waugh's kitchen before the events in question occurred. I suspect you may have seen something that you don't realize that you saw." He removed his glasses so I couldn't avoid the fierce look in his eyes. "If you don't mind, I'd like to review your experience during those days."

"Now?" I asked.

"If you don't mind," he said. "If it's not inconvenient."

He couldn't seem to help a little sarcastic inflection on the last word. I slid into the passenger's side of his cruiser and he maneuvered the laptop computer protruding from under the dashboard out of my way.

"So, Ms. Waugh called you to come and observe her kitchen," he began.

"No." I shook my head. "Wally told me that my assignment was to do a piece on this new chef who was quite well-known in New York City. I was to write about the restaurant she was opening in Key West. It was only later that I learned that she had asked for me." I paused for a moment, puzzled. "But how did the assignment come about in the first place?" I wondered aloud. "It couldn't have been that Ava wanted the feature on Edel's place. Ava definitely didn't want me writing the piece. Maybe worth looking into that," I told Bransford. "Maybe she hates her for some reason. Although, in my experience, she dislikes about eighty percent of the people she runs into." I frowned. "But, on the other hand, my opinion is colored by the fact that I'm one of the people she can't stand." I stopped to draw a breath.

Already he was looking annoyed. "Okay, your boss didn't want the feature. But you went over there, anyway."

"Wait a minute," I said, "before you start assuming

I do whatever I want, no matter what the people in charge think."

"That sounds about right," he said.

I looked away, my hand on the door handle. "I have two bosses. Wally Beile is the editorial director. He's the one who assigned me the piece."

"Go on," he said.

"So I went to the restaurant, as I was asked. Edel was preparing for what she called a soft opening. She showed me around and had me observe for a couple of hours and then fed me dinner, along with the rest of the staff. Spaghetti Bolognese," I added, "in case you're interested." Which I doubted he was. He was not the kind of man to slow down and swoon over the subtle meld of pork and beef, tomatoes and milk and fresh basil, all simmered for hours. And then nestled on top of authentic Italian pasta and sprinkled with freshly grated Parmesan cheese. Or, I wondered, had she made the pasta herself right there in the restaurant? I remembered an incredible chewy texture and the way it had perfectly soaked up the sauce. But I hadn't seen a pasta machine.

"Earth to Hayley," said Bransford.

"Sorry. I was having a foodie moment." I grinned. "So, then I learned that after Wally made the first contact, she asked for me specifically on account of the problems that she was having in her kitchen. I told you guys all of that. And the second day I visited was when she threw a fit over the change in cooking oil."

"What kinds of reactions did you notice from the staff?" Bransford asked.

"They couldn't get away from her fast enough," I said. "She was scary, screaming at the top of her lungs. I mean, I understand why she was upset. A person could have died."

Bransford broke in. "A person did die. In fact, it was her husband."

"Her ex. But I know very little about that," I said. "We did not discuss her personal life the two nights I was in her kitchen."

"And you never saw him come by?"

"Never. I don't even know what he looks like. I assumed he was still up north." I pressed my hands to my cheeks. "That's not quite it—I didn't assume anything because his presence or absence didn't cross my mind."

"And you know nothing about their relationship."

I squirmed. "We talked about it a little after the fire. And I did some reading. I'm sure you saw the Page Six article, too."

Bransford studied me, his lips twitching. "Listen, we've had our disagreements, you and me. And I understand how you react if you think someone is trying to influence you. Truth is, you're the most stubborn girl I've ever met."

"Oh, how you flatter me," I said, blinking my eyes like a debutante.

He did not smile. "But you really don't know what you've gotten into this time. This is a ruthless woman. If she's killed once and tried to hide it, she would do it again in a heartbeat. If she feels threatened. And you probably make her feel threatened. Because you are nosy and relentless," he said, ending that speech with a sputter.

"Why, thank you," I said. "What a lovely description." I pushed open the car door and sprang out. "I know. I know. Don't hesitate to call if I think of anything else."

I rattled off his phone number, which I wished I could erase from my brain at the same time that I eliminated Chad Lutz's number from my memory. Then I poked my head back into the cruiser.

"And since you'll probably hear this, anyway, you might as well hear it from me. Edel and her ex-mother-in-law are coming to my mother's home for dinner tonight. My mother is fully in the loop. Whether Edel killed him or not, both she and Juan Carlos's mother are desperately grieving. And for the record, I don't believe she did kill him. I think she still loved him. I believe she was devastated by his infidelity."

He shook his head, looking beyond annoyed. "Honest to god, you make me want to throttle you."

"So unprofessional," I said, gritting my teeth and smiling. Wondering how I could taunt him back. "Since our boundaries are loose today, anyway, would you like to come for dinner, too?" I slammed the door and stalked off to my scooter.

He rolled down his car window and called after me. "What time?"

18

She ripped open the cellophane bag and even though it was before dinner, they both sat there, eating cookies and not talking, ruining their appetites and not even caring.
—Caroline Leavitt, *Is This Tomorrow*

With my hands still trembling from the dustup with Bransford, I punched my mother's number on speed dial. "I'm afraid I just invited another mouth for dinner," I said when she answered. "The rest of his body's coming, too."

"Wonderful! I'd love to spend more time with Wally."

"Unfortunately." I paused and cleared my throat. "It's not Wally who's coming, it's Detective Bransford."

Mom was stunned to silence for a moment, which doesn't happen often. "Well, honey, if that's who you like now, why, we'll try to like him, too."

"I don't like him," I said and started to describe how the invitation came about. But how to explain that I felt like he'd been needling me so I needled him back? And then why in the world had he turned the tables and accepted my offer, which I'd not really meant? "Bottom line is I think he believes Edel killed her own husband but he can't quite nail her. I think maybe he hopes she'll say something to incriminate herself."

"Odd," said my mother, but she sounded distracted. "We'll figure it all out when he arrives. And if he acts rude, we'll ask him to leave. Wait until you get here—the sauce smells divine. Could you possibly find something to fill in for dessert at Fausto's? I'm running a little behind."

"I've got cookie dough in the freezer on the houseboat," I said. "I'll bake some up this afternoon and get Miss Gloria to help with the decorating."

"Sam wants us all here by six," Mom told me. "He's making special cocktails and he says he has a surprise."

After hanging up with Mom, I tried to imagine who might know more about Edel and Juan Carlos than I'd found out so far. I tapped through my apps until I found the WhitePages. Then I typed in Mary Pat Maloney and found her address, located in a small neighborhood in New Town, just ten minutes from where I was standing. How could it hurt to swing by and have a chat with her?

I started up my scooter and headed south on Duval Street toward the Atlantic Ocean and then took a left on South Street. As the holidays got closer, the hordes of tourists seemed to grow larger. Was it my imagination or were more of them Asian, speaking in languages that sounded utterly foreign? I had to wonder what they made of our little island, and whether this was the only place in the United States that they were visiting. If that were true, what a peculiar sense of our country they would be taking back with them.

I found Mary Pat's home in the small neighborhood

a stone's throw from the Publix supermarket. New Town is still Key West, but set outside the district of wooden homes with eyebrow windows and gingerbread trim that constitutes historic Old Town. Also set outside of HARC, the Historical Architecture Review Commission, with its strict guidelines. These houses were mostly built of concrete, with small yards of thick spiky grass, shaded by palm trees and prickly bougainvillea hedges in full pink bloom.

The trunks of the palm trees in Mary Pat's yard had been wrapped with red and green Christmas lights. Inside her picket fence, enormous blow-up figurines of Santa and his elves had pride of place. Every window, door, and roofline was draped with blinking icicle lights, and the outline of Santa fishing flashed on the roof. Three towheaded boys wrestled in the yard in front of the plastic Santa. I stopped outside the gate.

"Hey, guys," I called, "is your mom around?"

The boys paused for a minute to look me over, then the middle boy hollered, "Mom! A lady wants to talk to you."

Mary Pat came to the door, a denim apron hanging around her neck and tied loosely around her waist. Both she and the apron were dusted with flour, and she clutched a spoon dripping with some kind of batter. The incomparable scent of baking cookies wafted out behind her.

"Oh my gosh," I said, "it smells divine. Gingerbread?"

Mary Pat squinted as she studied me, but finally she nodded. "We're going to build our gingerbread house this afternoon."

"We're making a castle!" screeched the two bigger boys in unison.

"With a moat," added the smallest one.

"And knights and warlocks and cowboys and Indians," shouted the others.

Mary Pat shrugged and grinned. "You see what comes of not producing a daughter?"

I smiled back. "I guess it's not the best time to bother you, with a castle in the oven," I said, "but could I come in and ask you a few questions? I won't take long. But it's really important. You know about Edel's husband by now, I assume."

She pinched her lips together with her left fingers and wiped her face with her right arm, leaving a sweep of flour across her forehead. "I don't have much time."

"I swear it will be just a few minutes," I said, sniffing the air. Was something burning?

She rushed into her house and I followed. The screen door banged closed behind us. "Boys," she called back over her shoulder, "stay in the yard."

Her kitchen might have been eligible for disaster assistance—the counters and sink stacked with pots and pans and bowls and dishes, all spattered with butter and sugar and flour. A battered copy of *The Joy of Cooking* lay open on the kitchen table. She hurried across the linoleum floor, flung open the oven door, and yanked out a tray of cookies in the shape of castle building blocks, with the edges crisped almost to black. She sighed.

"At least these pieces are the roof. They'll be covered in white icing, so a little extra brown along the edges won't hurt a thing. So, what did you want to know?" she asked.

I tried to frame my questions carefully. Here was a woman accustomed to making the best of situations that weren't perfect. And yet she'd made that comment a few days ago about her dreams getting trashed.

"I wondered how long you've known Edel and her

husband. How did you start working for them? And how did it happen that you made the move from New York City to Key West?"

"That's three questions," she said with a smirk. Then she began to roll out more gingerbread dough on the one clear counter that had been sprinkled with flour. "I met them years ago when they were down here on their honeymoon," she said. "That was BK."

I looked puzzled.

"Before kids," she said. "Life was a lot simpler. I was a newlywed myself, working for Blue Heaven back then. I was semifamous for creating a beautiful tropical salad. At the center was a pan-fried grouper, surrounded by mango and avocado slices and then drizzled with the most amazing lime vinaigrette."

"Sounds glorious." My mouth was watering. "What kind of vinegar did you use in the dressing?"

"Trade secret," she said with a laugh. "Edel and Juan Carlos asked their waiter the same question. When he couldn't or wouldn't answer, they asked to meet the chef responsible for such a masterpiece. So when the lunch rush was over, I came out from the kitchen. At first they tried to wangle the recipe out of me. When I refused to hand it over, they started talking about the restaurant they had opened in New York. And how they were always looking for the best of the best to come and work for them, and would I be interested in joining them? What did I have to lose?"

She heaved an enormous sigh and began to scrape the gingerbread forms onto an oiled tray. Then she slid the tray in the oven, set the timer, and plunked onto the seat across from me. She dipped her finger into a bowl of green icing. "Ahhh . . . Sugar. Want a hit?"

"No, thanks." I watched her lick the icing off her fingers like a grooming cat. "I'm going to be blunt. Do you know of any reason someone would have had it in for Edel? Had she ruffled feathers getting her new restaurant off the ground?"

Mary Pat unloosed the band that held her ponytail, then smoothed her hair and gathered it back up. "I'll tell you this because you'll find it out, anyway. I really got along better with Juan Carlos. But, on the other hand, I was dying to get back to this island. During our eight years in New York, my husband and I had the three boys, and we were all squeezed into a one-bedroom apartment." She jerked her thumb at the front yard. "I thought we could make a better life for them if we could get down here. I didn't know that my husband wouldn't be coming along. We didn't have a big blowout or anything; he's a musician and he just wasn't prepared to leave New York."

"I'm sorry to hear that—you've suffered a loss, too." I rested my chin in my hand. "And raising the boys alone—that sounds hard. How do you manage?"

"My mother lives in the back bedroom—it's her house, anyway. She's here whenever I'm working. Or whenever I was planning to be working. I don't know if that darn place will open, the way things are going."

"But you'll find work, anyway." I smiled. "The island was probably devastated when you left with your vinaigrette recipe. Did Juan Carlos object to Edel establishing her own restaurant?"

"He was a fiery man with flashes of brilliance and also flashes of idiocy," said Mary Pat. "The ladies loved him. And I think he expected that Edel would stick with him no matter what he did on the side. He didn't even imagine that she could get along without him." She shook her head. "And to come back to Key West without him, his island paradise . . ."

I screwed up my nerve. "Were you involved with him?"

She scrunched up her face and almost spat the green frosting out. "You've got to be kidding. Where would I find the time between working sixty hours in the kitchen and raising three boys?" Her voice was irate.

"Sorry—I had to ask." I ducked my head. "I'm just trying to figure out who she angered—who didn't want her opening. Who might have wanted her to fail? And could it have been Juan Carlos himself?"

The timer chimed and she pushed away from the table, grabbed a pair of oven mitts, and pulled the cookie sheets from the oven.

"Juan Carlos would not try to destroy her. He wasn't that kind of man. And, besides, he did love her." She ripped open a bag of gumdrops, dumped them into a glass bowl, and brought them to the table. "Boys!" she yelled out to the yard. "Ten minutes and we'll put this damn house together."

"But why was he here?"

"You'd have to ask her that," Mary Pat said. "And while you're at it, ask her neighbors on the bight what it was like to have a pushy New Yorker sail in and try to take over the harbor. They've had colored lights and flashing reindeer and lighted beer cans and everything else for years. And suddenly she wants them to put only white lights up? Ridiculous! That's all I have to say." She clamped her lips, stood up, and stomped outside.

I scored one red gumdrop and followed her to the yard, where she was herding her boys back into the kitchen. "Thanks for chatting," I said. "And good luck with the gingerbread house."

I mounted my scooter, reminded by Mary Pat's gingerbread that I'd promised to bake cookies for dinner. I dialed up Miss Gloria and asked her to pull the cookie dough and the icing out of the refrigerator and the freezer. Then I made my way across town, trying not to get annoyed at the holiday traffic. Parking in the Tarpon Pier lot, I could hear Schnootie the schnauzer's hysterical barking all the way up the finger to our houseboat.

Mr. Renhart poked his head out of their living area and yelled to his wife. "Could you shut that fool dog up? Or I'll take the thing back to the pound."

Mrs. Renhart gathered the animal into her arms. "Daddy doesn't mean it," she whispered to the quivering dog. "It's just that he's working the night shift this week and he's tired and crabby." They disappeared into the cabin, both of them sniffling.

On the counters of our tiny galley, Miss Gloria had laid out the sugar cookie dough, the colored icing, and the colored sprinkles, and she'd preheated the oven. I washed my hands and rummaged through the drawers to find my heavy-duty rolling pin and the new cookie cutters I'd ordered from Sur La Table. Miss Gloria danced across the room to turn on her favorite CD of Christmas carols.

"I love this season," she said. "Almost enough to make me want to go back up to Michigan for the holidays. The snow was so pretty." She laughed. "But the winds off the lake were wicked—more than an old lady who's thin as a spare rib can bear."

I laughed along with her and whirled her off her feet. "And we would miss you so much! And your sons are coming next month, right?"

She nodded. "I tried to get them to come for Christmas, but it's a devil of a time to travel. Prices are jacked up so high."

I began to roll out the dough, dip the cookie cutters in flour, and cut out the shapes of palm trees, sunglasses, iguanas, and roosters. Once the cookies were baked and cooled, we painted green fronds and white lights on the palms, red frames and white lenses on the sunglasses, and wild colors not seen in nature on the roosters and iguanas.

Outside, the not so dulcet barking of Schnootie the schnauzer had started up again, drowning out Emmylou Harris's version of "Silent Night." The racket went on and on. I packed up a dozen of the cookies for the Renharts and stepped outside to see if Schnootie had identified someone suspicious on the dock. Miss Gloria trailed behind me and settled into a deck chair.

The UPS man, wearing a holiday hat and jingle bells, was delivering a stack of packages to the boat at the end of the finger.

I waved down Mrs. Renhart, handed off the cookies, and tried to scratch behind Schnootie's ears. She whirled around, snarling, then resumed barking.

"I'm awfully sorry about the rumpus," Mrs. R said, shaking her head. "The busier the island gets, the more nervous is Schnootie. I think the renters who are staying on the two-story yacht at the end have gotten under her skin. And she really dislikes men with facial hair."

"No problem," I said, and added, "Merry Christmas."

"She's been barking her fool head off all day," whispered Miss Gloria when I returned. "Every delivery man on the island seems to think it's cute to wear a Santa hat." She broke into a big grin. "And it is cute— except for poor Schnootie's Christmas neurosis."

Connie and Ray came up the dock from the parking lot, carrying a toolbox. "Ahoy!" called Ray.

"Come and have some of our cookies," Miss Gloria suggested.

"No can do," said Connie. "We've been working on the decorations for Ray's boat for the lighted boat parade and we've run out of supplies. Gotta make a run up to The Home Depot. Remember you guys are invited to come with us tomorrow evening."

"Hot dog!" said Miss Gloria. "That'll be the best seat in the house."

"Bring Wally if you like," Connie said.

I rolled my eyes. "We're not really going anywhere together these days."

"Oh, Hayley," said Connie. "I thought you two were perfect for each other."

"In a perfect world we might have been," I grumbled. "But that perfect world wouldn't include Ava Faulkner."

19

Everything you see I owe to spaghetti.
                              —Sophia Loren

I double wrapped the cookies in tissue paper, zipped them into plastic bags, and strapped them into the basket on the back of the scooter. Then Miss Gloria and I donned our helmets, climbed aboard, and roared away. We stopped to admire the Christmas lights on Southard Street that had won second place in the town-wide competition. These decorations were a more expansive and sophisticated version of the lights I'd seen over in Mary Pat's neighborhood. A school of blue fish flashed by, lighting up in sequence across two sides of the home. Above the faux water line—a string of blue lights—Frosty the Snowman manned a rowboat, dipping his oars into the sea over and over. And finally at the far right corner of the house, Santa reeled in one of the bright blue fish. Every inch of the property was decked out with lights, ending with a carpet of white bulbs on the sidewalk that led to the street.

"Snow! I love it!" said Miss Gloria. "This one is so

amazing that it's hard to imagine what the first prize display looked like."

Then we crossed Duval Street, crowded as always, tooled through the Truman Annex gates past the gatehouse and down two blocks to my mother's street. Since I'd visited on her first day in town, she had wound lights and garlands of fresh evergreens around her porch pillars and along the railings. Candles flickered in every window and a big wreath dressed with a red bow and golden musical instrument ornaments hung on the front door. We parked in the shallow brick driveway to the right of the home and banged the knocker.

Sam flung the door open, a warm smile on his face. "Early Merry Christmas—come in, come in!"

He hugged us both, took the cookies, and ushered us inside. At the far end of the tropical-style living room towered an enormous fir tree, sparkling with white lights. I breathed in the heavenly evergreen scent. Around the base of the tree sat boxes of ornaments that I recognized from many trips up and down the stairs to the attic before and after holidays past. Labels on the brown boxes in my mother's neat script read: Fragile! Crèche and Train Set! Aunt Mary's Antiques! and Hayley's Homemade!

"How in the world did these get here?"

A wide grin split Sam's face again. "I packed them up and had them sent."

"That's so sweet!"

I dropped to my knees and began to peek into the boxes, feeling a wash of nostalgia. Here was the green glass good-luck pickle from the year I turned seven, and the pickles that followed every year until I turned fifteen. And here a piglet with her spider friend from *Charlotte's Web*, the year I was eight. And the set of perfect crystal snowflakes from the terribly imperfect Christmas after my father had moved out. Handel's *Messiah* played softly from the enormous Bose speakers and the sound of banging pots from the kitchen clanged in the background—a perfect accompaniment.

"Everyone's in the kitchen," Sam said, after I'd spent a few minutes rooting through the ornaments. "They say people will always gather there, no matter how nice the other rooms are."

"As good as this house is starting to smell," said Miss Gloria, "I am heading for the kitchen, too."

I tore myself away from my childhood memories and followed her. Standing at the center island, my mother and Cassie wore matching Christmas-themed aprons and Mom was instructing Cassie in the finer points of chopping vegetables for a salad. Joe sat at the kitchen table with Wally, drinking a beer. With Wally? My heart flip-flopped.

Right away, Wally noticed my chagrined look and shrugged helplessly. "I know this is a little awkward with all that's going on at *Key Zest*," he said, "but I ran into Sam here at Fausto's and he insisted that I come."

Mom looked over from her workstation, dried her hands on her apron, and hurried across the room to hug us. "We knew you wouldn't mind if Wally came to supper. I assured him that you can set aside the work stresses and just enjoy the evening," she whispered for my ears only. "Sam said he was about to buy the most pathetic-looking takeout. He couldn't just leave him there alone."

"If you say so," I muttered. I set the cookies on the table and Miss Gloria and I began to arrange them on a big green platter as the others exclaimed over our decorating skills.

"Cocktails and tree trimming before anyone gets

dinner," said Sam, when the prep work was finished. "Come on out to the living room and taste my special Christmas cocktail. I call it the Jungle Red." Sam motioned to us to pick up glasses and hefted a glistening pitcher filled with a dark pink liquid.

"What's in it?" asked Joe, looking at the pitcher with some suspicion.

Sam listed the ingredients—pomegranate juice, Prosecco, and orange liqueur. And garnishes of raspberries and pomegranate seeds and a lemon twist.

"I'll stick with beer," Joe said, backing away. He cracked open another bottle of Key West ale.

"Me, too," said Wally. He moved over to stand with Joe and they clinked their bottles.

Once we all had drinks, my mother and I began to unwrap the ornaments, and with the assistance of Cassie and Miss Gloria, hang them on the tree. When the boxes were emptied, we stood back to admire the results.

Mom sighed and slung an arm around my waist. "Like old times. Only better, right?"

I kissed her cheek. "Good new times."

Sam rummaged through the tissue paper in the box that had held the crèche. "There appears to be something you missed," he said, pulling out a small cardboard box taped shut. He handed it to my mother, who looked as puzzled as I felt.

"I've never seen this before," she said, turning to me. "Do you remember putting this one away?"

I shrugged. "Not really. But last Christmas was so hectic. Remember how I had to split my time with Dad and Allison and you guys and then get back down here for New Year's? Open it up and see what's inside."

Mom took the little package from Sam and used a pair of scissors to slice the packing tape. Inside was a green velveteen cube that looked suspiciously like a jewelry box. She peered up at Sam, her brows furrowed. Then she cracked open the box, revealing a ring, an antique gold band with an exquisite pattern of diamonds set into the gold.

"I was hoping this might be a good time to ask you if you'd marry me," Sam said, a tentative smile on his lips. His face had flushed pink and he looked happy yet vulnerable.

Mom's mouth opened and closed, opened and closed, opened and closed, like a hungry tarpon. "I hardly know what to say. You've caught me entirely by surprise." She took a deep breath. "It's absolutely lovely," she said, staring at the ring, without addressing his question in the slightest. She set the box on the coffee table, dialed up a big smile, and turned to me. "What are Allison and your father doing for the holidays? Did you say something about a cruise?"

I looked at her, whiplashed by the change in subject. "Rory is visiting his father over the holiday, so they're going to the British Virgin Islands for a few days."

Why was she bringing that up now? It was a rare thing for my mother to lack words suitable to a big moment. And it seemed rude and hurtful to sweet Sam. "The ring is stunning, Sam," I said, leaning in to get a closer look. "And now I suggest we vacate the premises and give you two some privacy." I tipped my head to the others and they leaped up and followed me to the kitchen.

"Sometimes surprises aren't what they're cracked up to be," said Cassie, glancing over at her husband. "We talked the idea to death before my sweetie proposed."

"I feel a little sorry for him," said Joe. "Since he gave her the ring so publicly, I bet he was thinking she'd accept on the spot." He squeezed Cassie's hand. "I suspect he's not used to someone else calling the shots."

Miss Gloria giggled. "He'd better get used to it. Strong women abound in this family!"

"I'll second that," said Wally.

We remained in the kitchen for the next ten minutes, trying to make ourselves useful. No doubt my mother would let us know when the coast was clear. The time lag did not bode well for Sam and his proposal. If she'd accepted, they both would have bounded into the kitchen to make that announcement and show off the ring for a second and more rousing round of admiration and congratulations.

I stirred the Bolognese sauce that simmered on the stove and took a taste, then adjusted it with a dash of kosher salt and a couple grinds of fresh black pepper. Cassie and Joe and Wally worked on putting together the salad, and Miss Gloria pressed two cloves of garlic and mashed them into half a stick of softened butter. We slathered the butter on a white country loaf from Old Town Bakery that had been cut in half lengthwise and then wrapped it in foil. Just when I had begun to wonder whether we'd be spending the night hiding out in the kitchen, Mom bustled into the room without Sam. Then the doorbell rang.

Mom frowned. "Who could that be?"

"I'll get it," Sam called from the front room.

My stomach twisting, I wiggled my eyebrows. "I mentioned to you that someone else might be stopping by."

"Well, I never imagined you were serious," said Mom.

"I never imagined he'd actually come. Maybe I'm wrong. Maybe it's the Fuller Brush Man," I muttered again, and went off to see.

But it wasn't Detective Bransford at the door, it was Chef Edel and her mother-in-law. Ex. They both looked pale and pinched, as though they'd been fighting. Or at least as though they'd been through a terrible war, which an untimely death could be considered. My mother and the others came into the living room to greet the newcomers.

Once I had introduced them around, Sam made quick work of providing drinks. Miss Gloria hurried over to the two of them with crackers and a bowl of smoked fish dip, a specialty of the Eaton Street Fish Market.

"This must be a terrible, terrible time for you," said my mother. "We're so glad you came by. Though I'm a little worried about my Bolognese sauce," she said to Edel with a smile. "From what my daughter tells me, it can't possibly live up to yours."

"I'm just grateful when someone cooks for me," Edel said. "It doesn't happen very often. People are intimidated by making dinner for a chef."

"Like when someone sings 'Happy Birthday' to a musician," said Miss Gloria. "No one but me will sing to my daughter in-law the opera singer, because they're so worried that she'll critique them for their range or their notes."

"Exactly," said Edel.

"She knows I can't sing," joked Miss Gloria. "So she braces for the worst."

My mother turned to Edel's mother-in-law. "We are just devastated about the news of your son's death. I told Edel yesterday how much we adored the restaurant in New York City. My ex-husband and I would go there for every special occasion." She threw back her head and laughed, her voice high and strained. "I even went there with a girlfriend to finally celebrate our divorce. That's the thing about a great meal: It's appropriate for any occasion whether it's happy or sad. And, my goodness, the sautéed spring vegetables on cheese grits with those Parmesan crisps?" She put her hands to her chest. "That dish was a dream come true. And the plate looked like an artist's palette."

"Thank you," said Juan Carlos's mother. "Though that particular recipe was Edel's, I believe. But I do appreciate your sympathy." Sam topped off her pink drink and she took a long sip, and I tried to think of another avenue of conversation. The doorbell rang again.

"My goodness," said my mother, fanning her face with her hand, "we are having quite a night here."

Sam strode across the room to answer the door. Detective Bransford followed him back in, bringing with him a blast of cold air. Which pretty much matched the expressions on the faces around me.

"The wind has really picked up," said Bransford. "We may need our down parkas by the end of the evening." He cracked a grim smile. "But good evening, all."

My mother moved forward. "I bet you haven't met everyone, Nathan," she said. "This is my friend Sam from New Jersey." She laid a hand on Sam's back, then yanked it off just as quickly, as if touching a hot griddle.

"I think we may have met last year with the Rory business," said Sam. "But nice to see you again."

My mother nudged Cassie and Joe forward. "And these are my niece Cassie, and her husband, Joe Lancaster. She's a golfer on the LPGA tour and Joe is her shrink."

Everyone laughed. "Not exactly," said Cassie.

I took a step closer to Bransford and took over from

my mother. "I know you've met Wally. And certainly you know Edel Waugh and her—Juan Carlos's mother."

"Yes." Bransford nodded. "Again, I'm sorry for your loss."

With no more introductions to give, an awkward silence fell over the room.

Sam clapped his hands together. "What are you drinking, man? Sorry to fall short on my duties."

"What have you got?" responded Bransford. Looking around the room at the women, he added: "Nothing pink, please. Do you happen to have a Diet Coke?"

While Sam rummaged in the cooler to find the detective a soda, my mother excused herself to finish getting the dinner ready. "Why don't you stay with the guests?" she suggested to Miss Gloria and Cassie. "Hayley can help me finish up."

In the kitchen, I fluttered around the table, adding enough place settings for the newcomers. And gritting my teeth to stay silent—waiting for my mother to comment about the marriage proposal.

"This is turning out to be a most unusual evening," she finally said from her place at the stove.

"You got that right. Did you give Sam an answer?" I hissed.

She waved her hand. "Later." But the grimace on her face and the empty ring finger told it all: There were no wedding bells in our family's immediate future.

Wally stuck his head into the kitchen, then motioned me closer and tipped his head at Edel, then Bransford. "Why is she here? Why is he here?"

"This has nothing to do with you or the magazine," I said. "I know you think I should keep a professional distance, but she's in mourning, as is her mother-in-law. And because my mother is a kind person, she invited them to join us." Which wasn't exactly the way it had gone, but why was it his business, anyway? "As for Detective Bransford—I have no control over where he goes or what he says. If you're uncomfortable with the guest list, I suggest you retire." I shook off his angry gaze and flounced out to the living room. "Dinner is served."

If there had been a more difficult seating chart in my mother's entertaining history, I don't know when it might have been or what warring factions were involved. But without looking flustered, she arranged everyone—Sam at the end in between Edel and her mother-in-law, Bransford at the other end, flanked by Miss Gloria and Cassie, the rest of us as filler to cushion the layers of tension. She served the spaghetti and sauce family style, piled high in two brightly colored Italian bowls. I delivered the salad and the garlic bread and grated cheese to the table.

"This is really lovely," Edel said, and her husband's mother murmured her agreement. "It has a little bit of sweetness—I think you must use a lot of carrots in your recipe. And maybe two kinds of wine?"

"You're amazing!" said my mother. "What a palate you have."

For ten minutes we ate, with only small talk to fill the space. And more red wine than was probably good for any of us.

"Do you have any idea why your son was in Key West?" Bransford asked Mrs. Alonso, after he'd wolfed down the mound of pasta on his plate. "Seems as though the holidays would be a busy time for his restaurant. Hard to get away."

"No idea," she said at the same time that Edel said, "He loved Key West. And I told you that he wanted to reconsider the divorce. More to the point might be:

Have you identified any suspects in the murder and arson?"

"Perhaps," said Sam in a genial voice, "we could save the interrogation until after dinner?"

"How long are you staying?" my mother asked Mrs. Alonso.

"Only until tomorrow. I'll have to get back and help with the restaurant—I suspect they're in chaos. And I'm planning a public memorial service for February. Juan Carlos would have been horrified if we canceled the holiday reservations that his customers made a year in advance."

Edel's face clouded. I wondered if she was wondering when her own restaurant might be allowed to open. That first night would be so important for the restaurant's future, along with those early weeks when her staff worked to get their sea legs. In the wake of the tragedies this week, they'd essentially lost their momentum. But maybe she wasn't thinking about the restaurant at all. Maybe she was remembering Juan Carlos. I recalled Eric talking about how grief can be so much more complicated when feelings about a relationship are unresolved before a death.

This conversation, these thoughts, were so inappropriate for a dinner table that my gut clenched with the tension.

Sam must have been thinking along the same lines. "Cassie, when is your first event on the Ladies Professional Golf Tour?" he asked as he got up to get another bottle of wine.

"We're talking that over," said Joe before she could answer. "She might go to the tournament in the Bahamas in January, but we're skipping Australia, Thailand, and Singapore."

"Don't you girls play in the US of A anymore?" asked Miss Gloria. She giggled as though she were tipsy, which she probably was. I had to hope she wouldn't drop off the back of the scooter on our way home.

"I don't know what I'll decide," said my cousin flatly. Joe reached across the table to take her hand, but she pulled away. After a moment, she pushed away from the table and stalked off to the porch. What was up between them?

"Well," said my mother in her brightest voice. "Shall we clear the table and serve the cookies? Miss Gloria and Hayley have outdone themselves in the decorating department," she added.

Bransford's cell phone buzzed. He glanced at the screen, muttered something unintelligible, and then stood up. "I have to get going. Thanks for dinner," he said to my mother. And more generally to the rest of us at the table: "I'll be in touch." Sam sprang to his feet to see the detective off, and Wally followed, saying his good-byes as he left.

"That's an improvement already," said Sam when he returned. "Sorry. That was rude. And I didn't mean to dis Wally." He grinned. "More wine, anyone?"

"We should be leaving also," said Mrs. Alonso. "I'm only now realizing how flat-out exhausted I feel."

"Do you need a lift?" Sam asked.

But Edel's mother-in-law explained that she'd rented a car and was staying at one of the hotels near the airport. I escorted them to the front porch and then returned to the kitchen, feeling pretty much like a wet sandbag, too.

"Has there ever been a worse dinner party?" my mother asked, nodding yes when Sam offered to fill her wineglass. "I feel like a terrible hostess, inflicting that cop on them in the midst of their grief."

"At least the food was good," said Miss Gloria.

Mom smiled, and then turned to me. "Why in the world did Bransford come, anyway?"

"I suspect his investigation is stalled. He was hoping Something Would Be Revealed." I wiggled my fingers in the air.

"Oh come on," said Sam. "He expected Edel to confess over a mouthful of pasta?"

Miss Gloria leaned forward, bright pink spots of excitement blooming on her cheeks. "I happened to be able to read the text that came in. Something about a Mary Pat."

"Mary Pat Maloney?" I asked. "She's one of Edel's line cooks. I spoke with her earlier today."

My mother's eyes bored in on me. "What do you mean, you spoke with her?"

"I swung by her place in New Town because I thought she might know quite a bit about the tensions in the kitchen at the bistro." I made a mental note to call Torrence tomorrow and see if he'd tell me what the cops really knew.

"And?" Joe asked.

"And she clammed up pretty quickly. That was after she told me flat out that she preferred Juan Carlos to Edel. So I can't imagine she killed him. Why would she?"

"Why would anyone kill anyone?" Joe asked. "Unless you're a sociopath who cares nothing for human life. Or"—he rubbed his chin—"unless you've been backed into a corner and strike out in desperation. I suspect that's why most murders occur. Someone makes a little mistake and tries to cover it up and the lies snowball . . ."

He sat back and sipped his wine. A smart man, just like my friend Eric. Except with his own wife, who seemed to be his blind spot. If I'd been in Cassie's position, mad at him for something, I'd have wanted him to come after me, comfort me, get me to talk about what was wrong.

But where did I get off critiquing anyone else's relationship when I was batting zero with my own?

20

"This is the Mr. Potato Head School of Cooking," he said. "Interchangeable parts. If you don't have something, think of what that ingredient does and attach another."
—Elizabeth Bard, *Lunch in Paris*

After spending most of the day poking around the houseboat—organizing, cleaning, and baking more cookies to try to keep myself from sinking into the doldrums, I walked up the dock to Connie's boat, where Ray would be picking us up for the lighted boat parade. Miss Gloria had decided to take a taxi up to the Truman Annex and watch the parade with my family from the less hectic viewpoint of Mallory Square.

First thing this morning, I had put a call in to Lieutenant Torrence, begging for any new information on the case. He hadn't returned it. Nor had Edel returned a text message asking if she'd heard when the restaurant might open. And my mother hadn't answered my text, either, in which I'd wondered whether she'd made up her mind about Sam's proposal. Worst of all, there had been no word from Wally about the status of the investors and Ava's plans for *Key Zest*.

Connie was out on her deck, watering her plants and picking off brown leaves from the undersides. "Ahoy!" she called. "So glad you could get away from work and family for a little relaxation."

"I desperately need the distraction," I said as I boarded. Her boat felt utterly familiar, as I'd lived with her for several months when I first arrived in Key West. I missed the day-to-day contact with my friend, but not my tiny closet of a bedroom, which had also functioned as storage space for the cleaning supplies for her business. The smell of Clorox and pine-scented industrial cleanser to this day made me feel a bit claustrophobic.

"There is no work to speak of," I added glumly. "If you have an opening for a house cleaner, I may be available." And then I filled her in on the upheaval at the magazine.

"What does Wally say?" she asked, a look of concern on her face.

"We had the dinner from hell last night," I told her, "and he hardly said a word except to question me about why Bransford and Edel were there, too."

Her eyes bugged wide. "Bransford? Edel? What kind of weird dinner party is that?"

I sighed and then welcomed the sight of Ray chugging up the channel toward us in his little motorboat. "I'll tell you later," I said. Listing all my worries out loud would only make them feel more real.

Connie ran inside to get her costume and equipment for the parade, while I moved to the back deck to grab Ray's bowline. As he glided closer, I noticed that on the bow's point he had wired a reindeer like the ones I was used to seeing adorning snowy front yards in New Jersey. The body and antlers were wound with blinking, multicolored lights. Pecking around the deer's hooves were three lighted chickens. More lights were strung up the poles that supported the Bimini top over his console. Ray himself wore a red T-shirt and a Santa hat that blinked in a cadence that matched the chickens. Christmas music pumped out over a hidden speaker. Ray had recorded himself singing "Rudolph the Red-Fowled Reindeer."

"Fantastic!" I cried, laughing so hard I could barely get the words out. "You've got a winner there."

"Strictly amateur hour," said Ray with a wry grin. "We don't really stand a chance against the sailboats with their big masts and riggings. But we had a lot of fun putting it together. Ready to go?"

I waved the elf hat I'd worn in the Hometown Holiday Parade and called back to Connie. "Captain says he's casting off."

Connie popped out of her cabin, dressed all in red and green, with a blinking hat to match Ray's and a blinking necklace, too. She carried a small cooler and a large flashlight. We scrambled onto the boat and Ray backed it up and turned it around. Then we exited Garrison Bight through the cut by Trumbo Point and chugged through the narrow sluice dividing Key West from Fleming Key, en route to the historic harbor. Dusk had fallen; the air felt chilly and lights sparkled all along the edges of the coast. I could almost believe it was the Christmas season.

"Do you miss being up north for the holidays?" I asked Connie.

"Not a bit," she said. "My father has left four messages inviting me to New York City for a weekend and it doesn't tempt me in the slightest."

"Not even seeing the tree at Rockefeller Center? Or the Rockettes? Maybe a little white Christmas?" But I knew what didn't tempt her—spending time with her father, who'd almost torpedoed her marriage before she and Ray had reached the altar.

"You sound homesick," Ray said, peering over the steering wheel to check out my face in the gathering darkness.

"I guess I am. A little. This has been a tough week. Besides the murder and my job—" I paused. This wasn't really my business, but it bothered me. I liked Sam. A lot. Once I got used to the shock of my mother dating, I hated to see her throw away a good chance at happiness. A lurking suspicion had started to take shape in my mind: Maybe she was as bad at accepting good fortune in the love department as I was. Maybe I had inherited the trait from her.

Anyway, since Connie was my closest friend and Ray was dependably closemouthed, I spilled the details about the dinner with the bereaved chef, Bransford, and Wally. And then I described the sweet gesture Sam had made buying the tree and shipping our ornaments down, the mysterious box at the bottom, the gorgeous ring, and my mother's tap dance around Sam's proposal.

"I know how it feels to be on his end of things," said Ray. "Horrible."

Connie gave him a playful punch in the ribs, a little harder than he expected. "I had reason to believe that perhaps you were not husband material." She turned to face me. "What do you think's going on?"

I merely shrugged.

"Did this happen at dinner last night? I can't believe your guest list. You fed all of them?"

"Mom did the cooking. And, fortunately, the Bolognese sauce recipe makes enough for an army regiment," I said, blowing out a big, tension-filled breath. "I was starting to tell you earlier—Sam invited Wally. And I invited Edel because she was so blue about her ex-mother-in-law arriving, and Juan Carlos's death, of course. And then Bransford was pushing me so hard about my connection with her that I told him to come see for himself. I never expected he'd actually do it."

"What's happening with his wife?" Connie asked, her tone a touch cool. She'd seen me through some disappointing times while I attempted to date Bransford last year. Like me, she hoped for the best until the worst was demonstrated. Which Bransford had done by resurrecting his moribund marriage rather than continue our relationship. At least this was "the worst" when seen through the eyes of my loyal friend.

"I haven't heard a peep about the wife."

Ray slowed the boat down and we circled outside of the dock where the Hindu and other day-tripping sailboats were docked. It was hard to hear over the noises of motors and the festive crowd gathering, so I turned away. Not that I wanted to continue that conversation, anyway.

Ray cut the engine and we glided into the historic harbor. There were dozens of boats lined up for the parade, which would wend past the crowds at Schooner Wharf and then around the point out to Mallory Square—assuming the weather held up. Ray had been right: Though his reindeer were definitely more original than some of the other arrangements, his decorations paled in comparison to the bigger boats. There were enormous sailboats with lights snaking up their masts, curving down their lines, and twinkling across their sails. There were motorboats carpeted in lights—blue, red, yellow, and green. And there were smaller boats with Key West–themed decorations—like Santa rocking in a hammock under lighted palm trees and leaping sailfish outlined in blue.

A man with a megaphone announced that all the boats should line up according to the number they had been issued when they signed up for the parade. We squeezed in between a Fury party boat and a small yacht that Ray estimated might have cost a cool million. Connie swayed in the bow, waving at the other participants, and Ray grinned like a monkey from his seat behind the console. This was the kind of night that made living in Key West worth every bit of the hassle: the traffic on Roosevelt, the tourists clogging Duval Street and all the streets radiating from it, the expensive or nonexistent vegetables. I snorted softly. Only my mother or I would add that last item to the list of island hardships.

I moved to the small bench at the rear of our boat and waved to the other contestants as they passed by. We motored slowly toward the Schooner Wharf Bar, where loud music piped from the rooftop speakers, and in the distance firecrackers popped. The tourists were piled up four and five people deep along the docks and sidewalks that lined the perimeter of the harbor.

A hollow cracking noise echoed above the holiday music. I felt a stinging, sharp and painful, in my left arm, almost as if I'd been bitten by an animal with big teeth. I looked down, puzzled. And dropped to the deck, woozy, when I saw that I was bleeding.

"Ray!" I screamed. "Ray! I need help!"

Just as it had taken me seconds to realize I was hurt, it took Ray time to understand why I was writhing on the deck of the boat. Blood gushed from my arm, seeping into the seawater that had splashed into the boat on the ride over, coloring the fiberglass a delicate pink. Feeling faint and weak, I dropped my head to my hands. Over my moaning and the Christmas carols pounding from the bar's speakers, I could hear Ray shout to Connie. Finally our boat swerved out of the queue and shot off toward a Coast Guard cutter that idled on the pier near a Key West Police Department cruiser.

"My passenger is injured!" Ray shouted.

Within minutes, Coast Guard personnel boarded our boat and helped Ray load me onto a stretcher, then transfer me and the stretcher to shore and then into a waiting ambulance. Connie scrambled in beside me, her eyes wide with worry. After a bumpy ride over the worst of the Roosevelt Boulevard construction, we arrived at the hospital on Stock Island.

Once we'd stopped moving, the paramedics whisked me through double doors to a big waiting room, which stank of antiseptic and fear. An orderly rolled me right past the intake windows and a white-coated clerk followed us to a treatment staging room. In answer to the clerk's questions, Connie found my insurance card and reeled off my important statistics: name, address, policy numbers, birth date, next of kin. The clerk tapped all of that into the iPad she carried.

Finally she looked up. "And what happened here?"

I rolled over a little so she could see the bloody shirt tied around my arm.

"I may have been shot."

She paled, thin fingers grazing her neck to pluck at a gold chain. "I think I'm going to be sick."

I groaned in response.

"Thanks a lot. How do you think she feels?" Connie said, stroking the curls back from my forehead. I croaked out a laugh.

After a few minutes, I was whisked through the next set of doors and ensconced on a hospital bed, separated from the rest of the room by an off-white curtain. In the adjoining cubby, I heard someone coughing hard enough to dislodge their tonsils, and farther down, the sound of a patient vomiting.

A nurse bustled in and took my vitals, tapping the results into a computer by the door. Then she unwrapped the bloody vestiges of Ray's shirt and the gauze squares that the paramedics had applied and examined my arm. "Looks like you got lucky," she said, swabbing the dried blood from my biceps. "It appears to have grazed the outside of your arm without nicking anything essential. Hang on. I'm going to clean it up a bit. Then we'll bring the doctor in to have a look, okay? He can decide whether you need an x-ray or a CT scan."

But I didn't get the idea she was asking my permission. I whimpered with pain as she cleaned the wound. Connie dropped my hand and sank into a chair at the edge of the cubicle.

"Sorry, Hayley," she said, "I've got a weak stomach. Not much better than the clerk." She jerked a thumb over her shoulder.

"Almost finished," said the nurse. "It's not as bad as it probably felt, but we'll call the doc in just to be sure." She had me hold a wad of clean gauze to the wound and she hurried off to find the doctor.

Connie tried her best to keep my mind off the throbbing and the fright of having someone shoot at me by chatting about the lighted boats and the silly costumes worn by the sailors. My mind pinged between fear, confusion, and outrage.

Finally the nurse returned, accompanied by a white-coated doctor with wispy blond hair who looked younger than any of us. "Gunshot wound," she told him. "It looks like it grazed the outer flesh of her arm. Fortunately, she's not that thin or I believe it would have hit bone and muscle."

He nodded hello, snapped on a pair of white gloves, and repeated the probing the nurse had done earlier, only deeper. Then he asked me to move my fingers as though I were playing scales on the piano, squeeze a fist, and lift my arm above my shoulder.

"Looks like you got lucky here, young lady," he said.

Twice they'd told me I'd gotten lucky. "Not sure how getting shot qualifies as lucky," I grumbled.

But the doctor barely smiled. "Let's bandage her up," he said to the nurse. And to me: "There are some gentlemen who would like to speak with you."

I groaned again. "I doubt they're gentlemen."

The doctor laughed and began scribbling notes on a prescription pad and tapping more notes into an iPad. "We'll give you something for the pain. Don't drive after taking it. And antibiotics, twice daily. Make sure you finish the whole bottle." He ripped off the top page of his pad and handed it to me. "You can change the dressing tomorrow. Have you had a tetanus shot recently?" I nodded. "Call us if you experience any excessive bleeding or swelling. Also if you notice pus or a foul discharge or you develop a fever. And follow up with your personal doctor in about a week. Questions?" he asked as he started out to the next patient.

"No." Wincing, I lay back on the bed, head against the flat pillow, to wait for the pain medicine he'd promised. I heard voices outside the cubicle; then Lieutenant Torrence and Detective Bransford pushed through the curtains, looking alternately solicitous and grim.

Bransford stayed near the foot of the bed, but Torrence came closer. "What's the report?" he asked.

"They think I'll live," I said. "But right now it hurts like hell."

"Let's review how this happened," said Bransford, his eyebrows arching to fierce peaks.

"We were riding in the parade," Connie explained, placing a protective hand on my shoulder. "We were focused on the activity around the Schooner Wharf because it was almost our turn to cut away from the flotilla and process in front of the judges. There were hordes of people on shore, a lot of them drunk and excited. Next thing we knew, Hayley was bleeding in the bottom of the boat. If there had been a shooter, I don't know how we would have noticed in all that chaos."

"But did you see anyone with a gun?" he asked me.

I shook my head, suddenly overwhelmed at the idea that there really had been a shooting and that I was the intended target. Obviously this had happened—I had the wound to prove it. But the meaning was finally sinking in.

"What direction would you say the bullet came from?" Bransford asked. "Where do you think the shooter might have been stationed?"

"We were headed into the harbor. So I'd say maybe it came from the left dock?" I looked over to Connie. "Does that sound right?"

She shrugged. "I was up in front, waving at the crowd, so I didn't notice anything. I didn't even know you'd been hit until I heard you screaming and saw the blood. There was blood everywhere," she told the cops with a shudder.

"Was anyone else hit?" I asked from my supine position. "Maybe someone on another boat saw this happen."

"Of course we're investigating the situation thoroughly." Bransford bared his teeth, his annoyance obvious. "But it's vital that you try to remember details. The question has to be asked: Was the shooter after you, or were you struck at random or accidentally?" He took a deep breath, clearly trying to rein in his impatience. "Have you had any threats? Was this a warning or an actual assassination attempt? Do you know of anyone who would want to hurt you? You would know the answers better than anyone."

"But I don't know anything about it," I squawked.

"Why would anyone want to shoot Hayley?" Connie's lips trembled. "It makes no sense."

"It's just possible," said Torrence in a soothing voice, "that this could be related to the fire the other night and the death of Ms. Waugh's ex-husband. Let's think about the possibilities before we get too excited, okay?"

Before we *freak out*, is what I imagined he really wanted to say. The nurse came in with a paper cup of water and a big pill and I swallowed it down.

Torrence turned away from Connie to focus his attention on me. "Who knew you would be involved in the boat parade?"

"My family, of course," I said, feeling a little tearful thinking of my mother and how distraught she'd be when she heard about the latest catastrophe. "Including my mom and her boyfriend and my cousin and Miss Gloria. They're all up at Mallory Square, watching the parade. They'll worry," I said to Connie, "when they don't see Ray's boat."

"Who else?" Torrence prodded.

I tried to clear my head of all the rubbish circulating and concentrate on his question. Had I discussed the invitation to ride in Ray's boat with anyone else? This sounded familiar, like a dim bell ringing—the echo of a conversation I'd had several days earlier. And then it came to me: Edel's kitchen.

The painkiller was taking effect, making me feel like the room was spinning and my brain was stuffed with cotton candy. "Edel's restaurant," I said. "A few days ago, when I was there to get material for my article. And then she asked me to help her out."

"Who else was in the kitchen?" Bransford asked sternly.

I glared at him, though his features were beginning to look fuzzy and my lips were beginning to feel tingly and thick like my grandmother's pink pincushion. "Pretty much the whole staff. Edel, of course. Her sous-chef, Glenn. Mary Pat Maloney, the line cook. The pastry chef. Rodrigo, the dishwasher." I was struck with the giggles. "It couldn't be the pastry chef. They're not all murderers."

Connie took my hand and squeezed it hard. "Take a deep breath, sweetie," she said. "You're getting hysterical."

I closed my eyes and breathed and breathed, trying to picture the scene in the kitchen—who had been there and what exactly I'd told them. "I was all excited about riding with Ray and Connie. I'd seen the parade last year but I knew it would be so cool from the water."

"And, so," said Torrence gently, "you told them what the boat looked like, maybe? Or not?"

"And the decorations," Bransford added. "Did you know in advance what the theme of Ray's lights would be?"

"Reindeer and chickens." My eyes flew open and my stomach lurched. "You think someone I know from Edel's kitchen was waiting for me and tried to pick me off?"

"It's a theory," Bransford answered.

"Something we need to explore," said Torrence.

The nurse bustled into my cubby, which made the space feel crowded to the point of claustrophobia. She noticed it, too, and shooed the cops out into the hall. "You can take her home now," she said to Connie as she handed me a sheaf of paperwork. She went over the discharge instructions and had me sign to say I'd been informed. "You'll want to review this reading material when you're at home."

I glanced at the papers—a treatise on puncture wounds, another on foreign bodies, and instructions for follow-up care and the possible side effects for the painkiller and antibiotics I'd been given. Not at all the kind of bedtime reading that would lead to sweet dreams.

21

We must have a pie. Stress cannot exist in the presence of a pie.
   —David Mamet, *Boston Marriage*

I woke up at nine a.m., feeling sore and uneasy. After one glance at the prescription pill bottles lined up on my bedside table, the night's events flooded my brain. I resolved to take Advil today, rather than the high-powered painkiller, as the drug had rendered my brain cells fuzzy and my dreams ominous. I stayed in my bunk for half an hour, listening to the wind rattle through Mrs. Renhart's chimes and thinking about who in the world would have tried to shoot me. And where he'd been shooting from. And why. A tap sounded on my door.

"You up?" asked Miss Gloria. "I come bearing gifts of caffeine and sugar."

"Come in!" I dragged myself up to sitting and both cats rushed in ahead of my roommate. She narrowly avoided tripping and sending the steaming mug of café au lait across my grandmother's hand-stitched quilt. We scolded the felines, who settled onto the bed at my feet, unrepentant. Miss Gloria fussed about, opening the blinds and uncovering a plate that held two of my favorites from Glazed Donuts, the shop near the Tropic Cinema—a plain glazed and a salted-caramel cake doughnut. Next to the treats, she had placed the *Key West Citizen*.

"Thank you, wonderful woman," I said, reaching for the coffee. First things first.

"Have you called your mother?" asked Miss Gloria, after everything had been arranged to her satisfaction. "She'll want to know about this." She gestured at my bandaged arm. "We were very puzzled when Ray's boat didn't come by Mallory Square."

I nodded, sipping slowly. I had texted my mother after reaching the houseboat last night, saying that Ray had had engine troubles and I'd phone the next day. But Miss Gloria knew the whole story. When I'd first arrived home, bandaged and half-hysterical, there was no way to hide the truth. I did play down the terror of the evening—the sharp pain as the bullet ripped through my flesh, the trip to the emergency room in the ambulance, the detective's questions and concerns. After some extended begging, she'd agreed not to call my mother in the middle of the night.

"I plan to talk to her this morning. There's nothing she can do about it and she has her own worries. Like what to do about that gorgeous ring."

Miss Gloria pursed her lips. "She ought to just go ahead and marry that man. Where is she going to find someone kinder and with money, too? But I suppose the only people who really know what's going on inside a relationship are those in it."

"I'm certainly in no position to give advice on love," I said, and tried to smile.

I thanked her for the breakfast treats and then

opened my computer and turned it on, hoping she'd leave me to sort out my troubles.

"I'll see you in a bit," she said. "I'm going to put some laundry in. Shall I leave the cats?"

I glanced at the felines, who were stretched out, grooming themselves at the end of the bed. Just watching them lick their glossy fur into submission brought my blood pressure down. "They're great. They'll keep me company while I work."

Spotting the sheaf of aftercare papers the hospital staff had given me, I paged through the instructions. Good gravy, I knew they had to warn patients about the very worst reactions that might occur, but the flood of medical jargon was truly terrifying. Especially for a person who leaned toward hypochondria in the first place.

After memorizing the side effects of the medications I'd taken, I skimmed the front page of the *Key West Citizen*. Then I turned the page, dreading the possibility of seeing my face in the crime report. It would be awful for my mother to read about the shooting in the newspaper—not to mention generally humiliating for me. Fortunately, my news had not made the crime column. I clicked on my e-mail box and scrolled through the stories sent by the Konk Life e-news blast. Nothing there, either. And no messages about progress in the case from either of my police friends—though Bransford hardly counted in that category.

I let the snapshots of the night before run through my mind. It had all happened so quickly—the shooting, the sharp pain, and then Ray turning our craft out of the flotilla toward the dock. And the crowd had been so thick in front of the Schooner Wharf Bar and so focused on the glorious lighted masts passing by, chances were most of them wouldn't have noticed the haphazard retreat of one small motorboat. Besides that, I remembered hearing fireworks before the parade, which would have disguised the sound of a gunshot. Still undecided about how much I would reveal, I dialed my mother's number. The frantic tenor of her voice made the decision easy.

"I'm over in Jennifer's kitchen," my mother said, her voice high and tight. "We've got two dinner parties and a cocktail reception this evening, and all hands are on deck. Would there be any possibility—" she broke off, and I could hear a conversation in the background.

"Never mind. Jennifer tells me her standby servers are coming in an hour. I'll call you tonight and let you know how everything goes. Okay, honey?" She didn't pause long enough for me to reassure her or confess. "Jennifer tells me that Edel's been given the go-ahead to open her restaurant this evening."

"Really? Tonight?"

My mother clucked sympathetically. "It will be good for her, take her mind off all the recent troubles. Her mother-in-law was a pip, wasn't she? Gotta go, sweetheart." She made a smooching noise and hung up.

Only then did it occur to me that she talked so fast because she had things she was hiding from me. I wasn't the only Snow woman with secrets.

After breakfast, with Miss Gloria's help, I wrapped my injured arm in plastic bags and took a shower, staying in the stall long enough so that the stream of hot water beat some of the stress balls out of my neck and shoulders. By the time I dried off and dressed in warm sweats, my phone blinked with a voice message from Edel.

"Any chance you could help me out in the restaurant today?" she asked. "The cops told me late last night that the bistro was good to go, so I ordered in all the fish and meat and vegetables, and they're promising a quick delivery. I'm going to try for another soft opening tonight."

I worked the fingers on the hand of my injured arm, opening and closing the fist and tapping them against my palm. The movement hurt a little, but not enough to keep me at home. Besides, Edel probably needed my observational skills more than my culinary expertise. Perhaps I had seen something during my hours in the kitchen last time that I didn't realize I'd seen. Something hidden in plain sight? And perhaps it was related to the shooting last night during the lighted boat parade. If I could pay attention to how each of her kitchen staff reacted when I showed up—very much alive—those tiny clues could unravel the mystery.

Or was she still hoping that I'd write a story on the bistro? At this point, that seemed like a more and more distant possibility—Ava certainly wouldn't publish it. And who else would, once they heard about my conflict of interest?

I debated whether to call Lieutenant Torrence and let him know where I was going. Chances were he would suggest that I stay home. And just as surely, I knew that I would not, could not, listen to him.

This time without Miss Gloria's assistance, I dressed in jeans, my most comfortable red sneakers, a white tank, and a long-sleeved yellow-plaid flannel shirt that would cover the bandage on my left arm.

"Are you certain you can manage on your scooter?" Miss Gloria asked. "Do you want me to drive you over? Or we could call a taxi." She fluttered around me like a hen with new hatchlings.

"I'll be fine," I said, and squeezed her hand with reassurance. "I really feel so much better. And helping Edel will get my mind off what happened. No one's going to come after me in a kitchen full of cooks. They all have ready access to sharp weapons." I didn't tell her that part of my reason for going was to watch the reactions of Edel's staff, looking for a possible murderer. Instead, I laughed at my attempted joke, grabbed my helmet and backpack, and headed out the door.

After a quick stop at the Cuban Coffee Queen for a large café con leche, I parked my scooter in the head of the alley behind Edel's restaurant, where all the fire equipment had been stationed several nights earlier. The place still reeked of charred wood, but the half-burnt fence and the remains of the little shed out back had been removed. I imagined it had been terribly painful for Edel to keep passing the very place where her ex-husband had died. And painful, too, to think that the last words between them had been ugly with anger. I squared my shoulders, checked that the shirt-sleeve covered my injury, and headed into the kitchen.

Inside, the space was already warm and scented with the delicious smell of frying onions, chopped ginger, and baking chocolate. Mary Pat Maloney was at her station, her fingers working furiously with a knife, a tall pile of slivered scallions in front of her. She looked up as I arrived, but did not return my friendly smile.

"Good morning," I said. "You must be working on that amazing fish special."

Her lips pinched, she dropped the knife on the cutting board and walked toward the big cooler.

"Morning, Rodrigo. Morning, Louann. Morning, Glenn."

"Morning, Hayley," said Louann and Glenn. Rodrigo gave a wave and a smile. Nothing in those reactions gave me any insight into the possible identity of the shooter.

I wandered through the small kitchen, admiring the

flaky pastry that Louann was layering into a buttered dish, and the pot of pale pink vodka sauce that Glenn was stirring. No one seemed unhappy to see me, but overall the atmosphere felt a little subdued, even angry.

The doors leading from the kitchen to the dining room swung open, and Edel swept in with Leo Mc-Cracken, the head waiter, on her heels. She clapped her hands and the clatter at the workspaces grew quiet.

"Listen, people," she said. "We have some big news. The food critic from the *New York Times* is vacationing in Key West this week with his family. Once he saw the news about the fire, he got interested in our bistro and he's coming for dinner sometime tonight. Or so we've heard on the coconut telegraph." She glanced back at Leo, who wore a sly smile.

"Speaking of the fire, I know I've spoken with all of you individually. I know most of you are deeply saddened by Juan Carlos's death." Her lower lip trembled. She glanced down, brushed an imaginary crumb off her white jacket. "I'm sick about it, too. You all read the stories about him . . . I know that. Just understand that most of what was printed was not true. And regardless of what the truth might have been, we loved each other dearly." She swiped at her eyes with the towel draped over her shoulder. "The best way I can think to honor his memory is to cook the most amazing dishes we can. Cook like we're on fire," she added fiercely.

I blanched at the unfortunate metaphor, but Edel didn't seem to have noticed. She glanced around the room, making eye contact with each of the staff. "Thank you for your support." She marched over to me and lowered her voice. "Are you going to be able to get your piece published in *Key Zest* this week?"

I gulped. Was this why she'd called me in? I thought I'd been pretty clear about my iffy status. "I'm kind of on hold," I told her. "Wally and Ava are negotiating with some possible investors and the entire direction of the magazine is in question."

I started to formulate the words to describe what I saw as the mounting conflict of interest, but the expression on her face darkened.

"I should say, I'm going to have everything ready to go . . . in case I get the go-ahead."

She stared at me as if I'd really let her down, then grunted and turned away. She walked from station to station, critiquing the work of her employees, from the number of custard and graham cracker crust layers in the key lime parfaits, all the way down to the spots left on the bottoms of several skillets by the Spanish-speaking dishwasher. When it became clear that she was too absorbed with her own staff to find something for me to do—and perhaps she'd never intended to let me work, I retreated from the heat and tension of the kitchen to the dining room. Leo and the other servers were busy wrapping silverware in snowy white napkins.

"Can I pitch in with something here?" I asked. "I came to help out in the kitchen but it looks like I'm in the way."

"If you could stay out of her warpath, I'd advise it," said Leo, crooking a smile. "I'm afraid she's not handling her grief all that gracefully."

"Who does?" I asked, as I sat and reached for a napkin. "Is such a thing even possible? She probably should have taken a few more days off."

"She processes everything by working harder," he said. "And when she works harder, we work harder. You should have seen her the night that Page Six broke the story on Juan Carlos and his paramour. We've never served so many covers. And the cooking was brilliant that night, brilliant. But we were worried that a couple of the staff would have to be hospitalized to have fluids forced. They were exhausted and dehydrated."

Startled by his chattiness, I decided to mine the lode of information while it was open. "Would you say she was surprised by his infidelity?" I asked.

"Perhaps not surprised, but definitely disappointed." He stood up and shouldered the tray of wrapped silver and then carried it off to a corner shelf that held water pitchers and extra vases of tropical flowers.

Once it became clear that he wasn't coming back, I got up and wandered outside to the walkway bordering the harbor. From this vantage point, I could trace the path in the water that the lighted boat parade had taken last night. Clutching my injured arm protectively, I started toward the Schooner Wharf Bar. In front of the bar, I scanned the edges of the harbor, looking for crannies where the gunman might have been hiding. It was difficult to believe that someone—anyone—would have shot at me. Was it to scare me away? And from what? Or had it been random bad luck?

I had been a small target in a chaotic night. If someone had truly wanted to kill me, he would have had to have been an incredible marksman. And the shot must have been taken from a hiding place above the water. I scanned the harbor's skyline again, noticing the second-floor apartment to the right of Edel's place, with its tiny deck out front.

If someone had been watching the parade from there, he might have also seen the shooter.

22

*I was not one to turn down a second din-
ner, as you could never be quite sure when
the next good one would be served.*
　　　　—Piper Kerman, *Orange Is the*
　　　　　　　　　　　　　　New Black

I retraced my steps along the dock, headed away from
the Schooner Wharf Bar. A set of rickety stairs clung to
the side of the building, leading to the apartment
whose windows I had noticed. I gazed up, trying to
decide whether I should call the police or feel things
out first. Pretty much the entire department had the
idea I was a hysterical fruitcake at this point. Calling
them with unlikely theories would not impress them
further.

Besides, a light glimmered at a desk or bureau in the
window overlooking the harbor. And possibly the shadow
of a human being hovered in the window, too. Strike
while the iron is hot. I heaved a big sigh and started up
the stairs, clutching the weathered railing with my good
hand. I paused at the top on a small landing ringed with
potted herbs. I recognized a bushy rosemary plant, a

basil plant bursting with fragrant leaves and flowers, and possibly two varieties of thyme. The sort of person who grew herbs was likely to be kind, not scary. "Besides, time is not on your side," I muttered, and rapped on the door.

After several long moments, I heard the tip-tap of approaching footsteps. A sixtyish woman swung open the door, blinking in the sudden light. She had hips that swooped into a wide pear shape, gorgeous curly graying hair, and an open face. She could have been Miss Gloria's younger sister, only with a lot more meat on her bones. And that resemblance gave me the courage to blunder forward.

"Good afternoon. Or I guess I should say good morning," I stammered, checking my watch. "You have a lovely view up here."

She squinted and looked me over from top to bottom. "Do I know you? I'm not prepared to buy anything today."

"Oh no," I said, reaching to touch her elbow to try to reassure her. She took a step back. "I was involved with the lighted boat parade the other night, and I was just thinking what a beautiful place this must've been to watch the action."

She nodded, the suspicion still clear on her face. So far I'd explained nothing.

"Spectacular. The rent's too high and the appliances are on their last legs and it's noisy at night, but when it comes to the view, this place has it nailed."

She stopped talking, leaned against the door, and tucked a springing curl behind one ear. "What do you mean, you were involved with the lighted boat parade?"

"My friend Ray—he's an artist—he decorated his little Boston Whaler, and I was along for ballast."

She nodded, her blue eyes still narrowed.

"May I speak frankly?" I asked, and continued on before she could answer. "I was hit . . . I was hurt—" I squirmed, trying to think how to dance around this. Coming up with nothing but the bare facts. "I was shot at the other night on a boat right over there." I pointed across the harbor to the approximate place where Ray's motorboat had been idling, and then toward the mooring where an expensive-looking fishing boat called the *Happy Hooker* waited. Finally, I rolled up my shirtsleeve to show her the bandage. Blood had leaked through the dressing and stained the gauze. She gasped, her eyes widening. "I'm okay now. But the thing is, as I was walking along the dock I saw your place. And I had to wonder if maybe you saw something that the police hadn't asked about yet. You said you were out on your deck last evening. Maybe you would've noticed something out of order. I know it was a crazy night and the crowds were incredible. And all those lights were flashing—like a discotheque, almost."

She nodded again, squinting now as she took in my story. "I get a reduced rent here because it's such a noisy corner. As you can imagine, it's not easy to sleep until well after midnight. And then in the morning the early birds start trooping along the harbor and workers clean the boats and empty the trash. If I was the kind of woman who needed a lot of sleep, I'd be psychotic." She grinned. "But you don't want to know about my sleep apnea." She thought for a few moments. "I watched the whole thing. A couple of my friends were here having a glass of wine and some cheese. We sat out on the balcony, enjoying this spectacular show. I'd say I saw just about everyone I know, and, of course, lots of folks I didn't recognize."

Her gaze lingered on my bandaged arm. "We did

see a boat race over to the far dock where the flashing blues were clustered. We wondered what was up. We figured someone had too much to drink, maybe even fell overboard." She shrugged. "There are so many strangers in and out of this town, it's hard to get too worked up about one more ambulance. One more tourist transported to the emergency room." Her eyes met mine. "I'm sorry. I didn't know it was you."

Of course she hadn't known it was me. She didn't know me. "Remember after that horrible bombing at the Boston Marathon? Remember how people recalled seeing those two men who left the backpacks—once they got over the shock of having survived the attack?"

She bit her lip. "I watched that whole thing unfold on television. My father spent some years living just outside Boston before he joined the military. Can you believe that kid was hiding in a boat in the backyard the whole time?"

I smiled with encouragement. "Think back to after you saw the blue lights—do you remember anyone running along the dock—away from the scene? Anyone who didn't look as though they belonged? Anyone shady or suspicious?" Which was a silly question—half the population of the island looked shady and suspicious.

"No one running." She shook her head.

"Okay, forget about the running part. If you could, just tell me who you might have seen. Maybe one of them would have some helpful information."

"I did see the fellow who cleans the Fury party boats every morning. He came by. But he was drinking beer with his buddies. Nothing out of the ordinary. And then the fellow who guards the parking lot just down the way on Greene Street. You always know him by his monstrous dog. No one is going to try to get a free

parking space with those two watching over the lot."
She chuckled at her own humor.

"Any other folks that you recognized?" I prompted
her, feeling rather hopeless. She unfortunately didn't
give the impression of someone who noticed details. She
saw what she expected to see and that was her story.

She rubbed her chin, paced over to the window as if
to reimagine the night's activities, and then continued
to free-associate. "And let's see, Wes Singleton, who
used to own the restaurant just up the block. He was
here. I know he feels bad about that New York woman
taking over the business that has been in his family forever. I see him a lot in the mornings, talking with
Glenn."

"Glenn?"

"Glenn Fredericks. He works at that new restaurant.
Tall, handsome guy with white hair." She blushed and
patted her stomach. "He's brought me a late-night
snack twice. I can't wait for that place to open. Do you
think she'll have the sense to offer a locals' discount?
Who does she think is going to keep the place afloat
when all the tourists have gone after the high season?"

I shrugged, my heart welling with desperation. "She's
pretty business savvy. So no one was carrying a rifle
with scope?"

"Sorry, no gun." She smiled, but weakly, a little
spooked by my intensity. "I'd follow up with those
people. I don't have anything else for you."

She edged toward the door and I got the message. I
thanked her and hurried down the stairs, trying to sort
out the whole bunch of nothing she'd given me. Coffee.
I needed coffee. The adrenaline I'd felt when I first
woke up had ebbed to nearly nothing.

*   *   *

Half a dozen people were lined up ahead of me at the Cuban Coffee Queen, and I almost decided to skip the stop. Until I noticed that the second person in line was the previous owner of Edel's restaurant. The man whom Miss Gloria's "twin" said she often saw talking with one of Edel's employees. He paid for his coffee and Cuban sandwich and carried the coffee to the bench underneath the pink blossoming bougainvillea to wait for his food. He pulled a pack of cigarettes from his chest pocket and lit one up.

While waiting to order, I studied the man's face and dress, while pretending to be fascinated by the birds chirping among the pink flowers and trying not to look obvious. His skin was weathered, with the look of a man who spent a lot of time in the sun, perhaps on the sea. I paid for my con leche and walked over to take the seat beside him.

"Beautiful day in paradise," I chirped, like one of those birds.

He slitted his eyes and glanced over. Was I for real?

"I have a feeling we've met here before." I thrust my hand toward him. "You look so familiar. I'm Hayley Snow. I write for *Key Zest* and drink as much Cuban coffee as I can manage."

He answered with half a smile but did not take my hand. "Wes Singleton," he said.

"Oh you were the owner of the Fishing Hole," I said. "I had a memorable meal there about eight months ago." I wasn't lying—I had had a meal there—memorable for the indigestion that followed.

"You surely won't be having anymore," he said, glaring at me now. "The powers that be decided that a local man struggling to make a living couldn't pay as much in taxes and fees as a New York outsider. I'm sure

they figure an outsider can be more easily fleeced, being more stupid and gullible than we locals are. I
guaran-damn-tee you that extra lease money goes right
to line the commissioners' pockets."

"Your specialty was fried fish and shrimp, from
what I remember," I said. "And those amazing double
cheesy fries." Thinking it might calm him down a bit if
I admired his food and his menu before I pursued his
rage-filled rant about the local authorities.

"We made the food that people like to eat," he blus-
tered. "And not just the damn tourists, either. I had a
crowd of locals who came every morning for breakfast—
best damn biscuits and gravy in the state of Florida,"
he said, smacking his lips.

My stomach growled and I wished I'd ordered a
sandwich along with my coffee. Miss Gloria's doughnuts had been delicious, but they weren't holding me.
"I love biscuits and gravy. As long as I don't think too
hard about the sausage grease where the gravy origi-
nated." I laughed but he did not. "How was your
restaurant doing?"

"It was doing just fine," he said, and crossed his
arms over his chest.

The worker at the little window called out his name
and he stomped over to retrieve his sandwich. Returning
to the bench, he pulled it out of the brown paper wrapping and took a big bite. Ham, cheese, pickles, and mustard, from what I could see through his non–Emily
Post–approved chewing. He swallowed, swiped a cheese-
greased hand across his lips, and took a slug of his coffee.

"They told me with only a week, maybe two weeks'
notice, tops, that they were doubling the rent on the
lease. Didn't give me the time to do any research into a
loan or anything. I went to one of those damn commis-

sion meetings that Tuesday and spoke my piece." His words picked up velocity. "And what do you think they said?"

I shrugged and widened my eyes to look interested. Actually I didn't have to pretend because I definitely wanted to hear the story. Maybe Edel was having a similar kind of problem with the city government.

"They told me thank you very much and they appreciated my family's contribution to the city of Key West over the years. And they were so sorry if my business had to fold, but a restaurant could expect some ups and downs." A little froth of bubbles appeared in one corner of his mouth. "My family paid good money to the government of this island for the past fifty years. I was born in Miami and moved here when I was two years old so my father and grandfather could open this restaurant. They would turn over in their graves if they could see what that fancy la-di-da New York lady plans to serve . . ."

"So, they thanked you for your service to this city," I said, wanting to get him back on track. "And what else?"

"And what else?" He slapped his leg with his free hand. "They said if I couldn't find a way to pay the rent and the higher taxes, I should find another place for my restaurant. Where the hell would I find a place to put a new restaurant? Maybe Stock Island, where there are no customers to speak of? Or along Roosevelt Boulevard, where the construction has just about killed the businesses over the past two years?" He sucked in the last pull on his unfiltered cigarette, almost burning his fingers. Then he dropped the butt to join the others littered underneath the bench and ground it into the asphalt with his boot. "If I had only thought about setting a fire, then I could have rebuilt the place and drawn in the crowd she's pulling in." He jerked his thumb over his shoulder, back toward Edel's place.

"It's tough to run a successful restaurant in this town," I said in a soothing voice. "It's hard anywhere, but especially on this island. Did any of your employees find jobs in the new place?"

"Glenn Fredericks," he said. "He's a wicked good cook. My main man. And now she's got him working like a McDonald's fry cook and she hangs over him every two minutes, correcting his technique. No wonder he's pissed."

The worker at the window called my name and I went to retrieve my coffee. I couldn't think what else I could get out of this man—not without working him into a lethal frenzy. He had one story line that he believed was the truth and there was no moving him away from it. Plus he seemed to be accusing Edel herself of arson. What would she have gained from that? The smart thing to do would be to call my friend Lieutenant Torrence and suggest that the cops swing by for a chat with Glenn Fredericks.

"It was nice talking with you," I said to the man. "How did you like the lighted boat parade last night?"

He looked puzzled. "I skip the tourist driven hokey holiday crap," he said.

As usual, it seemed, someone was lying.

23

[Rich Torrisi] went on: "That's the biggest misconception of being a chef: If you're not behind the stove, your restaurant's worse."

Or as Mr. [Mario] Carbone put it, "Do you think the C.E.O. of Bank of America is watching your checking account right now?"

—Jeff Gordinier, "The Red Sauce Juggernaut," *New York Times*

As I walked back to the area where I had parked my scooter, a text from Wally flashed onto my screen. *If available, good idea to show face at Key Zest. ASAP. If you can spare the time.*

I stuffed the phone into my pocket, feeling utterly annoyed. If I was available? Show my face? He acted as though I had been the one to choose unemployment, as if I couldn't be bothered to dabble in my work. I loved this job. And I'd taken it deathly seriously from the moment I landed it.

I texted Edel, telling her I'd be back sometime after five. As I motored across the island to our office, I wondered why Wally's attitude had changed. Had Ava's poison finally worked its way into his system? Why did he want me showing my face? I didn't have any assignments—she'd taken them all away.

My phone buzzed again, telling me that I'd received a voice mail. I'd turned off the ringer while interviewing the lady down at the harbor and forgotten to turn it back on. Wally had called, then left a voice message and then the offending text message when I didn't answer. I pulled over on Whitehead Street and, cringing, played the voice mail through.

"I'm having another meeting with the investors. You're not invited—that's not what I meant," he had added quickly. "But I'm thinking it won't hurt if you wander in. Or, take that back, walk in purposefully, as if you're working even while things are on hold. Because you're just that dedicated," he added with a forced chuckle.

Which made me feel sick to my stomach. Because I was that dedicated. But Ava couldn't see it and probably never would. I was beginning to wish I'd brought one of the painkillers that had been dispensed last night. Fuzzy edges might just help when facing my nemesis.

I drove the last few blocks, parked the scooter behind Preferred Properties Real Estate, and trotted up the stairs to our second-floor office. Through the clouded glass door, I could see the shadow of Danielle at the desk and hear the low rumble of voices from Wally's office. I brushed my fingers over my curls, squared my shoulders, and walked in.

"Good morning," said Danielle in a cheery voice, all while making a terrible face and pointing to Wally's office. She dropped her voice to a whisper. "The dreaded Ava is in session. With the investors. Did Wally tell you to come?"

I nodded. "What's going on?"

She shrugged. "Negotiations of some kind. He didn't want to tell me anything, at least not with her hanging over his shoulder." She dropped her voice even lower. "I took the liberty of doing a little research." She shoved a piece of white paper covered with block letters across the desk. *Did you know that Ava went to school with Palamina?*

"She told me that," I whispered. "Not Ava. Palamina. Ava wouldn't share information with me if we were the last two rats on a sinking ship."

Danielle laughed out loud, then clapped her hand over her mouth. But it was too late. The meeting had been interrupted by our hilarity. Wally stuck his head out of the office.

"What's so funny?"

"Just girl talk," Danielle said. "Hayley came in to catch up on some reviews. I was getting some snacks together for our guests." She gestured toward a white platter that held a selection of cookies. Honest to god, they looked like Double Stuf Oreos, Chips Deluxe Chocolate Lovers cookies, and store-brand caramel coconut Tim Tam knockoffs. Okay, we don't do cookies out of a package in this office—too much fat and sugar and not enough pleasure, except in a major emergency. This would count.

"Keep it down out there," Wally said, adding a pained smile. He turned back to his office and Danielle stood, preparing to follow him with the cookies.

"Store-bought?" I mouthed to Danielle, pointing at the trans-fat-laden orbs.

She raised her eyebrows and giggled.

"Hayley," Wally called over his shoulder, "would you mind joining us in fifteen minutes or so?"

I hurried down the hall to my writing nook and

spent the next fifteen minutes desperately trying to concentrate on the edits Wally had returned on the review of Latitudes, where I'd eaten with my family days earlier. It was hard to push away the memory of Edel's despair, that night when she heard that her precious new restaurant was burning.

I tweaked my lead-in paragraph, which was all about the setting: the short ride across the harbor to Sunset Key on the private people ferry, the palm trees wrapped in Christmas lights, the flickering torches lining the path that lead to the restaurant, the aura of wealth and privilege. Then I moved on to the amazing, spicy, condiment-laden Bloody Mary—thinking I could use one of them before facing Ava.

I had just begun to polish the description of the French onion soup, which I remembered as delicious though perhaps not remarkable, and the coconut-encrusted Key West pink shrimp, when Wally's voice echoed down the hallway.

"Hayley, could you join us?"

I swiped at the beads of sweat that had popped up across my upper lip and leaped up, slamming my knee against the desk on my way.

"Crap!" I hissed. And limped down the hall to Wally's office. I paused for a moment outside his door, practiced a grin that I hoped wasn't sickly, and stepped inside.

Wally said, "Of course you know Ava and Palamina and Marcus Baker. Hayley is our crackerjack staff writer. Have a seat," he said, "and please help yourself to Danielle's snacks."

The last thing I wanted was one of those cookies—it would sit leaden in my stomach, oozing sugar and preservatives. But I reached for one, anyway, so as not to appear snobbish or ungrateful. Wally flashed a smile, tight as the rubber band around a bouquet of broccoli.

"We're brainstorming ideas for the new Key Zest formula," he said. "Marcus was wondering what kind of readership we have for the restaurant reviews. How many hits and particularly comments have you noticed?"

Marcus leaned forward, palms on his knees. "We're wondering how often your reviews start a conversation. If we are to be involved in the new iteration of the magazine, it's important that we have a way for readers to speak to us. That they feel like we're inviting them to respond to what we write. It's very easy for writers to become solipsistic."

"Oh so easy," said Ava.

I cleared my throat, forcing myself to keep my gaze pinned on Marcus, away from Ava's prune-lipped grimace. Sweat ran in runnels down my spine and I knew my face must have reddened. The Jersey tomato look, my father used to joke when my mother or I got mad and he wanted to defuse our fury. His ploy never worked.

"I would like to think my readers always feel part of the conversation," I said. "I can't tell you how many people stop me on the streets to thank me for my opinions. My theory on being a restaurant critic is that I spend my money testing food so they don't have to waste theirs." I turned to Wally. "We have comments enabled on the blog already, don't we?"

"It's not simply a matter of enabling comments," said Marcus. "Periodicals that are successful these days are those that manage to develop a community around their product. So there should be an entire program of social media in place—a Facebook page, of course, for those trapped in the Stone Age."

We all laughed, though at *Key Zest* we relied heavily on Facebook to drive traffic. Or at least we thought we

were driving traffic. Or we hoped. We'd certainly noticed fewer hits and more requests for post-boosting
expenditures over the past year.

"And a Twitter feed," said Palamina. "But you need
to be a foodie and style leader, not just tweeting your
own links. You can hold chats and develop your Goo-
gle+ platform and Instagram, too. With teasers to your
lead articles."

"Pinterest, definitely," said Marcus. "With some group
boards. And Tumblr, maybe down the road."

Palamina turned to look at me, her expressive, bird-
like face drenched with sympathy. "You see," she said,
"our sense of *Key Zest* is that it needs a complete struc-
tural overhaul, not just a few cosmetic tweaks. If we are
to invest in the organization, we don't believe it will
work to apply plaster to the cracks to disguise the
weaknesses. We would propose taking apart the pieces
of the structure that are faulty and rebuilding for the
future. That, of course, will involve cost cutting, along
with really sharpening the focus."

"And, as Marcus said, figuring out the way to get
the readers dedicated and involved," Wally added.

"This also calls for a paid advertising program with
food establishments in this town," Ava inserted. "If the
restaurants have paid for ads, they are by definition
invested in our magazine."

I bit the inside of my cheek, trying hard not to snap
at her. She had brought up this possibility four or five
times over the past year and each and every time it
sounded dreadful. I waited for a moment to see if Wally
would respond to her. But either he had lost his concen-
tration or he had changed his mind and gone over to
the dark side.

"May I say something in response?" I said, horrified
that my voice squeaked as the words came out. "It

seems as though once you get restaurants paying to be featured or mentioned in the magazine, in exchange you have an obligation for a certain kind of review or coverage. The truth is sacrificed along the way. It's hard for me to be comfortable with that."

Ava put her hands out, palms facing to the ceiling, looking at the faces of Wally and the two investors. "You see what I'm trying to say. Our staff doesn't think big picture. They think about the small square inch of work directly in front of them and their own little niggling concerns. Very difficult to run a thriving business like that."

"You mean difficult to run a business with morals?" I snapped. Then I stood up and marched out.

24

I wouldn't feed you anything that would kill you. Just eat it and quit complaining!
—Dr. Kiel Christianson to his children

I collected my belongings from my office, blew past Danielle without explanation, and stormed out of the office. Most likely she would have heard the entire conversation, anyway—the walls are mandoline thin. And the volume had been ramped up pretty close to shouting by the time I finished. In my dreams, I might have wished that Wally would run after me, insisting that I had been right all along and that he'd ejected Ava for good—she was now out of the picture. The reality was different. I needed to suck it up and realize that this job was history. Possibly I could find another job related to food writing. Not likely I'd land another gig as a food critic, the position I'd dreamed about all of my short working life. But lots of people did lots of things that might not have been their first choice in order to stay on this island. I could do the same.

Assuming that I wanted to stay on the island, with or

without Wally. My heart started to beat faster and I felt my stomach pitch and roil. I needed to focus on something else or I would go mad. I yanked the phone from my backpack and started making calls. First one to Edel.

"It's Hayley," I said after the beep at the end of her message. "Just wanted to confirm that I will be back by five and ready to help in any way you can use me. But call me if there's any news on the fire or Juan Carlos's death, okay?" I hung up and dialed Officer Torrence. He didn't answer, either.

"Is there any news on the fire or the murder or the arson or the shooting? Are the police doing anything about any of this?" I took a breath. "Sorry," I added. "I know that isn't fair. I'm having a really lousy day. Call me when you get a chance?"

I got back on my scooter and buzzed down Southard Street past the Truman Annex gatehouse and left to Fort Zachary Taylor Beach. I needed to pull myself together before I talked to any other living being. After paying my token entry fee, I drove the half mile to the farthest beach, heading to the point where cruise ships make their turns into the channel leading to Key West. I left my scooter near the bicycle racks and trudged out to the beach.

As it was still early in the day, families gathered in town for the holidays had not yet arrived to spend hours baking in the sun. I took off my sandals and walked along the water. As I calmed down, I began to notice the line of Jet Skis bouncing along the horizon. And the waves crashing against the rocks a couple hundred feet off the beach. I'd heard that the snorkeling around them was amazing—my friends had reported seeing schools of colored fish darting through the water. I swore to myself that I'd get some goggles and go exploring in the New Year.

As my heart and pulse rates slowed, I forged a semblance of a plan. I texted Torrence and told him I would be coming by with a sandwich around one to apologize and chat. "Sandwich" would probably get his attention, though, in hindsight, "chocolate" would have been a surer bet. Then I tried to focus on exactly the questions for which I needed answers. Who had shot at me and why? That one I had a personal stake in. Who had set fire to Edel's restaurant? Why was Edel's ex-husband in her storage shed the night of the fire? Who was trying to sabotage her food? Was Edel having difficulty following the city's rules and regulations? Was she having conflict with her neighbors? And which of her employees—if any—might have wanted to see her fail? And was there anything I could do to save my job?

Once I'd ordered two Cuban mix sandwiches with extra pickles and BBQ chips from Coles Peace for pickup at noon, I perched on a picnic table under some trees a little ways from the beach. I started my search by Googling Ava Faulkner's name, grasping for anything that would help rescue my spot at *Key Zest*. I assumed she had not changed her surname, as this had also been the given name of her sister, Kristin, who had tragically died not long after I'd come to town. But that was a whole other story. Remembering that Palamina had told me that Ava and she went to college together at Columbia University, I began to Google their two names in tandem. The only connection I discovered was the mention of a sorority gala coordinated by Palamina Wells and Ava Faulkner. At least my trail was slightly warm. I could imagine the havoc Ava must have wreaked among her sorority sisters.

Then I started searching through the magazines for which Palamina had worked. On the masthead of a short-lived fashion magazine, I found the names of Palamina and Ava as staff assistants. But four names down from theirs was another I recognized: Edel Waugh. Bizarre. So Ava had to have known Edel years ago. Did she dislike her former colleague back then as much as she did now? I wondered if I could get Palamina to talk. Probably not. However, it did seem worth warning Wally about the connection. I hated to watch *Key Zest* take a direction that was based on Ava's grudges.

Wally answered his phone on the first ring. "I only have a minute," he said brusquely. "Still in a meeting."

"Understood," I said. "I thought you should know that Ava, Palamina, and Edel all worked on the same magazine in New York some years ago."

"And that's important because?"

"Because she seems to have you in a headlock and that's okay if it's really good for you and *Key Zest*, but what if she's making decisions based on old grudges rather than what's truly right for your magazine? I'm not so sure you're seeing everything so clearly right now. With your mom being sick and the investors waving money in front of your nose—" I stopped, gulping back the tears that took me by surprise. "You're vulnerable right now, that's all I'm saying. Be careful."

"I'll do that," he said, still formal and cool. "Thanks for the suggestion." The connection was severed. Probably in more ways than one. I blotted my face dry on my sleeve and headed off to get the sandwiches.

25

When I'm dead worn-out, in a reverie, I
often think that when it comes time to die,
I want to breathe my last in a kitchen.
　　　　　—Banana Yoshimoto, *Kitchen*

On the way back from the beach to the parking lot where I'd left my scooter, my phone rang—a call from my stepmother, Allison. Retracing my steps to a bench in the shade of some tall fir trees, I accepted the call. I hadn't spoken with her in a while so I might as well catch up now.

"Hayley, we haven't heard from you in forever," she said, sounding cheerful rather than accusatory, but a little concerned. "And usually that means you're either crazy busy or crazy worried, but don't want to bother us with the details."

"You know me too well," I said with a laugh. "How about both at once?" We'd grown a lot closer since the events surrounding Connie's wedding last spring. She gave me credit for persuading her ex to allow my stepbrother to live with my father and her this year, rather than be shipped off to a military academy. "How's Rory doing?"

"Absolutely thriving," she said. "He can hardly be bothered to sulk like a normal teenager. He just finished up with the cross-country season. For a kid without much experience in athletics, he did really well. And it even looks like he may be elected one of the captains. And his grades are all B or better."

"Wonderful," I said, really meaning it.

"Now you," she said. "Tell me the worried part. I can picture the busy. How's it working out to have your mom down there?"

I heaved a big sigh. "It's all fine. She's very busy, too, helping Jennifer with a million catering gigs." I paused. This wasn't really my story to tell, but Allison knew the players and might have some insight. "Can I trust you with a secret? No telling Dad."

"Of course," she said, adding a laugh. "His information is doled out on a need-to-know basis."

"Sam proposed," I told her. "In front of an entire dinner party."

"That was bold. And she said?"

"Nothing. She said nothing."

"Hmm," said Allison. "Can I be honest? She hasn't dated anyone else since the divorce, right?"

"Not worth mentioning." Not that I knew of. But her adventures on Match.com, where she'd met Sam, had all been a cold shock to me. Who knew how many dates she'd gone on before finding him?

"She's über-cautious when it comes to men," Allison said. "Maybe she's got a psychological block against considering a happy relationship. Maybe the idea is too scary."

I couldn't help defending my mother. "She planned

on her marriage to Dad lasting forever." Not that my parents' divorce had anything to do with Allison.

"I meant no criticism, just observation." Allison waited, then added, "A little bit like you, wouldn't you say? Or you're like her. She'll get around to it when she's ready. He's a lovely man; it would be a shame to cut him loose. Some other single woman would snatch him up."

"Exactly," I said. "Exactly."

"And how's Wally?"

"Deep in talks with investors who are interested in butting into *Key Zest*. Ava's behind it, of course. I'm not sure how long I'll even have the job, never mind the boyfriend." My voice caught in an embarrassing hitch. I tried to cover that up by segueing into the story about Edel and her ex, and the terrible, deadly fire. I described her staff and her fierce insistence on becoming a foodie star in the Key West scene, in spite of the very recent tragedy. "I don't believe she was involved in the fire, but the cops haven't come up with another good suspect."

"So, you're writing a piece on the restaurant?"

"I was. Until the fire and the death and the complications at *Key Zest*. What happened to Edel and her ex-husband was so sad. Their New York restaurant had been a raging success, but she pulled out after his very public betrayal." I explained more about the Page Six story.

"Was she angry enough to kill him?"

"I hate to think the worst of her, but that doesn't mean it isn't so." A heavy wave of sadness washed over me. Did most marriages end in disaster? Change the subject, Hayley.

"What do you have planned for Christmas?" I got

up from the bench and started to walk toward the parking lot as she began to tell me about their holiday plans with her sisters. "Sounds like fun. I'll miss you guys. Right now I have to go. I'm headed over to the police station. Maybe if I dangle a Cuban mix in front of Lieutenant Torrence, he'll tell me what they've learned."

"Maybe even better, just enjoy your lunch and leave the business of solving crimes to them?" she asked lightly. "But I know you better, so tell that sweet man Torrence I said hello."

Torrence had had a lot to do with saving Rory, and Allison would always remember that. I hung up promising to pass along her greetings and call again soon, feeling a mixture of relief and disappointment. Relief that she hadn't found out I'd been shot, because she'd worry herself sick. And my father even more so. And disappointment about the same. Much as I wanted to stand on my own two feet in this new Key West life, sometimes having a relative in your corner felt like a very good thing.

I buzzed up Southard, then over to Fleming and then Eaton, finally pulling into the busy parking lot at the Coles Peace Bakery. The lunch rush was in full swing, including a cluster of women ordering holiday pies and platters of Christmas cookies. I wormed my way to the counter, paid, and grabbed my sandwiches. The tantalizing smells of mustard and roasted pork and dill pickles called to me all the way over to the police station.

After picking up the phone on the wall outside the front door and stating my business, Torrence came to the lobby to get me. "A bribe," he said with a grin, and reached for the bag of sandwiches. "Come on in and tell me what's on your mind. How are you feeling? How's the arm today?"

"Just fine," I said, though, in fact, that whole side of my body had started to throb and I was dying to take a painkiller. I followed him into his office, where we spread out a layer of napkins, unwrapped the sandwiches, and began to eat. I opened the barbecued chips and tapped a few out onto a napkin. "Have you identified a suspect?"

"We've got guys canvassing the harbor and contacting all the boat captains who were in the parade. Nothing's turned up yet." He wiped his lips with a paper napkin and narrowed his eyes. "I don't suppose you've remembered seeing something new? Or thought of someone who might have it in for you?"

I ran my fingers down the length of the injured arm, feeling a ripple of the terror I'd experienced the night before. "No. I mean, nothing in my life is going really well at this point. But not awful, either. Nobody has it in for me in an 'I'm going to shoot you' kind of way."

I debated whether to tell him about the woman I'd interviewed this morning who lived in the apartment overlooking the harbor. He'd be annoyed. But, on the other hand, I was tired. And not feeling enough oomph to act like Hayley against the world.

"I did have one interesting conversation," I said to Torrence, not meeting his eyes. "There's a woman who lives on the second floor over the building next to the Schooner Wharf Bar. I saw her light on and I took a chance that she'd chat with me for a minute. But she really didn't have much to add other than steer me toward Wes Singleton." I squinted and risked looking at him dead-on. "You probably know him. He used to own and run the Fishing Hole on the bight. He spends a lot of mornings near the harbor. She thought he might have seen something."

Torrence set his sandwich down on the desk. "Haven't we been over this before? If the police are investigating a crime or an incident, the best thing for you to do is to mind your own business. Supposing this lady was willing to talk with one person but not more than one? You've already spoiled the possibility of a professional police interview by blundering in with your questions. Supposing she has taken the time between her chat with you and her chat with us to tweak her story?"

He was getting all wound up so I interrupted him to confess the rest of my transgressions. Why get yelled at twice? "Then I should also tell you that I spoke with Wes Singleton. But I couldn't help that. I was in line at the Cuban Coffee Queen and he was ahead of me. I couldn't be rude."

"And he said?" Torrence asked.

"That one of Edel's chefs, Glenn Fredericks, used to work for him. Apparently this man is sick to death of Edel's controlling nature. I didn't get much more, because then Wes went off on the city commissioners, along with the rest of the city administration. He's angry, of course, because he lost his lease on the restaurant that his family ran on the harbor for a million years. But he's got no beef with me."

Torrence nodded, picked up the sandwich again and began to eat. "We know all about him," he said. "He's a crackpot but harmless. Better use of your time would be to let us do the work and maybe you go bake a cake or something."

"I think you must be kidding, but those are fighting words," I said, starting to steam inside.

He laughed. "I'm kidding. But bring me a piece when you're finished. Red velvet, maybe. With cream-cheese frosting. That's my favorite. I always go on a diet after Christmas, but I'm not there yet."

"You're a comedian." I folded up my trash, including the section of the sandwich that I hadn't finished. I'd lost my appetite over the morning. In fact, the whole week had been enough to put me off my feed. A new kind of diet, I thought as I pushed through the front door of the station and went out into the bright light of the early afternoon. The "lose your job and your weight stress-and-gunshot" diet.

I tucked the sandwich into my basket and flipped through my messages while perched on the scooter. Edel had texted, inviting/suggesting/insisting that I be in the kitchen at five, ready to chronicle the opening minutes of her bistro's opening night.

I tried to imagine what it would be like to work on the line in her kitchen. I love to cook and to try new recipes and new combinations of food. But, on the other hand, the part of my job that feeds my soul is writing about food. Teasing out what makes one meal good, but another magical. Discovering a new chef or a new dish and describing my find to the world—or at least to other food-addled diners who'd go out of their way for something special. For me, the cooking itself was not so much the miracle. It was all about the eating. And then choosing the words that brought that food to life on the page.

A second message was from my mother, who was working in Jennifer's kitchen all day but would love to catch up when I had a minute. Why not now? I had nowhere else to be and nothing really to work on. The only downside was that it was difficult to obfuscate the truth when faced with my mother in person.

I texted her back and told her I was on the way over.

26

She turned back to the stove and stirred furiously, splashing bright red sauce over most of the stove. "I mean, what kind of a crazy person with mush for brains would look into the eyes of love and ignore it?"
—Suzanne Palmieri, *The Witch of Little Italy*

I located Jennifer Cornell's place off Roosevelt Boulevard, in the VFW building. The only glimpse I'd gotten into her kitchen previously was in an advertisement I'd seen in the free *Menus* magazine, featuring Jennifer herself in a white chef's toque and jacket, stuffed into an enormous stainless-steel stockpot. And grinning like a madwoman. She was not one to shy away from interesting publicity.

Inside, the air smelled like toasted coconut and fried seafood. Plus fresh garlic and basil and tomatoes and grilled onions. And maybe even ginger. A cornucopia of wonderful flavors. My mother, swathed in a white apron, stood before an eight-burner gas range, fishing shrimp out of boiling oil and placing them on paper towels to drain.

"It smells wonderful in here," I said. "What's on the docket tonight?"

"It's a wedding at the Oldest House on Duval Street," Mom said. "The bride is a woman after my own heart—after choosing her man, she's focused her heart and pocketbook on the menu." Then she looked away, making me think of Sam's proposal and the naked look of hopefulness on his face as my mother had opened the ring box. Mom clapped her hands. All business.

"Will you taste this sauce, honey?" she asked, clip-clopping across the kitchen in her green clogs to grab two bowls of dipping sauce. "Jennifer usually serves the coconut shrimp with mango chutney, but I was thinking something less sweet and more spicy might be a fabulous contrast."

She handed me a small plate containing a piping-hot shrimp coated in a crispy coconut crust. I dipped the shrimp in both sauces while she chattered about the plans for this reception and another luncheon tomorrow and a cocktail party after that. "These people down here in the high tourist season are on a treadmill of fun," she added.

"How about you? Are you having a good time?"

"I am having a ball," she said. "Everything I imagined and more."

But her voice sounded brittle and the smile on her face was not quite convincing.

I was about to push her harder about Sam when Jennifer Cornell bustled into the kitchen.

"I was just about to ask Hayley about Edel Waugh's new restaurant," Mom said, though we hadn't been talking about that at all.

"She's planning to open tonight, finally," I said.

"She's opening in spite of her husband's death?" Jennifer's forehead crinkled with concern. "I'm surprised that the cops are letting that happen. And, besides, how can she possibly cook under these circumstances? Sometimes I worry that if I have a sad day or I'm distracted, my feelings leach into my food. Those are times when I try to step away and let my assistants do the lion's share of the cooking. Those days, I stick with paying bills and working on advertising. Jobs that won't be affected by sorrow or a lousy biorhythm."

"Wow," I said, "you're exactly right. Though I hadn't thought of it in those words. But I'm sure she feels she can't bail out—she thinks the food critic for the *New York Times* is coming for dinner tonight."

"Huge opportunity. Huge risk." Mom turned back to the task of frying shrimp. Working on the middle island, Jennifer began to cut an enormous bag of tiny limes into halves.

"Dessert?" I asked.

She nodded. "Key lime pie. The bride wanted the whole meal to be tropical. To me that's fun."

"Back to Edel for a moment," Mom said. "I know we can't really get into her head, but why do you think she's pushing so hard? She's so ferocious about her food and her place. Why?"

"I've wondered, too," I said, and turned to Jennifer. "Some of it must have to do with going out on her own as a woman in this business. In the articles I've read, her husband, Juan Carlos, was usually credited for the magical combinations of ingredients and recipes. Edel was mentioned after him, the business tour de force, the sharp-edged negotiator, but also the woman behind the man and his cooking."

"I bet you that stuck in her craw like a chicken bone," Mom said, patting her neck with a paper towel.

"It's harder for a woman chef," Jennifer said. She tapped a fist on her chest. "I'm a little different. I don't take myself too seriously. If she wants to compete with the top restaurants—I don't mean just in Key West—she must be serious." She pointed to the newspaper articles pinned up over her desk: Jennifer in the stockpot. Jennifer in a mermaid's costume, including a big tail and a bikini top, posed with a dashing pirate. "I don't mind fooling around with things like this. I intend to have a successful catering business, not garner a James Beard award."

"Maybe that's why she can't serve her spaghetti Bolognese," I said. "It's too much like something an earth mother would cook, without enough manly pizzazz."

Jennifer began to crack eggs deftly, dropping the yolks into one bowl and separating the whites into another. "The bride says her new mother-in-law is allergic to anything citrus," she said. "So we'll have to make something chocolate, too. I was thinking of your Scarlett O'Hara cupcakes," she added, looking at Mom. "Unless that's too much to accomplish this afternoon?"

Mom shook her head and grinned. "There's nothing I'd rather do than spend the day here cooking. And I love the idea of those pink iced cupcakes at a wedding. They're so romantic. Did any raspberries come in the shipment this morning? If not, I imagine we could do something very similar with strawberries."

"I'll take a look." Jennifer headed off to the enormous refrigerators at the far end of her kitchen.

"Don't you and Sam have any plans?" I asked, once she'd disappeared, keeping my voice light and innocent.

"Sam's a grown man," Mom said. "He can take care

of himself." She fell silent and went back to plunging
the shrimp into hot oil, which sizzled and popped.

"Listen, Mom," I said finally, "I seem to remember
you telling Connie last spring that even though she had
to make her own decision about marrying Ray, as far as
we could see, they were a wonderful couple. I say the
same about you and Sam."

She did not answer.

I forged forward despite my mother's frostiness. "It
seems like something about his proposal has got you
spooked. Did he take you by surprise? Did you not like
the ring?" I snickered to let her know I was joking
about the jewelry. My mother had never in her life put
money or diamonds ahead of her connection with
someone, and I doubted she would do that now. But in
her current condition, I couldn't be sure.

"I'm just getting started making a life for myself,"
Mom finally said, turning the shrimp in the hot oil with
a pair of chopsticks. "I've never truly been successful
on my own." She waved off the protests that she must
have assumed were bubbling to my mouth. "Yes, I was
a good wife and a super mother. You turned out to be
everything I could have dreamed of in a daughter." She
flashed a tremulous smile. "But I never supported myself. I never had a career." She wiped the back of her
hand across her eyes. "Hayley, your career has gone
farther than mine ever did and I'm more than twenty
years older than you are."

"But, Mom—"

"Sam would take care of me. He *wants* to take care of
me. But I don't have the nerve to let go of what I'm
trying to do and trust the future with him. Trust that his
care would last forever. Trust that depending on him
would feel okay to me."

"But, Mom, surely he wouldn't ask you to give up

catering. He seems to love the fact that you're launching something new."

She tightened her shoulders and turned to face me, her eyes intense. "I don't have the nerves for it, Hayley."

I would have tried to argue if I could have thought of a strong rebuttal, but then her face froze in horror as she stared at my arm. I glanced down. Blood had seeped from my wound through the dressing and from there through my long-sleeved shirt.

My mouth working faster than my mind, I said, "It's not as bad as it looks. The bullet barely creased the flesh."

27

Pie solves most things.
            —Barbara Ross, *Clammed Up*

It took more than fifteen minutes to tell the details of the story of last night's incident to my mother's satisfaction: the lighted boat parade, the shooting, and the visit to the emergency room. Mom's gasps and outraged quasi-expletives slowed down the narrative.

"But why didn't you tell me?" she asked three or four times during my story. "We didn't see Ray's boat go by, but, my gosh, we never imagined you were in trouble. I wish you had called. I wish I'd been on the boat with you in the first place—"

"Mom," I said, turning off the burner under her frying pan and then taking both of her arms in my hands and pressing her onto a stool near the counter. "This is why I didn't tell you. Because I knew you'd get hysterical."

Mom turned to Jennifer, who was watching our exchange in awe and dismay. "Am I hysterical, Jennifer?"

"A smidge," Jennifer replied, holding her thumb and forefinger an inch away from each other.

"Maybe we should get started on the cupcakes while we're discussing this?" I suggested. "I'll work on the frosting."

"But you're bleeding," Mom said.

"It's just oozing. I'll show you later when I change the bandage. Seriously, it's only a flesh wound. They found nothing wrong with my bones—no nicks, no scrapes, nothing. There were no symptoms of any vessel damage. It's just ordinary, everyday bleeding."

"It's a gunshot wound," Mom said, her voice tight with worry. "There's nothing ordinary about it."

Jennifer called up the cupcake recipe on her laptop, and Mom began to stomp around, measuring the flour and the baking powder and sugar and cocoa powder. All the while, she interrogated me about what the police had said last night, what they learned about the shooting, and what kind of protection they were affording her daughter. Her only daughter. I wondered if Jennifer was worried about all this angst leaching into her bridal cupcakes.

"Of course they're canvassing all the boats that were in the parade," I said. "Plus they will send patrols around to talk to the owners of the bars and as many customers as they can get hold of. Bottom line? There really is no reason for someone to be shooting at me, which speaks to it being a random hit." I tried to sound measured and unconcerned and utterly confident that the cops would solve the question of who'd shot at me and why.

Mom's eyes widened, as if this was the first time she had considered a motive. "There might very well be a reason," she said. "What about Edel's situation and the fire? There is something very scary going on with that. For heaven's sake, her husband was murdered right on her property."

"We don't know that," I said sternly. "There are a million other ways it could have happened."

"How widely was it known that you were attending the boat parade?" Jennifer asked.

"It wasn't a secret," I said, then tried to reconstruct conversations I'd had about the event. The town locals had been talking about it for weeks—and I had, too. "I remember the day that I first showed up at Edel's restaurant, the kitchen staff was talking about the Christmas activities on the island. And I mentioned how much fun the boat parade was and that I would be riding in Ray's boat. He'd just invited me earlier that morning, and I was very excited."

"Who?" my mother asked. "To whom did you say that?"

"Pretty much everyone in the back of the house was there." I sighed. "Plus, certainly my friends at *Key Zest* know. And Miss Gloria. And that means everyone at Tarpon Pier heard about it, too. There's just no way to narrow it down."

My mother wrung her hands, her eyes a little tearful. "I am so, so sorry I ever said anything to her about what a good detective you are. This is all my fault, I know it—I've put you in danger."

"What are you talking about?"

Mom pressed the GO button on Jennifer's monstrous KitchenAid mixer. I turned the machine back off, feeling stunned and confused. "You'd better explain."

She dabbed at a splatter of batter on the counter. "Edel mentioned she was having some trouble in her kitchen. And I said how perceptive you were and how you'd helped solve some other cases."

"When did you have this conversation? Why were you even talking to her?"

My mother put a hand to her cheek. "Because we

invested in her new place. Or Sam did, anyway. You know how I've always loved her food. And I was so excited to hear about the bistro, and then Sam had the idea of backing her."

"So that's why she keeps calling me," I said, hardly knowing what to feel about this new information. Like the kaleidoscope I'd had as a child, the knob had been turned and all the events of the past few days looked different.

"It doesn't really change anything," Mom said. "She respects you for you. I'm just sorry I dragged you into a dangerous situation." She turned the mixer back on.

While the oversized beaters mixed the batter, Mom began to drop cupcake liners into a row of pans on the counter. When the liners were all in place, she turned off the mixer and parked her hands on her hips. "I think we should call Lorenzo and see if he has time to give you a tarot card reading. I can't get away right now, but I'll tell him you want to meet him for coffee or lunch."

I could have argued but what was the point? Besides, talking with Lorenzo almost always calmed me down. I rely on him when the going gets tough. Mom loves him, too. For me, absorbing his measured words works like yoga or tai chi or meditation—or even psychotherapy—does for other folks.

Mom got off her phone after a short conversation. "He's going to meet you at the Coffee Plantation on Caroline Street in half an hour. I promised him the snack of his choice." She kissed my cheek. "Go ahead, honey—it's my treat." She pressed a crumpled twenty-dollar bill into my palm. "I've got to stay here and finish the cupcakes. And for the love of Pete, be careful!" She pushed me toward the door. "And call me right away to tell me what he said."

I motored across the island to the coffee shop on Caroline, a little white clapboard house with green shutters. Lorenzo hadn't arrived yet, so I dropped my backpack at a table on the porch and went in to order. Inside, brightly colored walls were hung with cheerful local and Cuban paintings. Books from local artists were displayed around the room. I approached the counter and asked for a latte. The almond cake dusted with powdered sugar sang to me, so I ordered a slice of that, too.

"A friend will be joining me shortly—I'm treating," I told the clerk.

Back outside, I sat at the table overlooking the street, determined not to process my mother's confession until I'd fortified myself with caffeine and sugar. Despite the fame rendered to it by a popular Jimmy Buffet tune, Caroline Street, with its busy traffic and the construction of a new hotel a block away, did not afford the quietest respite on the island. But it was a great spot to watch the world go by.

Did it really matter, I wondered, that Sam and my mother were backing Edel's restaurant? I was glad for her that she had them in her corner. But I felt silly, thinking she'd called me for help because of my reputation both as a food critic and a puzzle solver when, in fact, the whole thing had been set up by my mother.

Ten minutes later, Lorenzo took the seat beside me, carrying a cup of tea and a slice of pie. His dark hair curled like mine in the humidity, and he wore Harry Potter–style round glasses and red clogs. I felt instantly calmer in his presence.

"I was hoping you weren't on a diet," I said, pointing at his plate.

"The cards say, 'Never pass up key lime pie,'" he told me as he swallowed the first creamy bite and rolled his eyes with ecstasy.

We chatted for a few minutes about the politics of the street performers at Mallory Square and their difficult negotiations with the city about a new lease. I wasn't the only person struggling with a crazy workplace.

"I got worried this week when we cruised through Sunset at Mallory Square with Mom's guests and you weren't there. There was another tarot card reader where you usually sit," I said, lifting my eyebrows. "Is she your new competition?"

"It all depends," he said. "Do you want a performance? Or a reading?" He placed his deck of cards on the little table between us.

"A reading. Definitely. No drama." I began to shuffle the cards. "I've got enough of that in my own life."

He smiled warmly and dealt out three cards. A look of alarm crossed his face, erased as quickly as it had appeared. "Hmm." He leaned across the table to take my hand. "We'll get to these cards. But I sense danger for someone close to you. Possibly a woman. Someone needs to keep her channels open—she may not be able to see things clearly. Does this sound right?"

"Not exactly, but I'll think about it." Besides me getting shot at, Edel, of course, sprang to mind. Had someone been targeting her personally when the fire was set? None of the other women in my life were in any physical danger. Emotional danger, though, that was always a possibility.

"Stay open to your senses, okay?" he said.

I nodded, feeling the light-as-air almond cake churn in my stomach as I glanced down again at my cards. The Tower for the past, the Eight of Swords for the present, and the Page of Wands for the future. Upside down.

"Let's take the present first, the Eight of Swords. You've drawn this before, remember?"

Too well. I disliked the message then and I didn't like it any better now.

"It's hard work to change," he said, "when you feel trapped by a situation. But no one can rescue you from said situation, whether it's real or whether it's something in your head."

Who in the world used the phrase "said situation" in normal conversation? I knew I was getting scared and cranky when I started critiquing his way of speaking. But I tried to set aside the negative internal chatter and really listen.

"If you are feeling powerless, it may be time to question your assumptions. Get ready to open yourself to change. To new possibilities. Remove the block and the energy can flow."

He tapped my third card with two fingers—the card that had been dealt out upside down. The drawing was of a handsome golden man carrying a large staff or walking stick that sprouted leaves at its tip. Buff, I would have said, if it had been a live man instead of a drawing. The figure gazed off into the distant mountains on the card. "Page of Wands," Lorenzo said.

"He's cute, isn't he?" I quirked a smile, trying not to show how on edge I was feeling.

"I see a lot of craziness, maybe at work. But maybe at home?" He cocked his head and studied me. "You'll suffer if you don't articulate your thoughts—if you try to protect other peoples' feelings at the expense of your own." He placed his hand over mine, squeezed gently, and then shifted his attention to the first card in my sequence.

The Tower. Too many times I had drawn the Tower and I disliked the news that it trumpeted every time. "Any chance you could remove this from the deck next time I come?"

He shook his head. "There's change ahead. Up-heaval. You may feel trapped by feelings and emotions that no longer serve your current purpose," he said. "You may feel that you're out of control, but this will help you evaluate the ways you feel trapped. Don't let yourself remain in the position of refusing to see the truth."

There were so many ways I was feeling stuck and out of control—my job, my love life, just to mention two. Lorenzo paused, still studying the cards. But it seemed as though they had given him all they had to say. And I needed to do some serious thinking, alone.

"How are you aside from the Mallory Square business?" I asked Lorenzo.

"I'm good," he said. "I'm busy. I'm feeling calm and centered."

"I'm glad someone is," I said.

"Just remember, there are two worlds—a world of love and a world of fear. You choose where you want to live, okay?"

We chatted a bit about holiday plans while I finished my coffee and the half slice of cake that I had planned to take home to Miss Gloria. She wouldn't miss it if I didn't mention it. Sometimes hearing about the future demanded more sugar.

We gathered our trash and stood up. "Are you sure you're okay?" he asked.

"I'm fine," I said, thinking he'd held back on some-thing terrible during my short reading. I suppose I needed to know. "Why?"

He pointed to my shirtsleeve. "Is that blood?"

I breathed a sigh of relief. "Just a scratch. Nothing to worry about."

I grinned and hugged him good-bye and hurried off. Once balanced on my scooter, I called my mother.

"Everything looks fine to him," I said. "No problems, nothing out of the ordinary. Change is coming, of course. See the truth; don't stay stuck."

"Change?" Mom asked.

I added quickly: "I drew the Tower in my past position."

Mom groaned. "The Tower again?"

"I'm not worried about it," I said. "Neither is Lorenzo. Listen, I wish you'd told me about Sam investing in Edel's place. I would have handled that just fine. Just as Sam can handle your career if you two get married. Each of us is stronger than we think we are."

"I'm sorry," she said. "Maybe."

"Anyway, I'm exhausted. I'm going home to the boat to take a short nap before I have to leave for Edel's place tonight. Try not to worry, because I'll be fine. I'll take no chances. You've got plenty to manage on your side. Be nice to Sam, whatever you tell him."

"Of course," she said, her voice a little distant. "I'll talk to you later or tomorrow."

"Tomorrow will be fine."

Loud noises banged, coming from behind the fence surrounding the construction site in back of the Coffee Plantation. I glanced over, noticing how the rooftops of the new hotel could have offered an excellent staging platform for the shooter as he studied the harbor, looking for his target.

28

He had seen a girl with a sandwich in her hand and fallen in love with the part of her that made sense to him, that fit the partic-ular story he knew how to read.
— Erica Bauermeister, *The Lost Art of Mixing*

I grabbed a quick nap and then played with Evinrude for half an hour, throwing his KITTY CAN'T COPE catnip sack over and over until he tired of the game. He had been acting standoffish in the face of my recent ab-sences from the houseboat, and I knew too well that an angry cat could wreak some ugly vengeance. Finally I took a shower, washed my hair, and enlisted Miss Glo-ria to rebandage my wound.

"It's healing quickly," she said, when all the dress-ings had been removed. I winced as she patted antibi-otic cream on the wound with a sterile pad. "Are you sure you're up for going back to Edel's kitchen?"

"Are you kidding? This could be my only chance ever to see the *New York Times* restaurant critic in ac-tion." Miss Gloria doesn't usually go all parental-worried on me, but obviously this incident had thrown her, too.

"Did you tell your mother?"

"I definitely told her," I said. I did not add that she'd wormed it out of me only because the bandage was leaking. And that she'd spilled her own secret about backing Edel's new restaurant.

Miss Gloria tried one more time to persuade me to relax at home, abandon my station at Edel's bistro tonight, and forget about the conflict at *Key Zest*. But part of growing up meant figuring out when a little mothering became too much. And how to mother myself.

"How did Janet seem?" Miss Gloria asked.

"Jennifer's got her so busy," I said, "that she doesn't have much time for anything else, even worrying. And that includes Sam and his proposal."

"Lucky for me," said Miss Gloria, "I never had to go through a divorce. I imagine that changes your faith about marriages being happily ever after."

"It sure did a number on my mother," I said as I unrolled my shirtsleeves and buttoned the cuffs. "So, you're planning a quiet night?"

Miss Gloria laughed, a lovely silver tinkle. "As quiet as I can manage with that crazy schnauzer for a neighbor. I'm going to watch the sunset out here with the kitty cats and have a teeny-tiny glass of wine, and then eat some of your leftover stew and watch TV. This time of year is so hectic, at my age I have to watch getting overexcited and overtired."

"At your age?" I said with a big grin. "You have more energy than most of the people I know that are my age. You're a role model for all of us."

I gave her a one-armed hug; grabbed my phone, my helmet, and a notebook; and headed out to the scooter. Only when I was halfway down Southard Street did I remember that I had not taken any anti-inflammatories or painkillers. The prescription stuff would have made me fuzzy and woozy. But a couple of ibuprofen might help get me through the night. I veered right on Simonton Street and pulled my scooter onto its stand in the lot next to Fausto's Food Palace.

The wide glass doors slid open as I approached the store and I ducked inside. A collection of tourists and locals were busy shopping for their night meal. As the only true grocery store left in Old Town after the demise of the Waterfront Market, Fausto's does a good business. In fact, if I'm not baking, I've been known to peruse their dessert counter for treats home baked by Chef Jeffrey Smiley. I hurried down the aisle displaying toiletries and over-the-counter medications and grabbed a bottle of ibuprofen. At the far end of the row, I saw my cousin Cassie, her husband, Joe, and poor hung-out-to-dry Sam standing by the meat counter. I went over to greet them.

"We wondered when we would see you next," Joe said. "How was the lighted boat parade? Cassie and I started over last night, but once we got to Greene Street the crowds were so thick. We couldn't see much so we opted for gelato from Duetto and then saw the end of the parade from Mallory Square with your mother. Not your boat, though."

"There were some gorgeous entries," I said, working to keep my voice light. "We couldn't provide much competition in a little motorboat, even though Connie and Ray went all out with their lights. And you were right, it was hectic. We cut out early, too."

They would hear soon enough from my mother about the shooting. I preferred not to rehash the incident at the meat counter, where half the island's locals might be listening.

Sam added, "We're having to fend for ourselves tonight, so Joe's offered to make his beef stew. I'm springing for the wine. They carry a lovely selection right here. Imagine finding a French rosé in downtown Key West." He held out a gorgeous bottle of pale pink wine.

"And I am in charge of dessert." Cassie grinned and showed me a clear plastic container that held half a key lime pie and a large chunk of coconut cream layer cake.

"Those two are definitely my favorites," I said. "It didn't take you long to catch on."

"Can you join us?" Sam asked.

"Oh that sounds so good. And so relaxing. But I told Edel I'd be there tonight for her opening."

"Was there news about Edel's husband?" asked Sam.

"Nothing on that," I said. "But supposedly the critic from the *New York Times* food section is coming to review her restaurant tonight. They're all very excited and that helps a little bit with the sadness."

Sam gave me a big hug, squeezing my sore arm, and I tried not to wince. "Maybe that restaurant critic can take a few tips from you. I think you're the best writer in the business." He pulled me a few steps away from the others. "Have you heard anything from your mother?" he asked in a low voice.

I cleared my throat, wondering how much to say. "I checked in with her at Jennifer Cornell's kitchen." I toyed with my small gold hoop earring. "Here's what I think: be patient. Give her some space. You know it's not you, Sam," I said, grabbing his elbow and giving it a little shake. "She's got some things to work out in her own brain. You're the best thing to come along in her life in a long time—she knows that, but she's scared."

Joe accepted the package of beef tips that the butcher handed over the counter, and he and Cassie came over to join us.

"Did you ever follow up with that Mary Pat person?" Joe asked.

"The one whose name came up on your handsome detective's phone," Cassie added.

Why did every member of my family persist in referring to him as "my" detective?

"Not yet," I said, "but I'm glad you reminded me." I blew them a round of air kisses and retreated to the checkout, grabbing a Coke from the cooler nearest the cash register—for the caffeine and the sugar and to swallow my pills.

29

And lobes of dismal-flavored sea urchin served over thick lardo and heavy toast were just dreadful: the eighth band after Nirvana to write loud-soft-loud music and call it new.
—Sam Sifton, "Imperial No. Nine,"
New York Times

Over at the harbor, Edel's kitchen was buzzing like a video on fast forward. I imagined it would be hard to slow down and sleep after a night at this pace. People say that becoming a chef requires a complete shift in biorhythms. And a shift in social life, too. While we customers in the front of the house are unwinding from our hectic days and enjoying the wonderful food, the cooks in back are working at peak velocity. When we're tumbling into bed after a great meal, the kitchen staff is hitting the town to unwind.

I melted into a corner by the desk and bookshelf where Edel planned her recipes and menus and paid her bills, to be out of the way of the workers. And to have enough space to observe how they were working together. I wished I could tease out the stress of opening night from the strain of the recent tragedy—and the possibility that someone was trying to hide his involvement in several very serious crimes.

Edel bustled in from the backyard and the tension in the room kicked up a couple of notches.

"How are you feeling? Everything okay here?"

She shrugged her shoulders, looking tightly wound. "We've taken reservations for every seat in the house, from opening moment to closing time at ten. It's just a matter of whether this staff can manage the heat. If you don't mind," she said, "I prefer that you sit out back or in the dining room for a bit while we get the preparations completed."

"Okaaaay," I said, drawing the word out and trying to figure out what the heck was the subtext of her message. Besides *"Get lost."* This was the first time I'd been banished. "If you're sure there's not something I can do to help. I'm pretty good with a knife and very good at stirring—"

"I would just as soon any nonessential, nonprofessional personnel move out of the way for a while," she said, not meeting my eyes.

"Have you heard anything more from Paul Woolston's staff?" Paul was the critic for the *New York Times*. Having him come all the way to Key West to critique Edel's food was a huge deal. He held an enormous sway over foodies across the country, with an emphasis on the tristate area around New York City. He was not known to be soft or subtle with his criticism.

"Nothing new, nothing different," she said, "but I'm pretty sure he's coming. And if he does, I would love for you to go out and chat with him. I don't need a sycophant or a cheering section, just a friendly Key West welcome. And I'd rather it didn't appear to be set up.

Maybe more like you happened to be dining here, too, and you recognized him and wanted to say hello." Offering a very thin smile, she turned away to shout orders at Glenn, the sous-chef. Nothing he was doing at the stove or the counter appeared to be up to her standards. Honestly, if I'd been him, with the way she talked, I'd have been tempted to quit. Walk straight out the front door, opening-night jitters or not.

"I'll be out in the back if you need me." I gathered my backpack and phone and slipped through the swinging screen door. Maybe that was the real reason she'd asked me to be here tonight: not to help out in the kitchen or watch her back, but to help handle the most important restaurant critic in the world.

I retreated to a stone bench in the rear yard, which seemed to serve as the staff's smoking and break station, based on the cigarette butts clustered on the surrounding dirt. The faint odor of burned wood from the big fire still lingered. And the not so faint memories of Edel's beleaguered ex-husband with it. I pulled out my phone and began to formulate the opening paragraph for a story about Bistro on the Bight. If I no longer had a job at *Key Zest*, perhaps I could use this piece as a sample of a profile in food journalism when I applied somewhere else.

> It's not easy to leave an environment where your food is well-known and wildly successful. Nor is it easy to leave a partnership that has those same qualities. But Edel Waugh was determined to do both. "I adore Key West," Waugh said in an interview days before the opening of her new Key West establishment, Bistro on the Bight. "I don't know how well anyone can ever know this island—she's a tropical beauty, but mercurial, multilayered, fickle, and quirky. I had vis-

ited many times over the past two decades and I was
pretty sure I could cook here in a way that I would be
able to cook nowhere else. I intend to make dishes that
reflect this island's Caribbean roots and her migrant
past. But I will also cook dishes from my own past,
dishes that reflect the best of my influences."

That was the easy part of the article. Next I'd have to
talk about whether Edel had been successful in the task
she'd laid out. No question in my mind that the food
would be successful—but whether the woman and the
restaurant would make it in Key West was up for de-
bate.

The screen door squeaked open, then slammed shut
behind Rodrigo, who carried two enormous black bags
of garbage to the Dumpsters a hundred feet away. He
lingered at the end of the alley, lit up a cigarette, and
leaned against the wall of the building next door, which
housed the public restrooms. At first glance, I thought
he was killing time, looking at nothing in particular—
the sky, the diesel tanks, the weeds bordering the open
space behind the Bistro. Probably relieved to be out of
Edel's spotlight for a few peaceful moments. But then I
noticed the flowers laid out on the ground. I got up and
walked over.

"*Hola,*" I said when I got nearer to Rodrigo. Pathetic,
but the only Spanish I knew.

He startled, then grunted a greeting in reply.

When he leaned to straighten a paper weighted
down by several pieces of coral rock, I realized he'd
been standing over a mini shrine to Juan Carlos: photos
of the man in his New York restaurant, toasting the
cameraman with a glass of wine and a cigarette, and, at
the bottom, a photo of him and Edel, arms around each
other. In earlier, happier times. And in front of the pho-

tos, a pile of wilting flowers—roses mostly, with a few carnations mixed in.

"Good man," Rodrigo said, his words perfect though his accent was heavy.

"Did you know him long?" I asked.

"Twenty years New York. Then I followed her." He jerked his head toward the restaurant. "Hate cold. And my family's Miami."

"Did you see him before the fire?"

He glanced behind him, looking both ways, as if he worried that I'd set a trap. "No cops?"

I shook my head and held my palms open. Which could have meant anything, but if he told me something that would lead to the killer or a shooter, I wouldn't keep it to myself.

"They fight," he said. "Like always, only worse."

"A physical fight?" I asked.

He put his hands around his own throat and squeezed.

Edel stepped onto the porch, beckoning frantically for me. "Hayley?"

I patted Rodrigo's shoulder and trotted back to the restaurant.

"What was all that about?" Edel's eyes had narrowed, her hands on her hips.

"I think he's in mourning," I said. "He was talking about Juan Carlos." I did not mention the pantomimed choking. Not yet.

"Paul Woolston is in the house," Edel said, after one final glare in Rodrigo's direction.

The *New York Times* critic. I felt a little frisson of excitement—a current of the same seemed to be running through the kitchen staff, too. They were working faster, their faces intent, chattering about the meaning of the visit—the possible benefits. And costs, if he didn't like the food. What would he order? Should they send him something extra? Who had come with him?

I peered through a crack from the swinging door leading from kitchen to dining room. Woolston had been seated at a table for two near the window overlooking the harbor. Despite his sway in the world of food-obsessed Americans, he looked like an ordinary diner, maybe a little too recently deplaned from New York to have relaxed completely. His companion, a middle-aged woman with streaked blond hair, was dressed in a black shift with pearls and kitten heels. Woolston himself wore sharply creased khaki trousers and a long-sleeve button-down shirt, also neatly ironed.

An amber-colored cocktail sat in front of Woolston, and something pinkish—a cosmopolitan, maybe?—in front of his companion. Leo McCracken, Edel's head waiter, was hovering near the table with a wine list and two leather-bound menus. Edel pushed the door closed, nearly pinching my fingers.

"Wait a while until he's had a chance to order his starters," she snapped. "I don't want it to look like I've set the dogs on him." She grinned, baring teeth like a stray dog herself, a mutt that you couldn't be sure was smiling or growling.

Leo burst through the door into the kitchen, still holding the menus. "He knows we're onto him," he said. "He told me nothing extra from the kitchen. He wants what everyone else is getting when they order and nothing special."

"What did he order for starters?" Edel asked, her face relaxing a little.

"They weren't ready," Leo said. "They wanted to enjoy their cocktails."

Edel took a small white bowl and filled it with her

smoked fish dip, then centered it on a plate and surrounded it with toast rounds. She shoved the finished plate at me. "Will you take this out? I'm too nervous to talk to him. I can't bear to know they're sitting there with nothing to eat."

So I stumbled out of the kitchen and over to the water-view table, a frozen smile on my face. "Hello, Mr. Woolston. I'm Hayley Snow, the food critic for the local style magazine, *Key Zest*. This dip comes with compliments of the chef. I know you said nothing special, but she couldn't help herself." I shrugged and grinned and slid the plate onto their table. The toast rounds shifted. I reached over to straighten them, then snatched my hand away. Good gravy, who would want my fingers all over their snacks?

"Paul," the woman said, "why don't we ask Ms. Snow to join us?" Her eyes twinkled and a friendly smile played across her lips. "As long as you're no longer incognito."

"Waiter!" said Paul, snapping his fingers at Leo. "This lady is joining us." And to me: "What are you drinking?"

"Are you sure?" I asked. "I would kill to . . . let me try that again. I didn't mean to insert myself into your dinner . . ."

"Since my cover appears to be blown already," he said, pushing the third chair away from the table and motioning me to sit, "we might as well get some local insights."

"A glass of the Paco and Lola Albariño," I told Leo as I took the seat between the food critic and his wife.

"Never mind the wine just yet," said Paul to the waiter. "This looks like a woman in need of a martini. Do you mind?" he asked me. "I'd like to sample something else from their bar without sliding under the table before the entrées arrive."

"Absolutely," I said. "Lots of olives. Make it dirty." Which I'd seen on bar menus but never actually sampled.

Leo scurried off to fill the order while Mrs. Woolston chatted about the amazing weather and the sharp contrast with the polar vortex in New York.

Within minutes, the martini was deposited in front of me. "Cheers and welcome to Key West," I said, then clinked their glasses and took an esophagus-burning gulp. "I adore your column in the food section," I said. "I so admire both what you say and the way you say it. Honest to god, if I could write a review like that . . ." I trailed off, horrified to find tears filling my eyes.

The woman patted my hand. "I'm Margaret, by the way, the great critic's wife." She grinned. "You should call him Paul. Believe me, he didn't always write like that and he's had some excellent editing across the years."

"She knows how to take a man down a few pegs if his head swells too big," said Paul with a chuckle. "She's also in charge of exercising me, because, as you've probably discovered, spare tires around the waist are a serious side effect of the job." He patted his belly, which had a pleasing roundness without wandering into a pot.

"Now tell us about Key West. What should we see while we're in town?" He spread a spoonful of Edel's fish dip on a crusty piece of bread and popped it into his mouth. "This is very good, by the way, Margaret," he told his wife. "The smoked fish is outstanding. But the dip has a nice bite to it, too. Tabasco and lime zest?" he asked me.

"I can't tell you her secrets, but doesn't it taste like a

dash of Old Bay Seasoning?" I said with a grin. "And a squeeze of lemon."

He tasted the dip again. "And maybe a bit of horse-radish? I should have known. What else should we not miss on the menu?"

So I told him about Edel's signature yellow snapper, and the spaghetti Bolognese that wasn't listed but he could request it, and the key lime parfaits. When we'd gone over the entire menu, he signaled for Leo and or-dered the dishes I'd mentioned, plus half a dozen oth-ers.

"Now," said Margaret, "where should a brand-new tourist begin to explore this island?"

"I always recommend that folks start with a ride on the Conch Tour Train. Don't be put off by the crowds, because the ride gives you an overview of the island. And later you can go back to visit the places that catch your eye."

Then I began to describe my favorite tourist attrac-tions—the Hemingway cats, the Custom House Mu-seum, the sunset celebration, Truman's Little White House, Fort Zachary Taylor park. I barely registered that Leo had brought a second round of cocktails and then set up a wine cooler to the left of the critic.

But I did notice that I'd begun to feel tipsy, which made me garrulous. And bold. "Tell me about Juan Carlos's restaurant in New York," I said. "My mother was a huge fan. And you must have eaten there many times."

Paul exchanged a glance with his wife.

"At least a dozen times over the past ten years," he said, scratching his head with two fingers. "In fact we visited a couple of weeks ago, and, well—" He shrugged and sighed. "I was rather appalled at the de-terioration in his dishes."

"In New York circles, Juan Carlos had always had the reputation for being the cooking genius of the pair," Margaret added, her voice barely above a whisper. "I suspect some of that was old-fashioned sexism. But this visit got us wondering whether, in fact, Edel had been the more brilliant chef of the couple all along."

"What kinds of changes did you notice in the food?" I asked.

Leo approached the table to show the wine bottle to Paul, who nodded briskly. Then the waiter opened the bottle, poured a taste for Paul to approve, and filled our glasses. *"Bonne santé,"* said Leo as he whisked away the empty cocktail glasses.

I was careening toward a whopper headache tomorrow, but I sipped the wine, anyway. This was way too much fun to stop.

"A couple of the items on his menu were over-salted," Paul continued. "The fish was overcooked, and Margaret even felt that the bouillabaisse tasted the tiniest bit fishy."

"You know what I mean," Margaret added. "Fish is fish, but fresh fish is vastly different from sea creatures who have lingered a day too long in the cooler."

"The restaurant was rather well-known for offering an unusual special any day you visited. At least one or two new dishes a week," Paul said. "But the last time we dined there was absolutely nothing new. We asked our waiter about specials and he said no, Chef was concentrating on the standards."

"More like worn standbys." Margaret laughed. "Like the old moccasins I can't get my husband to throw away." She winked at her husband.

"I was literally appalled by some of the dishes I sampled. I was going to give it another shot," he added, "because of their history. I hated to publish a critical

review. After all, maybe I'd caught them on a particularly rough day. But then this tragedy happened."

"And that's what gave him the idea of coming here,"
said Margaret. "We could pay tribute to Juan Carlos at
the same time we tried his wife's new restaurant. We
managed to get a flight at the very last minute. I have
never turned down a trip to the tropics. But we've gone
on too long," she said, placing a manicured hand on
my wrist. "Do tell us about your job."

If I hadn't been so far into a big glass of Spanish
white after two brain-numbing martinis, I would not
have told the truth. As it was, I spilled everything, from
how I'd followed a man to Key West and how quickly
that relationship soured to how that led to my dream
come true—my job as food critic at *Key Zest*.

"But now," I said glumly, "it looks like my run is
over. One of the co-owners of the magazine has invited
some investors and they want to revamp everything.
Including firing staff and soliciting ads from the restaurants where we do our reviews."

"But that's completely unprofessional," Margaret
exclaimed.

"I think so." I shrugged. "Of course, this is a small
town and I can't expect to be anonymous the way you
are," I said to Paul.

"In most cases, anyway." He broke into a wide grin.
"Your man Leo was onto us the moment we sat down."

"Oh it wasn't just that," I said grinning back at him.
"We knew you were coming yesterday. You've got a
leak somewhere in your system."

"Probably one of these transplanted New Yorkers
working in the kitchen," said Margaret. "They all stay
in touch, working their fingers on their phones like de-
ranged monkeys. But enough about the famous critic.

Why can't you keep your job and work with the new investors?"

"The owner can't stand me," I admitted. "If she manages to raise enough money to buy out my boss—or buy his silence—I'm finished."

"That's too bad," said Paul. "I bet you'll find something else. This is a goofy business, anyway, eating for a living."

My heart plummeted. Had I really imagined that the *New York Times* restaurant critic would magically rescue me from my disastrous life?

Then the food began to arrive at the table and it was hard to remain depressed. Who could maintain glum spirits in the face of a perfect Caesar salad or a yellowtail snapper pan-fried in butter and garnished with crispy scallions and julienned carrots and a whisker of ginger? Who could feel sad in the presence of shrimp and grits starring local Key West pinks?

Paul dictated notes into his iPhone as he ate, and I overheard phrases such as "fresh and sweetly crisp" and "animated and lush, with a lingering burn." And then the idea came to me for the perfect article about this night in Edel's restaurant: a day in the life of the *New York Times* restaurant critic. I could talk about the food, but the food as seen through his eyes. And his life, bounding from one meal to the next, seldom at home with his own family, almost always eating more than he should. A meta review. If *Key Zest* didn't wish to print it, someone else surely would. I explained the concept to Paul and he didn't say no. So I pushed ahead, feeling absolutely gleeful and trying not to let that show.

"I'll text or e-mail you this week with a draft."

"Don't feel obligated to show me what you write,"

he said. "Most publications don't want their subjects' input. They tend to want all the juicy stuff removed." We exchanged contact information as Leo returned to the table.

He cleared the plates and ran through the dessert options.

"Anything's fine with me," I said to Paul. "I so enjoy watching you work—seeing what you choose and why you choose it."

"As I'm sure you know," he said, "my selections can't just be about me and my tastes. Or even Margaret's." He chuckled and reached across the table to squeeze her hand. "I'm always thinking about my relationship to food—as in, Do I need comfort today or am I feeling adventurous?—because that affects the mindset I carry into a meal. And then I try to set my own feelings aside and imagine how my readers might be approaching the restaurant."

After a few words about seeing dessert as the meal closer—the last opportunity a chef has to make memories—Paul chose the key lime parfait, lime-scented pastry cream layered with buttery graham crackers and accented with raspberries, plus the standard key lime pie and a chocolate layer cake.

"Who is this monster boss of yours, by the way?" asked Margaret, while we sipped coffee and waited for dessert to be served. "Is he someone local?"

"Actually not—a New Yorker. And it's a she, not a he." I snickered. "Though maybe 'it' is a better description. Ava Faulkner."

Paul's eyes widened and he looked at his wife. "Not the same Ava Faulkner who used to work at *Brilliance Magazine* with Edel?"

"If there's a god somewhere, there wouldn't be two women with that name." I laughed again and the des-

sert arrived. The Woolstons declared the key lime parfait to be sinfully rich, the chocolate cake worthy of a
grandmother, and the pie serviceable.

After the dessert plates had been scraped clean and
the bottle of wine emptied, we left the restaurant,
stuffed and woozy with food and wine. I walked Paul
and Margaret out to the dock and said good-bye. Once
they were out of sight, I returned to the kitchen. Every
staff person stopped what she or he was doing and
turned to stare at me.

"Well?" asked Glenn. "You're killing us here. What
did he think?"

"He loved everything," I said, cracking a wide smile.
I'd tell Edel about the key lime pie another time. The
kitchen broke into a madhouse of whistles and cheers,
except for Edel, who looked shocked.

"I'll never get used to this part," said Edel when I
went over to hug her. "It feels so stressful. And it's always a crapshoot."

"Not the way you cook," I said. "You are brilliant."

30

*For a heart that is open, room can always
be made for new cookware.*
                                    —Jenn McKinlay

I left the restaurant feeling wobbly and exhausted, and
decided that I'd be better off walking home than negotiating even the back streets by scooter. In the busy pre-
holiday season, the cops would be patrolling in full
force and I did not need a DUI on my record.

As I reached Eaton Street, my mother called.

"How was the opening night?"

My earlier annoyance with her evaporated in the
glow of the moment. "Glorious! You won't believe this.
I actually had dinner with Paul Woolston and his wife."
My words tumbled out as I explained how this had
happened and how much they loved Edel's food and
my idea for the new article.

"What fun! I'm so glad you had the chance to meet
them. You sound a little tipsy," Mom added. "Are you
okay to drive?"

"Don't worry. I'm walking. It's not that far and the
night air will do me good. But tell me about the wed-

ding and the Scarlett O'Hara cupcakes. Was everyone happy?"

"It was a magical night. The bride was delighted with the way her party turned out," Mom said. But she sounded a little sad. "We've got another one tomorrow and more after that. This island is a virtual wedding machine—three-quarters of them are second time around: the triumph of hope over reality."

"Oh you don't mean that," I said.

But she had no comment.

"What about your arm? Have the police made any progress identifying the shooter?"

I scrolled through my text messages before answering. Miss Gloria was hitting the hay early. And Danielle wondered if I'd heard anything new about our jobs. But no phone calls from the police and nothing from Wally.

"I'll call Torrence tomorrow," I said, "and report back to you." As soon as I hung up, the phone rang again. The name WOOLSTON flashed on the screen.

"Hello?" I asked, breathless, sure he was calling to weasel out of my article.

"It's Paul Woolston. We enjoyed our dinner together very much. Margaret suggested I call you and she was right as usual." He chuckled. "Just one more word about Ava Faulkner. Don't get in the middle of anything with her. We've known her a long time. Keep your distance, even if it means your job." He cleared his throat. "That's all." And he hung up before I could ask anything more. Not that there was more to ask—I'd known all along that she was bad news.

I finished the trek home in silence, absorbing the sounds of night in the city—sirens blaring in the distance, snatches of rock bands from the harbor, and the traffic whooshing over the bridge on Palm Avenue and out to Roosevelt Boulevard. A barking dog, a crowing rooster with a confused time clock, a flock of birds uttering mournful cries.

By the time I reached Tarpon Pier, I was tired and a little achy from the day's activities, but just the right kind of sleepy. As Miss Gloria had warned me, only the outside light on our deck was on, along with a small nightlight in the kitchen. I boarded the houseboat, hearing Schnootie woof a few desultory barks from inside the Renharts' cabin. I headed directly to the bathroom to wash my face, brush my teeth, and pop two more Advil, then got into pajamas. After plugging in my phone and turning off the ringer, I climbed into my bunk, where Evinrude and Sparky were curled up, already sleeping. Sparky woke and began to pace across my chest, purring and meowing.

"Shhhh," I whispered, rubbing his head. "We're all beat tonight." Within minutes, I faded into sleep.

About an hour later, I bolted upright, wide awake, uncertain what had woken me. If I'd heard a noise outside while sleeping, it was quiet now. If I'd had a bad dream, I could no longer remember a snatch of it. I wrestled to straighten the bedcovers and stroked Evinrude until he rumbled, but finally had to admit I wasn't returning to sleep easily. I got up, used the bathroom, and shuffled into the kitchen to consider a snack. I wished I'd brought a serving of the key lime parfait home. But how could I even be thinking of food, as much as I'd consumed over the night?

Sparky wove around one of my legs and then the other, crying his most piteous meow. I dropped a few kibbles into his bowl—hush money—and noticed that Miss Gloria's enormous tin of black pepper—the one her son in Michigan had sent as an early gag gift for Christmas—was missing from the counter. Then I saw the black powder tossed across the white linoleum and the canister itself kicked to the little hallway that led to our back deck, where Miss Gloria kept her houseplants. Cat footprints tracked the pepper to my bedroom door and Miss Gloria's. No wonder Sparky was unhappy, if he'd been licking pepper off his paws.

I flipped on the overhead light, ready to comfort the cat and clean up the mess. But I noticed more things out of place: the wooden chair tipped over in the living room and a braided throw rug tangled up in a heap. Now feeling worried rather than just annoyed and perplexed, my heart rate lurched higher. I hurried over to Miss Gloria's door and tapped on it. The door swung open. My roommate was not in bed. Though from the condition of the rumpled bedclothes, she had been at some point this evening.

"Miss Gloria? Miss G?" I called. No answer.

I trotted to the back porch—perhaps she'd slipped out there, seeking a dose of night air or a look at the brilliant swath of stars that I'd noticed walking home. And then perhaps she'd fallen into a deep sleep. But the chairs were empty. Had I missed her snoozing on the front deck in our one comfy recliner? I tripped back through the houseboat, both cats on my heels. That chair was empty, too. I grabbed my phone, switched it on, and called her number. Straight to voice mail. Now I was really worried.

I seized the yellow rain slicker hanging on a peg by the door, pulled it over my pj's, leaped onto the dock, and dashed to the Renharts' boat. Schnootie began to bark in earnest. Mrs. Renhart stumbled to the door, sleep in her eyes, the barking dog in her arms.

"Have you seen Miss Gloria?" I asked, my voice trembling.

"Earlier this evening. She was tippling a little glass

of wine on the deck." Schnootie licked Mrs. Renhart's chin.

"She's missing," I croaked.

Schnootie woofed.

"Did she have plans to go out?" Mrs. Renhart asked. I shook my head.

"Did you check the Laundromat?" she asked. "Sometimes if I can't sleep I'll go down the end of the dock and wash my clothes. Believe me, there's no competition for machines in the middle of the night. And watching the clothes go round and round is better than a sleeping pill."

"I doubt it. She did laundry early this morning." But I spun around and jumped from their boat to the dock. "Wait. I'll go with you," Mrs. Renhart said. She snapped a leash on the schnauzer, slipped into a pair of orange gardening clogs, and clumped along with me to the laundry building at the edge of the parking lot.

I held my breath. What were the chances of Miss Gloria doing the whites at two in the morning? Not good. But my mood sank even lower when her absence was confirmed.

"I'm calling the cops," I said, already dialing as we headed back to my houseboat. The dispatcher took my information and promised she'd send a patrol car right over. Within minutes, two police cars with lights flashing pulled into the lot. Lieutenant Torrence and a young woman I didn't recognize emerged from the vehicles, and jogged down to where we waited.

I hugged Torrence, feeling grateful and relieved, and explained the problem.

"Did she say she was going out?" he asked.

"No, she specifically told me she was going to bed early."

"Schnootie and I saw her earlier, maybe around

eight," Mrs. Renhart inserted. "I'm Schnootie," she added in a high-pitched voice, waving the dog's paw at the cops.

"Let's take a look around," said Torrence, ignoring the dog introduction. He and the woman officer switched on their torches and swept around the outside of the boat. They found nothing.

"Show me her room," he said.

Schnootie had begun to bray like a donkey and struggle to get out of Mrs. Renhart's arms. "We'd better wait outside," said Mrs. Renhart, finally seeming to absorb the hostile glances from the young cop. "Schnootie is so sensitive. If anyone's feeling distressed, she starts to feel anxious, too."

She kissed the top of the dog's head and they retreated to the deck while I led the cops to Miss Gloria's cabin and showed them the bed with its rumpled sheets and quilt. "Her cat was sleeping on my bed when I arrived around eleven, which should have alarmed me. But I'm embarrassed to say I'd had a couple of martinis at dinner and I wasn't as sharp as I should have been." I pressed my hands to my cheeks to keep from crying.

"Any friends she might have gone out to visit?" Torrence asked.

"It's two in the morning," I said, suppressing an accusatory wail. He was trying to help. I took a deep breath. "She's close to eighty. She has plenty of friends but she doesn't have an active nightlife. Not after ten p.m., anyway."

"Could there be a man friend?" asked the young cop. "Perhaps someone she hasn't mentioned to you?"

I glowered. "Absolutely not."

"Take a look around the room," Torrence suggested gently. "Without touching anything, if possible. Tell us if anything's missing. Anything that seems a little off. And what she might be wearing."

So I crept around her bed and opened the door to her little closet. "Her robe is here." I pointed to a fuzzy yellow chenille shape that hung on a hook in the closet. "But only one bunny slipper. She wears them every night. I can't imagine why she'd go out with only one." Staring down at the nubby ears and pink whiskers, I felt like weeping. Things were getting worse and worse.

"What else?" asked the lady cop.

So I inspected the nightstand, where a cozy mystery starring a psychologist with a talking cat lay open, face-down. I tugged my sleeve down over my fingers and opened the drawer. "Her purse is here."

The policewoman donned purple gloves and began to flip through Miss Gloria's bag, reporting aloud what she found. "License, library card, Medicare card, family pictures, and two hundred in twenty-dollar bills."

Dropping to my knees to look under the nightstand, in the light of Torrence's powerful beam, I saw a glint. Miss Gloria's glasses were there, the wire rims bent and one lens shattered. Now I felt literally sick. She simply didn't see well enough to go anywhere without her glasses. Unless she was forced to. And then I remembered Lorenzo's warning about keeping channels open, and how someone couldn't see. Although he hadn't wanted to alarm me, perhaps this was the danger he'd sensed—and more concrete than I'd ever imagined.

"Something terrible has happened. She's blind as a bat without these."

Torrence radioed the dispatcher at the station, and several more uniformed policemen were called in to assist with the search. I phoned Connie, and she and

Ray came over to help me wait. The cops worked up and down our finger, blue ghosts knocking on doors and inquiring about whether anyone had seen Miss Gloria leave Tarpon Pier. The neighbor at the end closest to the street, who had moved in last month and hadn't responded to anyone's friendly overtures, reported seeing a woman get into a pink taxicab sometime between eleven and one o'clock and then tear off toward town. He could not remember how she was dressed or any other details about her physical appearance.

At the water end of the dock, Mrs. Dubisson, Miss Gloria's best friend, said she'd spoken to my roommate around nine p.m. They were looking forward to breakfast at Harpoon Harry's in the morning. Once a month seniors were given fifty percent off anything on the menu and they hated not to take advantage of the price reduction. But as far as she knew, Miss Gloria had no other plans. The cops moved on to the other docks in the houseboat neighborhood, and I sank to a chair on our deck.

"They'll find her," Ray finally said. "And if they don't, we'll mount a search around the bight the minute it gets light."

Torrence returned, sat next to me, patted my knee. "I'm sure there will be a reasonable explanation. Please don't assume the worst."

But my mind had already rushed to the worst: that Miss Gloria had been attacked and abducted, or even thrown overboard. Where she would have sunk to the sea bottom like a little white stone.

"Can we get the Coast Guard looking? Maybe she's in the water somewhere. Maybe she's found a little piece of Styrofoam or something and is bobbing around, waiting to be rescued." I sniffled and tugged at his shirtsleeve, and then turned to Ray. "Can we take your boat now and go out looking?"

"I've called the Coast Guard," Torrence said. "Best if you stay put in case she comes home. We'll find her if she's out there."

31

He has even begun to receive confessions, as if he had ascended to a sort of food priesthood. "You don't have to tell me if you like your Cheetos," he said. "That's between you and your cardiologist."
—Emily Weinstein about Michael Pollan, "Pots and Pans, but Little Pain," *New York Times*

I woke as dawn broke, confused to find myself curled up on our couch, my neck cricked at an awkward angle, and both cats crying for breakfast. It took me a minute to remember that Miss Gloria was missing.

I leaped up, threw aside her hand-crocheted afghan, and roared into her bedroom. There were no signs of her having returned. I scrolled through my voice mail, e-mail, and text messages. No news there, either. I left a voice mail for Torrence, asking for an update, and texted him to be sure he paid attention, and then turned to the ugly task of calling my mother—Mom adored Miss Gloria, and vice versa. Even worse than informing Mom would be telling Miss Gloria's children.

"I'll help with that," said my mother briskly after she'd absorbed the news of the night. "Wait a little bit in case she shows up. I'd hate to scare them for no reason. Sam and I will be right over."

By the time I'd showered and dressed and started a pot of coffee, my mother and Sam had arrived at the boat. We hugged and cried a little, and I poured the coffee and we sat on the deck. "I feel so helpless," I said, popping up to pace back and forth and back and forth across our little space. "I know it's the right thing to stay here in case she calls, but I'm going crazy."

"We could go nutso watching you," Mom said, with a sympathetic smile. "We all feel the same way. Why don't you head over to the Cuban Coffee Queen and get us something stronger than this," she said, raising her coffee cup to show what she meant. "Sam and I can wait here in case there's news of Gloria. Get us Key Wester sandwiches while you're there. We need protein, and it doesn't look like there's much in your refrigerator."

Which was a strange turn of events for me. Like Mom, I pride myself on always being prepared to whip up something delicious in times of trauma. But this week had gotten away from me. Sam insisted on pressing two twenty-dollar bills into my palm. I took the money because I could see it was the only way he could imagine being helpful.

I grabbed my helmet and trotted down the finger to my scooter, calling in the order for three large café con leches with one sugar, and three Key Westers, one with ham and two with bacon. Then I zipped across the island to the CCQ. In spite of the early hour, there was already a line. I paid my friend Josh at the counter and then took a seat to wait. Wes Singleton, the previous owner of Edel's restaurant space, was also waiting for his order, smoking his usual cigarette.

"Busy day," I said, moving to the bench across from him to avoid the fumes.

He grunted. "These damn tourist people oughta turn around and go the hell back home." He dropped his lit cigarette, ground it into the bricks, and kicked it aside to join a growing pile of butts near the wall. As he yanked the packet of Pall Malls from his left back pocket to light up another, a ratty Santa hat fell out of the other side, the MADE IN CHINA label exposed.

"Don't you hate that?" I asked. "Why can't we make things that sell at reasonable prices in our own country?"

He said nothing, just looked at me like I'd lost my mind. He looked a little more disheveled than he had even the day before, his eyes red rimmed as though he hadn't slept, and four days' worth of patchwork stubble on his chin. To be truthful, he looked as though he'd caught a wicked case of the mange. I pinched myself inwardly; chances were even though I'd showered, I didn't look much better. Josh finally called my name from the take-out window, and I loaded the coffee and sandwiches into the basket of my scooter and buzzed back to the houseboat.

"You didn't miss anything," said Mom when I arrived. She took the bag and distributed the loot to Sam and me. "No calls, no nothing."

"It just kills me to think about where she might be—who's got her and whether she's hurt." I unwrapped my egg, bacon, and cheese sandwich, and took a big bite so I wouldn't cry, distracting myself by savoring the crispy bacon and soft egg and melted cheese. "I'm going to have to call her family in a little while and tell them that there's no news at all."

"You can't feel responsible," said Mom, patting my back. Sam patted me from the other side. "You're supposed to be her friend and roommate, not her body-guard."

But I did feel responsible. And sick with guilt. And truly sad. Miss Gloria was like the grandmother I no longer had, plus a dear friend, plus a wise little Yoda/ Buddha figure, all rolled up together in one adorable, funny, loving package.

"Yoo-hoo," Mrs. Renhart called from the dock. "Permission to board your craft?"

I waved her forward and she picked up Schnootie and climbed onto our boat. As I began to explain that there was no news, and that the police would be canvassing more neighbors today to ask what they might have seen or heard, Evinrude strolled by, all attitude, with his tail switching and head held high. Schnootie started to bark like a maniac, struggling to get out of her mother's arms. She leaped down and burst through our screen door, into the living room, and down the hall, after the cat.

"I'm so sorry," said Mrs. Renhart. "I don't know what's gotten into her these days. I'm starting to call it the Santa syndrome. I finally figured out that she hates men with beards and hats."

I gave a halfhearted laugh and followed her into our place. Neither of our cats were wearing Santa hats this morning—or ever—but Schnootie still had it in for them.

Just past the living room and the kitchen, Schnootie had planted herself in the hall leading to the back deck. The cats were long gone but she was still yapping hysterically.

"What is the matter with that animal?" I heard Sam mutter as I hurried toward the dog.

"She has a few issues left over from the animal shelter," Mom said, following me down the hall. "She's got a good heart. We need to give her lots of time to get adjusted."

Then I realized the dog was standing on the trapdoor that led to the mechanical crawl space underneath the kitchen. I'd never seen the space but remembered Miss Gloria explaining about the bilge pump and some other functions I hadn't registered at the time.

"I hope we don't have rats," I said. But a horrible idea came to me, and based on the look on my mother's face, she had thought of it as well. "It can't be . . ."

I grabbed a kitchen knife from the drawer next to the sink and tried to pry open the door. The knife blade snapped in half. Sam appeared behind my mother. Schnootie lunged at all of us, yipping with excitement.

"Could you get that damn dog out of here? Please," he added with a tight smile in Mrs. Renhart's direction. She grabbed her dog's collar and dragged her away.

"Do you have a toolbox?" Sam asked me.

"Miss Gloria does." I raced into her room and yanked open the closet door.

I returned in seconds with the box, and Sam rattled around until he found an enormous flat-head screwdriver and a hammer. He banged the screwdriver into the crack in the floor and pried the door open. We peered into the musty, dark space.

"Your bilge pump must be down here," Sam said. "Not much call for it if the boat is staying put—and not sinking."

I tapped on the flashlight app on my phone, illuminating a reach of blackness and highlighting something pink and fuzzy. My heart lurched: Miss Gloria's missing bunny slipper. Then I saw the skating figurines on Miss Gloria's pajamas, then the tape holding her hands and feet together and slapped over her mouth. Last I noticed her terrified eyes, and salty channels where her tears had dried. More tears leaked down her face, collecting in her hair and her ears.

"Call the police," Sam yelled over his shoulder to Mom, his voice as sharp as I'd ever heard it. "Tell them to send an ambulance." He reached a hand down to Miss Gloria. "We're coming," he told her in a soft voice. "You're going to be fine." He turned to me. "If you could just lean down and try to loosen the tape. If it doesn't come easily, we'll have to wait. I'm afraid to move her until the paramedics arrive. If she's broken anything, we could make things worse."

Only minutes later, we heard the wail of sirens, then the pounding of boots on the dock. Two paramedics burst into the houseboat and instructed us to clear away. With tender expertise, they lifted her out of the bilge-pump compartment; cut the tape binding her hands, feet, and lips; and loaded her onto the stretcher.

"I'll go with her," Mom said. "You meet us at the hospital?"

32

His tyrannical, tantrum-throwing tenden-
cies are encouraged; they make him all the
more compelling to watch. Quietly, on an-
other channel, Nigella the home cook lov-
ingly frosts a cake for her child's birthday,
with a little swivel in her hips.
—Charlotte Druckman, *Gastronomica*

By the time I reached the hospital, which had become
altogether too familiar lately, Miss Gloria had been seen
in the emergency room and whisked into a regular patient room. She was hooked up to IVs and scary-
looking, beeping monitors that reminded me of my
stepbrother's coma last spring. But my mother assured
me she was sound asleep and not expected to stay longer than overnight.

"Fastest service I've ever seen," said Mom. "Her vital signs are spectacular. But they thought it best to observe her for twenty-four hours just because of her age
and her size and the general trauma of being taped up
and stuffed in that hole."

"Was she able to say who did it?" I asked, feeling

irate and sick to my stomach all at the same time. "Who would do such a thing to an old lady?"

"She wasn't really in any shape to be interviewed, though she mumbled all the way to the hospital." Mom shook her head. "'At least I got the bum with the closest thing to pepper spray that we have in this house.' That's all I could make out."

Slightly hysterical at the idea of poor Miss Gloria trying to defend herself with a tin of black pepper, I couldn't help snorting with laughter. I quit laughing and told Sam and my mother the other not-so-good news. "Miss Gloria's son is on the way down from Michigan. I know he's going to move her away from Key West. I'm a terrible failure as a protector."

"It's not your fault," Sam began.

"But it is my fault if the attacker meant to hurt me but got her instead," I said. "And that's the only logical conclusion to draw."

"It could have been a random robbery," Sam said. "Someone looking for drug money."

"Why in the world would a robber stuff her into the bilge-pump cubby?"

"They'll do anything to anyone who gets in their way, those druggies," Mom said. "It doesn't have to make sense."

I stayed around for another half hour until my mother insisted I was driving them crazy with my jiggling knees and texting fingers. "We'll call you the minute she wakes up, I promise," she said. "Why don't you go back to the houseboat and clean up? Get things in order for when she comes home."

"Don't you have to work today?" I asked.

"I called Jennifer and explained what happened. She told me not to come back until the day after Christmas. So we'll enjoy the holiday and then I'll go back to slaving in the kitchen. Should I roast turkey or beef for our Christmas dinner?"

"Both," said Sam with a big grin. "I hope you invited Gloria's family to stay with us. Let's make a list for the grocery store. Sounds like we're having a celebration!" He kissed my cheek and pushed me out of the room.

So I roared back to Tarpon Pier on my scooter and spent the better part of an hour straightening up, mopping the floor, making the beds, and feeding the cats. All the time fretting about who tried to hurt Miss Gloria and why. Then the idea of tracking down my homeless friend Tony came to me—maybe he would know something about the attack. He hears almost everything there is to hear on this island, though he's not always willing to share.

I drove over to Rest Beach, where Tony and his gang often spend afternoons at picnic tables near the water. The wind had picked up enough that white caps dotted the ocean and the sand beach was deserted. Tony raised a hand in greeting as I approached the coconut palm–shaded table, but, honestly, he looked less than thrilled to see me.

"Could I speak to you alone for a minute?" I asked.

He stood up and shuffled behind me until we were out of earshot. "What did I do this time?"

"Not a thing. I'm just wondering—" I flashed a tremulous smile and explained what had happened to my roommate. "You hear things . . . and maybe someone might have bragged or slipped up or something." I studied his face, which was utterly impassive. "Never mind—it was a long shot. I'm just feeling helpless. And guilty. I suspect she was hurt because of me, and that makes me feel just awful. Thanks, anyway." I turned to go.

"Why do you think she was hurt because of you?" he asked.

I swiveled back. "You know how badly things are going at Edel's Waugh's restaurant. I've spent a fair amount of time with her lately. I'm just wondering whether someone thinks I saw something or I discovered something about the fire and the murder. Maybe one of her employees has it in for her. It sounds dumb, doesn't it? But I know you were eating there for a while. Out in the alley, I mean," I added, feeling ridiculous. He ate discarded leftovers in the alley; I ate with the *New York Times* food critic at the best seat in the house.

"I'm not seeing the connection," he said.

I rolled up my sleeve and showed the residual bandage. "Someone shot at me. During the lighted boat parade. I don't think the two events are coincidental. And now Miss Gloria." Tears filled my eyes.

He nodded, then tapped a cigarette from a pack he fumbled out of his chest pocket, and then cupped his hands to light it. "They came after you and she got mixed up in it?"

"She tried to fight him by throwing black pepper in his eyes. And the schnauzer next door to us went crazy during the night. She hates men with beards and Santa hats. If only the neighbor had let her out—" I could feel my eyes widen to saucers as the pieces began to fit together: the cigarette butts in the alley near Juan Carlos's pop-up memorial and at the Cuban Coffee Queen, the mangy beard, the Santa hat from China, the watery eyes. "Do you know Wes Singleton?"

Tony nodded, blew out a cloud of smoke. "He's taken a big fall the past few years. And he has no idea that he's responsible for where he's landed. Don't you even think of going after him by yourself. Call your pal Torrence." And he stood there watching until I dialed.

When the lieutenant answered, I told him everything I suspected—that Wes blamed Edel for taking over his lease. That somehow he was behind the mischief in the kitchen and maybe even the fire, though I wasn't sure how. And that maybe he'd thought I was onto him and tried to take me out during the boat parade. And that perhaps he'd planned to finish me off on the houseboat, but Schnootie had rattled him, and Miss Gloria had fought him like a banty rooster.

"That's a lot of maybes, but I'm going to send someone out to pick him up for questioning," Torrence said. "I'm glad you called instead of trying to handle this yourself."

Tony was grinning ear to ear when I hung up.

"I had no intention of trying to tackle him alone," I said.

"Right," Tony said, and ambled back to his friends at the picnic table.

I headed back to my scooter, feeling relieved. But one loose end still bothered me a lot. No way Wes could have gotten into the kitchen to substitute the oil and ruin that lovely vodka sauce. He would have stuck out like a greasy hamburger at a four-star restaurant. He had to have an accomplice inside. I phoned Edel and gave her an update on the events of the night before.

"You sure you don't have a more personal connection with Wes?" I asked. "Can you think of anything that would have made him this angry at you?"

Her denial sounded absolutely sincere.

"Okay, another question: You and Ava Faulkner and Palamina Wells all worked together at *Brilliance Magazine*. But then Ava dropped off the masthead. What happened?" I asked.

After a few silent moments, she said, "Ava was accepting money from advertisers under the table. And then she pitched them as feature stories and wrote them up in glowing terms. It was bribery, plain and simple. And we'd all signed contracts stating we'd have no contact with our advertisers because it would be construed as a conflict of interest. I tried talking to her about it first, but she blew me off. So I had no choice—I took the evidence to the editor-in-chief, who allowed Ava to resign. The understanding was that if she left without a fuss, he wouldn't take it any further."

"And she knew you turned her in?"

"She knew," Edel said.

"Could she have gotten into your kitchen and made those switches?"

"I don't see how I would have missed her," Edel said. "Though she's absolutely capable of paying some-one else to do her mischief."

"Like whom?"

"Glenn's the one I've been hardest on," she said with a sigh.

I got back on the bike and motored over to Mary Pat's mother's place in New Town. Mary Pat worked in the front line with all the players. Before I talked to the cops, I'd like to find out what she knew.

She came out of the house onto the sidewalk as soon as she saw me pull up. "I figured you'd be back."

"Tell me what happened," I said, leaning against her picket fence. Behind her, the giant, cartoonish Christmas balloons drooped on the stubble of grass in the yard. "Was Glenn Fredericks involved in sabotaging the kitchen?"

She shook her head, and I suddenly realized this was not Glenn's story—it was hers. "I told you my husband left us," she said, the expression in her eyes flat. "How much money do you think a line cook makes?" She smoothed a lock of hair into her ponytail. "And the cost of living on this island is horrendous."

I said nothing.

"Singleton pitched it as a practical joke. For five hundred bucks, all I had to do was make sure a few things went badly in the kitchen. I had no idea he'd push it so far."

"And the fire?"

"I never, ever would have set the place on fire. I loved Juan Carlos. Loved him." Her voice broke. "I'll go to the cops and tell them what I know." She started back to the house.

"Wait!" I called. "Was Wes working alone?"

She stared at me for a minute. "Tell them to talk to Ava Faulkner, too."

When I got to the end of the block, I called Torrence again. "You were absolutely right," he said, before I had a chance to speak. "Singleton squawked like a parrot as soon as we picked him up. He went to your houseboat last night—he says just to scare you. But Miss Gloria fought him and he panicked and taped her up. He claims he meant her no harm, but I doubt the judge will see it that way."

"I figured out another piece of it," I said. "One of Edel's sous-chefs, Mary Pat Maloney, switched out the oil and salted the sauce. You probably want to talk to her yourself—in fact, she swears she's coming down to the station right now. But she says she didn't set the fire and I absolutely believe her."

I waited a few minutes, holding my phone out from my ear, while Torrence ranted about my meddling.

When he seemed to be finished, I told him the rest. "And, by the way, she thinks my boss, Ava Faulkner, could be connected to this. And I believe that, too. The tarot card guy as much as told me to watch out for her, and so did the restaurant critic from the *Times*." I cackled. "As if I needed help seeing that she was a witch."

"We're going to pick her up and bring her back to

the station for questioning," he said. And after a beat: "And this once, if you want to listen in, you can."

Fifteen minutes later, after promising to let them ask the questions, I was seated at a conference room table with Ava, Torrence, and Detective Bransford.

"Why is she here?" Ava asked, stabbing a finger in my direction.

Both men ignored her question.

"Edel Waugh deserved what she got," she finally said. "She didn't deserve to land on her feet here. My island. My space."

"She deserved to have her restaurant set on fire?" Bransford asked. "Did Juan Carlos deserve to die?"

"I never suggested that dunce Singleton torch the place," Ava said, slumping back in her chair. "You might have noticed that's he's carrying a grudge that's made him a little crazy. He's a regular nut job," she added with a smirk.

I felt a flicker of rage catch fire in my stomach and push up to my throat. "What about Miss Gloria? She could have suffocated in that cubby."

"He's an idiot," she said, flicking the air with her fingers. "I never asked him to do that, either. Or shoot you." She smirked. "I might be blamed for bad judgment hiring him to do pranks in the kitchen. That's it," she said, smoothing an imaginary nick in one red-painted nail.

"That's all for now, Hayley," Torrence said gently. "We'll take it from here."

I started for the door, but then turned around to face her. "You should know: They don't do manicures in the big house."

33

If you're seized with terrible, unprintable rage towards someone you love, a ripe, velvety avocado can send you over the edge with its innocent bystander meekness.
—Kate Christensen, *Blue Plate Special*

The next day, with Miss Gloria settled back on the houseboat with her sons, and the grocery shopping completed for Mom and Sam's Christmas dinner party, I couldn't help gnawing on the last unanswered question: How had Juan Carlos ended up in the fire? Neither Wes Singleton nor Ava Faulkner claimed to know anything about it. Rodrigo's description of the dead man's last fight with Edel kept surfacing in my tired brain. What could he have wanted so badly from her that he traveled to Key West and snuck into her shed?

Her recipes, of course.

I found Edel in her kitchen at the bistro, alone. She was paging through her recipe bible, taping the edges that I thought might have been torn in the struggle with Juan Carlos. She looked up, her eyes haunted with sadness.

I leaned against the wall, my arms crossed over my chest. "So, he was looking for the recipes you two had developed," I said. "In the safe that you said did not exist. I would have thought he'd made copies. Or at least committed them to memory. You, too," I added.

"I wanted to keep them safe," she said. "They were trade secrets. We had tried a number of brand-new ideas right before I got fed up and left New York," she added. "Neither of us have the kind of mind that retains every detail—not until we've made the dish half a dozen times. Even then . . ." She spread out her hands. "We've got hundreds of recipes in the file." She tapped the book, her eyes filling with tears. "I've made lots of notations along the sides of the pages. What worked especially well. Substitutions to consider. Tweaks on the temperature and how to plate the final product. Side dishes—everything that fleshes out a recipe draft and transforms it into a signature dish."

"But wouldn't he have had those on a computer at the New York restaurant?" I asked.

"Some of the ones we were using in New York, yes. But it wasn't only the dishes we'd worked on together over the years—I would have shared those with him in the end. I'd developed a lot of new ideas for the bistro. Fresh takes on old favorites. Ways to set my restaurant apart from everything we'd done together. It was the only way I had to prove to the world—and to me—that I was capable of standing alone in the kitchen. Without him." Her eyes grew moist and she pressed her lips together, tightened her jaw. "Moving past our history so I could be a chef myself—not the woman behind the famous man."

"So, it meant a lot, him coming down here and trying to steal the book."

"Everything," she said, softly. "Everything. It meant his needs were more important than mine. And that the garbage he'd come spouting was really that: garbage."

"What did he say?"

"When he first arrived, he begged me to come back with him. He was sure we could get our magic back. I said I'd have to think it over." She fell silent again.

"But?" I nudged.

"But he kept calling and calling. And it sounded like he'd been drinking. I told him to go to wherever he was staying and sleep it off. I didn't care if he spent the night in the mangroves with the other bums; I'd talk to him again the next day." She began to straighten the canisters of spices on the counter, then wiped the surface clean with a big sponge.

"And that was Monday," I prompted. "The day the restaurant was closed."

She tossed the sponge into the sink and perched on a stool. "I came back over here because I was nervous about the opening. And upset about the things that had been happening in the kitchen. Someone was undermining me. I'd risked everything for this new restaurant. I couldn't relax."

"But once you got here . . ."

"He had already broken into the shed. Yes, I had a safe there, where I kept the recipe bible." Her eyes flashed a warning. "You think I was being paranoid, but there was a lot at stake."

"Obviously," I said.

"He'd already opened the safe because I'm a fool and I used the same combination I've used all my life, starting with my high school locker. Of course, Juan Carlos knew what it was. In all the hustle of getting the restaurant ready and preparing for our opening, it simply didn't occur to me to change it. It never crossed my mind that he'd be desperate enough to steal from me." Silent tears ran down her cheeks.

"So, you went to the shed and—what?" I asked.

"Honest to god, I caught him red-handed, with the safe open and the book tucked under his arm. He was utterly soused, as has so often been the case in the past few months. I was furious. Livid. We struggled. He was reaching to choke me, so I picked up the rolling pin lying on the shelf and clunked him on the head. He went down like a sack of turnips, looking so surprised."

"You knocked him out?"

"That's the funny thing—he was still talking, blabbing about how we were so good together and he wanted only the best for me . . . I took the book and told him I was locking the door and leaving. He should pull it closed when he got himself together. I wanted him gone, off the island and out of my life. That's the last I saw of him." She suppressed a sob. "Between the clunk on the head and the alcohol, he must have passed out. I hid the recipe bible in the deep freezer and left for Sunset Key." The shuddering sobs came hard and fast. "And then someone set the place on fire . . ."

I waited a few minutes, patting her back as she cried. "I'm sure your name will be cleared. It was a horrible coincidence, nothing more."

She ran her sleeve over her eyes. "I was so focused on getting away from him and back to my condo. You have to understand that his betrayal shook me to the core. But now I wished I had stayed with him, made sure he was okay." Her shoulders slumped a little lower.

I couldn't think of way to argue that with her, so I rustled in my backpack until I came up with my copy of the *New York Times*. "Did you see the review this morning? Paul Woolston went crazy for this place. Let me read you my favorite part." I opened up the food section until I found his review of the Bistro.

Chef Waugh's version of spaghetti Bolognese (which, sadly, is not a regular offering on the menu—yet), was bold, rich, and possibly the best pasta sauce I've eaten since a trip to the northern part of Italy more than ten years ago. This dish not only proves that Waugh's cooking comes from the heart, but her recipes can more than hold their own with any top restaurants in the business—including those of certain well-known Italian chefs brimming with testosterone and hubris. She could braise shoe leather and we'd gladly gnaw it down, all while bowing to her artistry and praising its texture and robust flavor.

She took the paper from me and scanned the article, a big smile lighting up her face by the time she'd finished reading. "I'm thinking of adding the spaghetti Bolognese to the permanent menu after all. If Woolston of the *Times* says I can cook whatever I want and get away with it, why would I argue?"

Before zipping over to my mother's house to help with the feast preparations, I made one more quick stop—at *Key Zest*. Wally was in his office, as I'd hoped. I'd called him the night before and left a message with all the news, including Ava's arrest for arson and attempted murder.

"I'm really sorry about the way things have gone," he started as soon as he saw me. "And I owe you and Danielle an apology. I shouldn't have allowed Ava to bully me into taking on those investors." He pushed his glasses up the bridge of his nose. "Marcus Baker bailed out yesterday when he heard about Ava's role in sabotaging the bistro. But Palamina wants to pick up the slack where Ava left off. Money-wise, I mean. She's not sure she wants a hands-on role with the content, but she wants to invest. She likes what we're doing and she's itching to help with our social-media campaign. She loves you and your work and wants to see you gain a bigger profile." He grinned.

I grinned back—a grin so big it felt like it might split my face wide open. "Better than I could have dreamed."

"Me, too," he said, but then his face fell. "Except you were right: My mom's illness has really affected me more than I admitted—even to myself."

"I wish you wouldn't apologize for that," I said.

"It's important to me that you understand," he said.

And then he told me what it had been like sitting with his mother as the stew of chemical poison dripped into her system. How he could literally see her rosy complexion turn bluish white as the IV emptied into her veins.

"I'm so sorry about that," I said. "I don't know how to say it better than that." Tears welled up in my eyes and I reached over to take his hand. "If it had been my mother, I'm not at all sure I could have been as brave as you."

"You find that you do what's needed," he said quietly. "But it changes things. There are no guaranteed happy endings, you know?"

He planted a kiss on my forehead and picked up the suitcase that I hadn't seen next to his desk. "I'm off to spend the holidays with her. I'll be back after the New Year and we'll get to work."

34

Deliciousness is in the details.
—Betty Fussell

Christmas flew by in a happy blur. Because Miss Gloria asked, we all attended the Christmas Eve service at the Key West Metropolitan Community Church, where Lieutenant Torrence served as pastor. After the lessons and carols and the most beautiful rendition of "O Holy Night" that I'd ever heard, we retired to Mom and Sam's place for a magnificent feast.

Mom had talked Sam into saving the roast beef for New Year's, but we decimated a twenty-pound turkey, along with corn bread and sausage stuffing, mashed potatoes and turnips, corn pudding, brussels sprouts roasted with maple syrup, and a river of gravy.

"We should have done this before we ate, but better late than never," my mother said. "Let's go around and say what we're thankful for this season. I'll start." She squeezed Sam's hand with her right hand and held up her left to show us the ring. "Thanks to my daughter's wise counsel, I'm getting married to the sweetest, kindest, most patient man in the world."

Sam grinned at her and then me, and everyone at the table broke into cheers and congratulations.

"I know I've been a little crochety this week," said my cousin Cassie, when her turn came. "It's a weird time for me. I so admire how Hayley has made a new life with so many new adventures and new friends." She turned to look at me. "You have so many wonderful things ahead of you. While I, well, I'm having a baby." She burst into tears.

"It's an adjustment," Joe said. "Because we know how it will change our lives. And that's scary."

My mother got up and circled the table to give Cassie a hug. "Honey, becoming a mother has been the absolute high point in my life. I just know you'll find that to be true. And golf will always be there waiting." Cassie smiled through her tears and returned my mother's embrace.

"I'm grateful to be here with all of you and not rotting away in the bilge-pump cubby," said Miss Gloria, beaming. "And grateful for that silly schnauzer."

"Ditto," said her son Frank. "Listen." He pointed at me. "I know you feel responsible for what happened, but you needn't. Our mother has never seemed happier than this past year, living with you, at least not since our father died. She's got new friends and new interests—heck, we can't get a word in edgewise when we call her."

"Wait just a minute," she said, but he kept talking.

"She wants to tell us everything about what you're cooking and where she's going with you or Janet. She looks and sounds ten years younger than the last time I visited. I wouldn't dream of forcing her out of here. As long as you're willing, the houseboat is your home and she is your roommate."

"And now," said my mother, "it's time for dessert!"

*   *   *

On New Year's Eve day, Mrs. Renhart emerged from her living room to her deck with Schnootie, both of them in costumes. Schnootie's outfit was a full-body, soft-sided felt bun with the tips of brown hot dogs poking out of each end. A large band of yellow felt imitating mustard squiggled across her back. Mrs. Renhart's costume was only a hat, but some hat—a two-foot-long stuffed hot dog in a bun that perched atop her head like William Tell's arrow through an apple, only with a mustard squiggle that matched Schnootie's.

"Oh my gosh," I said. "You two are hysterical! Where are you headed?"

"The Dachshund Parade," Mrs. Renhart replied, grinning like a monkey.

"But isn't Schnootie a schnauzer?" Miss Gloria said, her brow furrowing into puzzled lines.

"Of course she is," said Mrs. Renhart. "But all kinds of dogs march in this parade." She waved us over to her deck, more animated than we'd ever seen her. "I've been working on the costumes for months. And Schnootie and I have been practicing so she doesn't try to scrape it off while we're walking down the middle of Duval Street."

Miss Gloria and I disembarked from our boat, walked the few yards up the dock, and boarded hers. We oohed and ahhed over the hand stitching, the remarkable likeness between the two costumes, and the subtle line of relish made of green sequins that she'd added to Schnootie's hot-dog bun only the night before. I avoided meeting Miss Gloria's eyes, for fear we would burst into uncontrollable laughter.

"Are there prizes?" I asked. "You will surely be in the running."

"No prizes," she said. "But I've always wanted to have a dog I could take to this parade." She swooped up the schnauzer into her arms and kissed her on the lips.

I had to look away. She was so happy, it was painful. But funny as heck, too.

"I made a hat for Mr. Renhart, too, but he went off fishing." She held up a large felt hamburger and bun, and this time Miss Gloria and I dissolved into helpless giggles.

"Maybe we'll buzz up later to take a look," I said, when I caught my breath.

Mrs. Renhart's cell phone rang. She put down the dog and took the phone from her pocket. Her face fell as she listened.

"Right now?" she asked. "Can you get anyone else? What about Jonette? Or Al?" She listened again, the smile fading from her face. "Okay. I'll be there in fifteen."

"Oh dear, what's the matter?" Miss Gloria asked.

"I can't go," she said, pulling the hot dog from her head. "I've been called into work. Schnootie will be so disappointed. We've looked forward to this forever."

I doubted that her schnauzer cared a whit about marching around the block with a bunch of similarly clad hot-dog imitations, but I nodded sympathetically. Schnootie was, after all, the heroine of houseboat row.

"Unless . . ." Mrs. Renhart's face brightened as she looked at me. "Would you be willing to take her? It's a lot to ask, but . . ." Her voice quavered. "I would be glad to lend you my hat." She held out the stuffed hot dog, her smile tentative.

"I'd pay good money to see that," Miss Gloria piped up. "Just try it on. I'll wear the hamburger."

I backed up a few steps toward the dock, unable to see myself doing something quite that foolish. But Mrs. Renhart looked so mournful. Even the dog at her feet dressed in that silly costume looked sad. "I'd love to help out but I have no way to get down to the Courthouse with the dog. I wouldn't trust myself on the scooter with an animal."

"But you forget—I have a car!" Miss Gloria cried.

With Miss Gloria in the front seat and Schnootie in the back, we drove down Fleming until I spotted a parking space and jockeyed Miss Gloria's land yacht about a foot from the curb. I hopped out for a look—not my best parking job. "That's the best I can do."

"It's fine," said Miss Gloria as she sprang out of the car. "I never get closer than this. Besides, we don't want to miss the parade."

I hooked Schnootie to her leash and we waded through the massive New Year's Eve traffic streaming across Duval Street. When the tourists saw the hot dog on my head and the second wiener strapped onto the schnauzer's back and, finally, the hamburger perched atop Miss Gloria's white hair, they parted ways to let us through. We reached the Courthouse Deli just as a small white van with AUDIO VISUAL IN PARADISE painted on its side panels began to pipe "Who Let the Dogs Out?" over their speakers. Even I began to feel jaunty.

We forded into a sea of dachshunds dressed in tutus and wings and tiaras and devil costumes, and even a small mutt wearing a white box that had the words MY GIRLFRIEND IS A DACHSHUND written on it in large black letters. Schnootie snarled and snapped at a few of the dachshunds. Finally the stimulation seemed to overwhelm her and she relaxed and began to enjoy the parade. Our cavalcade lurched up Southard Street, following the van, which followed three police officers on horses who cleared the way, towering over the little dogs. The sidewalks of Duval Street were crowded with tourists three or four deep, all the way to Appleruth Lane. Ahead, the white van's speakers blasted Elvis Presley singing "Hound Dog."

"Look!" said Miss Gloria. "They're taking videos of us. Maybe we'll be on the news tonight! I feel like a movie star."

Maybe Lassie or Mr. Ed, I thought to myself but didn't say. In our faux-dachshund attire, we were clearly the biggest spectacle for blocks, possibly the entire parade. As we drew near the finish line, Mom and Sam and Joe and Cassie waited outside of 2 Cents restaurant, hot dogs in one hand and beer in the other. Except for Cassie, who held a bottle of water up to me in a toast. Then I noticed Wally, standing beside Mom, his arm linked through hers.

"Happy New Year, darling!" she called to me. "You are the most beautiful hot dog in all of Key West."

"And that's saying something today," Wally added with a laugh. "Happy New Year!" And then he blew me a kiss that set me quivering from my head to my toes.

Recipes

Lucy's Scarlett O'Hara Cupcakes

Ever since reading Elinor Lipman's novel *The View from Penthouse B*, I've had the urge to bake Scarlett O'Hara cupcakes, like one of her characters did. But what exactly is a Scarlett O'Hara cupcake? A red velvet base seemed like a shoo-in. But what kind of icing would show Scarlett's sass? Ginger? Peach? Chocolate ganache? Lemon? Cinnamon? Jalapeño? I settled on a raspberry cream cheese frosting. These may not be authentic, but they taste wonderful and they are showstoppers, too.

CUPCAKE INGREDIENTS
2¼ cups unbleached all-purpose flour
1½ teaspoons baking soda
¼ teaspoon salt
2 tablespoons white vinegar
1 cup milk
2 teaspoons vanilla extract
2 large eggs
2 tablespoons cocoa powder
2 tablespoons red food coloring (one 1-ounce bottle)
12 tablespoons unsalted butter (1½ sticks)
1½ cups granulated sugar

To make the cupcakes:

Preheat the oven to 350°F. Place 20 to 22 cupcake liners in two cupcake pans.

In a medium bowl, whisk together the flour, baking soda, and salt.

In a large glass measuring cup, make a buttermilk mixture by adding the vinegar to the milk. Let it sit for about ten minutes. Whisk the buttermilk with the vanilla and eggs.

In a small bowl, mix the cocoa with the food coloring until they form a smooth paste.

In a medium bowl, beat the butter and sugar together until fluffy, about 2 minutes, scraping down the bowl as necessary. Add $1/3$ of the flour mixture and beat on medium-low speed until just incorporated, about 30 seconds. Add half of the buttermilk mixture and beat on low speed until combined, about 30 seconds. Repeat with half of the remaining flour mixture, the remaining buttermilk mixture, and the other half of the flour mixture. Add the cocoa mixture and beat on medium speed until completely incorporated, about 30 seconds. Do not overbeat.

Distribute the batter into the cupcake pans and bake until a toothpick inserted in the center comes out clean, 18 to 22 minutes. Allow the cupcakes to cool for 10 minutes, then remove the cupcakes to a wire rack to cool completely.

FROSTING INGREDIENTS
1 stick unsalted butter, softened
8 ounces cream cheese, softened
1 cup confectioners' sugar
1 teaspoon vanilla extract
1 pinch salt
About 40 raspberries

To make the frosting:

Beat the butter and cream cheese together until smooth. Beat in the sugar and then the vanilla. Set aside the

20 best raspberries, and beat the remainder into the frosting.

Frost the cupcakes and decorate each with a raspberry. Refrigerate the cupcakes if you aren't serving them right away.

Cassie Burdette's Hot-Dog Casserole

1 medium onion, chopped
1 small green pepper, chopped
Olive oil
6–8 best-quality hot dogs, sliced into rounds*
1 (28-ounce) can B&M Baked Beans
2 tablespoons Dijon mustard
3 tablespoons barbecue sauce or ketchup
2 tablespoons molasses or brown sugar
Worcestershire sauce

Sauté the onions and pepper in a small amount of olive oil. Set aside.

Sauté the hot-dog slices until brown. Remove and discard the pork fat from the baked beans. Mix the baked beans with the hot dogs, onion, and pepper. Add the mustard, barbecue sauce or ketchup, molasses or brown sugar, and Worcestershire sauce to taste. Mix and pour into a greased 9 x 11 inch casserole. Bake at 350°F until bubbly.

You should probably serve this with something green.

*Use your judgment on "best-quality hot dogs."

Chef Edel's Cheesy Polenta with Spring Vegetables and Parmesan Crisps

VEGETABLE INGREDIENTS
3 carrots
2 radishes
1 small white onion
A big handful of snow peas
1 cup broccolini or broccoli florets (or asparagus,
* fiddleheads, or green beans)*

To make the vegetables:

Clean all the veggies and cut them into bite-sized pieces. Set aside.

PARMESAN CRISPS INGREDIENTS
2 oz. fresh Parmesan, grated (use a block of cheese, not the
* stuff in a green container)*

To make the Parmesan crisps:

Heat the oven to 400°F. Grate the Parmesan using the large holes of a grater. Cover a cookie sheet with parchment paper and grease the paper, or use a SILPAT liner on the cookie sheet. Drop the grated cheese into small mounds, about 1 tablespoon each, leaving an inch or more of space between them. Bake at 400°F for 4 to 5 minutes, watching carefully so they don't burn. At first the cheese will melt and bubble; then it will gradually turn golden. Take them out FAST!

CHEESY POLENTA INGREDIENTS
2 cups chicken broth
1 cup water
1 cup cornmeal grits or polenta
1 cup cheddar cheese, grated
2 tablespoons butter

To make the cheesy polenta:

Bring the water and the broth to a boil, and slowly add the grits or polenta. Reduce to low heat and simmer about ½ hour, whisking often to keep lumps from forming and to keep it from sticking to the pan. (Take care, because the grits will pop and can burn the chef.) Mix in the cheese and butter, and set aside.

Quickly stir-fry the vegetables in olive oil until tender but still crisp. Serve them on the hot polenta, garnished with Parmesan wafers.

Janet Snow's Spaghetti Bolognese

This recipe makes a lot of sauce—enough for a generous dinner and then some to freeze for another night of pleasure. I like to put it all together on one day, and finish simmering the next.

2 tablespoons olive oil
1 large onion, minced (about 1 cup)
1½ cups carrots, minced (about 6 carrots, can be done in a food processor)
2 large cloves garlic, minced
1 pound lean ground beef
¾ pound ground pork
½ cup red wine
½ cup white wine
2 (28-ounce) cans whole tomatoes
1 (6-ounce) can tomato paste
½ teaspoon dried oregano
½ teaspoon dried basil
1 cup milk

Heat the olive oil in a large stockpot over medium heat. Sauté the onions and carrots in the oil for about 5 minutes. Add the garlic and cook 30 seconds more. Scrape the vegetables out of the pot onto a plate. In the same pot, brown the beef and pork, breaking up the meat into crumbles. Drain the fat. Add the veggies back into the pot with the drained meat. Add the wine and cook this down a little. Add the tomatoes, breaking them up in the pot as you stir. (I like to make sure little hunks of skin are not left on the fruit before I add them to the pot, but you be the judge of whether skins in the sauce will annoy you.)

Add the tomato paste and the herbs and stir. Stir in the milk. Simmer about two hours, until the alcohol has evaporated and the flavors have blended.

Serve the sauce over the pasta of your choice with freshly grated Parmesan cheese, and a green vegetable on the side.

The Jungle Red Cocktail
(Courtesy of Susan Elia MacNeal)

1 part pomegranate juice
½ part orange liqueur (Susan likes the spiciness of Créole
  Shrubb)
3 parts sparkling wine (or ginger ale)
Lemon twist, pomegranate seeds, and raspberries, for
  garnish

Mix the first three ingredients. Serve over ice and garnish with a lemon twist, pomegranate seeds, and raspberries.

Decadent Key Lime Parfaits

BEEP! BEEP! BEEP! A calorie alert has been issued for this recipe. You should not go in with the idea that a Key Lime Parfait is a light dessert because of the citrus.

Also be forewarned that although key limes have a lovely flavor, they are small and a bit of a nuisance to juice. Be patient—it might take a pound of key limes to produce the juice you need.

5 whole graham crackers, crushed (about 1 cup)
2 tablespoons melted butter
1 tablespoon brown sugar
2 cups heavy or whipping cream
¼ cup powered sugar
1 teaspoon vanilla
1 (14-ounce) can sweetened condensed milk
½ cup key lime juice
Key lime zest

Preheat the oven to 350°F. Crush the graham crackers by sealing them in a ziplock bag and rolling them with a rolling pin. Mix the crumbs with the melted butter and brown sugar. Spread the mixture on a foil-covered baking sheet and bake for ten minutes or until golden. Let it cool, then break it into crumbs again.

Meanwhile, in a large bowl, whip the cream with the powdered sugar and vanilla until soft peaks form. Set half of the cream mixture aside for the topping.

Mix the condensed milk with the lime juice. The citrus will cause the milk to thicken. Gently fold in one cup of the whipped cream.

Set out eight parfait or martini glasses. Reserve a couple tablespoons of the crumbs for topping. Layer some of the baked crumbs into each glass, then add some of the key lime mixture. Repeat. When you have distributed all the ingredients, top with dollops of whipped cream and sprinkle with reserved crumbs and some zested lime if you want a stronger citrus flavor.

Read on for a sneak peek at the next
Key West Food Critic Mystery,
coming in summer 2015 from Obsidian.

The first time Miss Gloria almost died, she came out of the hospital rigid with fear.

The second time, just before Christmas, she came out fighting. In spite of having been jammed into a small space for hours, with hands and feet bound and mouth taped shut, she was determined to embrace life with all the risks that entailed. For weeks she'd brushed off my concerns about conserving her energy, going out alone at night, and piloting her enormous Buick around the island instead of calling a cab. Good gravy, wasn't she almost eighty-one years old? And, besides that, she could barely see over the steering wheel.

I took a deep breath and lowered my voice so the entire marina wouldn't hear us squabbling on the deck of her houseboat. "Your sons will have conniptions if they hear you're driving again," I said. "Lots of things can go wrong. The traffic is terrible this time of year—"

"When you look at it without your blinders on, Hayley Snow," she said, "isn't life just one big series of close calls? We all have to go sometime," she added with an impish tilt to her head. "And I've realized that I don't want to go feeling any regrets. And I'd definitely regret spending the rest of my life acting like a scared old lady." She grinned and patted my hand. "My training shift at the cemetery starts at three. You're coming for a tour at four so I can practice, right? How about we compromise and you'll drive me home? That way you can walk over to the cemetery, burn off a few calories, and earn points with your gym trainer," she finished with a sly wink.

I sighed and nodded my agreement. I'd been had and we both knew it.

She hurried down the dock to her metallic green car and I buried myself in my work in order to avoid watching the big sedan back and fill. When she'd extracted the vehicle from its tight parking space, she pulled across the Palm Avenue traffic, tires squealing and horn blaring.

I plugged my ears and tried not to look. I had my own problem to attend to: roughing out a plan for my latest restaurant-review roundup, tentatively called "Paradise Lunched." My new boss, Palamina Wells, was a lot more hands-on than any of us working at *Key Zest* had expected when she assumed half ownership of the magazine in January.

"I'll back off once I get a handle on things," she told us in a staff meeting yesterday. "In the meantime, let's work on making our lead paragraphs truly memorable. Think tweetable, think Buzzfeed-able, think Instagram envy. Let's make them irresistibly viral, okay?"

Irresistibly viral felt like a lot to ask from an article on lunch.

At three thirty I put my overworked, underperforming first paragraph aside and told the cats I'd be back in an hour, lord willing that Miss Gloria allowed me to drive home. If the lord didn't will that, I couldn't promise anything.

By the time I fast-walked from Houseboat Row to the Frances Street entrance of the cemetery, I was sweaty and hot, which meant my face had to be its most unattractive tomato red. I took a selfie on my phone and texted it to my trainer, Leigh, as proof of my aerobic exertion. She had been on the money last week when she pointed out that my fitness program had lots of room for improvement. "Increasing zero miles per week walking to any positive integer would be good," she'd said, snapping her iPad shut with a flourish.

The Key West cemetery sits in the center of the island, where it was moved after the hurricane of 1846 washed the graves and bodies into the Atlantic Ocean. Because of our high water table, most of the burials are now handled in aboveground crypts, which makes for an interesting and spooky landscape. That—along with some interesting inhabitants—makes the cemetery one of the biggest tourist attractions on the island.

I'd put off agreeing to this tour for as long as I could. It's not that cemeteries scare me exactly. It's that the idea of people dying makes me sad. People like Miss Gloria, who's probably closer to that transition than most of the people I know. And I love her like a grandmother, only more so, because she's a friend, too, without the baggage that family can bring. And now here she was, training to be a volunteer guide at the cemetery, where it would be all dead people, all the time.

She was waiting for me at the gate, positively vibrating with excitement. "How much time do we have?" she asked. "I've learned so much. I'd like to tell you all of it."

I laughed. "I have to be at the city commission meeting by six, and I dare not be late. And I definitely need something to eat before—the commissioners have a reputation for running hot and late. So, let's say half an hour?"

She straightened her shoulders, the serious expression on her lined face not a match for her cheerful yellow sweatshirt, which featured sweet bunnies nibbling on flowers. "In that case, maybe we'll start in the Catholic part of the cemetery, since it's closest." She pushed her glasses up the bridge of her nose. The hinge at the left temple, still held together with silver duct tape, caught on a clump of white hair. She had gotten the lens replaced after it was crushed in the scuffle last December, but she refused to spring for new frames. "I like old things," she laughed. "They go with me." She waved me forward. "So, we'll start on the right. Then we can work our way around the edges and I won't forget where we left off."

"How long are the tours you'll be giving once you're finished with your training?" I mopped my face with my sleeve and paused in the scanty shade of a coconut palm.

"It depends if it's a special event. In that case I could be here two hours. But most tourists don't have that kind of attention span. They want to see the gravestone that says 'I told you I was sick.' And maybe the double murder–suicide grave."

"The double murder–suicide?"

"Yes." She nodded enthusiastically. "He shot her and then killed himself. And the poor woman is stuck in the same grave site with him for eternity. What's up with that?"

"Somebody with a sick sense of humor made that decision," I said. "Though Eric always says you never know what's going on in a marriage unless you're living in that space. I guess it's possible that she drove him to it." My childhood friend Eric is a psychologist and, besides that, the most sensible man I know.

She cleared her throat and started to speak in a serious

public-radio kind of voice. "Okay, in this right-hand corner that runs along Frances and Angela streets, you will find the Catholic cemetery." Miss Gloria wove through the mossy stones, pointing out the plot for the Gato family, prominent in cigar-manufacturing days, the English family plot honoring the first African-American man elected to the city commission, and a gravestone reading DEVOTED FAN OF SINGER JULIO IGLESIAS.

She adjusted her damaged glasses again. "I hope you'll find something more personal to say than that when my time comes."

"Definitely," I said. "'Miss Gloria, spark plug, wonderful roommate, and mother of fabulous sons.' Let's see, that's too wordy. How about, 'She was up for anything'?" Then I glanced at my watch, hoping to change the subject. "It looks like we have time for one more."

"Oh, I have to show you this one, then," she said, and led me to the grave of Mario Sanchez, an artist who had recorded scenes of early Key West in his folk-art woodcut paintings. "His artwork's shot up in value. Can you imagine, I had the chance to buy some of his pieces twenty years ago?" she said. "But my husband thought two hundred dollars was out of our price range." She looked up at the sky and shook her fist. "Honey, you weren't right about everything. Those pieces are selling for close to a hundred grand now."

Then she hustled up ahead of me. "Here's one more. Isn't it amazing? Their monument looks like a wedding cake. But apparently these two families were feuding. Maybe they bought the plot before they started to fight? But, anyway, now they're stuck next to each other for eternity, with only this metal-spike fence to separate them."

As we headed out of the graveyard to her car, Miss Gloria darted ahead of me so she could slide into the driver's seat. She waved me to the passenger's side. "Since I'm thinking of driving more often, maybe it's a good idea if you check out my technique."

Crossing my fingers behind my back, I got into the car and fastened my seat belt. Then I gripped the handle above the door with my right hand and the seat with my left. She looked over at me and laughed.

"I swear it won't be that bad." She put the key in the ignition, turned on the car, and revved up the big engine. We jolted away from the curb on Olivia Street and headed up toward White. Cars, bicycles, and scooters roared by in both directions. The town definitely felt busier than usual, but with Miss Gloria at the wheel, all my senses were heightened. She turned on the radio and scooched up the volume so I could barely hear myself worry.

"I'm going to take a right here," she yelled over the Beach Boys singing "Fun, Fun, Fun." "Because I'm afraid turning left will make you too anxious."

"You could be right," I said with a pained smile.

She drove the few blocks from White to Truman without incident and pulled into the left-turn lane. "See, now," she said, craning her neck around to look at me. "I'm putting on my directional signal. And my hearing is perfectly good, so I'm not going to leave it on after I turn, like the other old people do." She cackled out loud, but I kept looking straight forward through the windshield, praying she'd get the message and do the same.

"Green arrow!" Miss Gloria sang out, more to herself than to me. She piloted the Buick like a boxy Carnival Cruise ship from the left-turn lane onto Truman Avenue and lurched across the intersection to the right lane. "What are you working on today?" she asked.

I tried to ungrit my teeth and relax my jaw. "It's an article on lunch," I said. "I'm planning to include Fire-fly, and maybe Azur and the Café."

"What about Edel's bistro?" she asked. "Aren't they serving lunch?"

"Everyone knows Edel and I are well acquainted af-ter all that publicity," I said. "I'm going to give her place a rest for a couple months." Edel Waugh had opened a bistro on the Old Town harbor last December. A fire and a murder had almost tanked the restaurant. I'd been a little too involved to be considered a disin-terested party. "Besides, she's gotten so popular lately, it's hard to get a table."

"Jesus lord!" Miss Gloria yelped, and leaned on the horn as an unmarked police car cut in front of us. She slammed on the brakes and rolled down her window. "Where did you get your license—Kmart?"

"That's a cop car," I muttered. "Roll up the damn window and keep driving."

"I don't care who it is. He's driving like a horny high school student late for his date."

I goggled at her in amazement. As we reached the intersection of Truman and Palm Avenue, where an-other left turn led to our marina, I noticed the flashing of blue lights from the water.

"The cops," said Miss Gloria. "Let's pull over and see what's happening."

Before I could protest, she had hurtled up onto the sidewalk, thrown the car into park, and scrambled out. A tangle of orange construction webbing floated in the brackish water closest to the new roadway, dotted with assorted trash and a lump of something bigger. Three or four policemen stood on the sidewalk, looking down, seeming to discuss how to get the whole mess ashore. One of them glanced up and then hurried toward us, scowling.

"Get back in the car and keep moving, ladies. This isn't a sideshow. And you're blocking traffic, ma'am."

"Let's go," I said, herding Miss Gloria to our sedan. "You can watch them from the back deck with the binoculars."

"I swear, Hayley," she said, turning to look again, "I think they've snagged a body."

ALSO AVAILABLE
FROM NATIONAL BESTSELLING AUTHOR

Lucy Burdette

An Appetite for Murder
A Key West Food Critic Mystery

Hayley Snow's life always revolved around food. But when she applies to be a food critic for a Key West style magazine, she discovers that her new boss is Kristen Faulkner—the woman Hayley caught in bed with her boyfriend. Hayley thinks things are as bad as they can get—until Kristen is killed and the police pull Hayley in as a suspect. Now Hayley must clear her name or the only restaurant she'll by reviewing is the prison café.

**"Food, fun, and felonies.
What more could a reader ask for?"
—*New York Times* bestselling author
Lorna Barrett**

Available wherever books are sold or at
penguin.com

facebook.com/TheCrimeSceneBooks

ALSO AVAILABLE
FROM NATIONAL BESTSELLING AUTHOR

Lucy Burdette

Topped Chef
A Key West Food Critic Mystery

Hayley Snow loves her job as the food critic for
Key Zest magazine, tasting the offerings from
Key West's most innovative restaurants. She would rate
her life four stars, until she's forced into the spotlight—
and another murder investigation.

When Hayley's boss signs her up to help judge the Key
West Topped Chef contest, she's both nervous and
excited. But when a fellow judge turns up dead, Hayley
has to find the killer before she's eliminated from
the show...permanently.

**"The victim may not be coming back for seconds,
but readers certainly will!"**
—*New York Times* bestselling author Julie Hyzy

Available wherever books are sold or at
penguin.com

facebook.com/TheCrimeSceneBooks

OM0123